Joan Shirley-Davies lives in Shropshire with her actor husband. She always wanted to be a writer and an actress, as she loves to entertain and communicate with people. Although Joan loved acting, she hated the life, so she wrote plays instead. This book marks her transition from playwright to novelist.

Dedication

To my husband, John, who mopped up tears, made me tea, comforted me when I was rejected and bought me champagne when I wasn't.

Joan Shirley-Davies

MONEY IS EASY

AUSTIN MACAULEY PUBLISHERS™
LONDON • CAMBRIDGE • NEW YORK • SHARJAH

Copyright © Joan Shirley-Davies (2018)

The right of Joan Shirley-Davies to be identified as author of this work has been asserted by her in accordance with section 77 and 78 of the Copyright, Designs and Patents Act 1988.

All rights reserved. No part of this publication may be reproduced, stored in a retrieval system, or transmitted in any form or by any means, electronic, mechanical, photocopying, recording, or otherwise, without the prior permission of the publishers.

Any person who commits any unauthorised act in relation to this publication may be liable to criminal prosecution and civil claims for damages.

A CIP catalogue record for this title is available from the British Library.

ISBN 9781788231466 (Paperback)
ISBN 9781788231473 (Hardback)
ISBN 9781788231480 (E-Book)

www.austinmacauley.com

First Published (2018)
Austin Macauley Publishers Ltd.
25 Canada Square
Canary Wharf
London
E14 5LQ

Acknowledgements

Paula Peplow-Freer
Ian Andrew
Ian Shirley

Chapter One

'You've what?' Shaken to the core by her sister's news, Lizzy began to pace about in the Merevale Hotel foyer. Her fingers gripped her cell phone as she squeezed her voice through her tight, aching throat. 'That's a joke—right, a sick, cruel joke.'

'No, I really mean it.'

'So, after all that planning, you think you can just...' Her voice caused somebody to look around so she spoke quietly. 'Just leave me to get on with it on my own?'

'C'mon, Lizzy, I've explained why.'

'Two or three weeks, Carrie, you told me two or three weeks. The delay was bad enough. I was so frustrated I had to go out jogging every day before I could face my work.'

'You'll be OK.'

'How can you say that? I've got six months, for goodness sake. Just six months to repair the damage, otherwise I'm finished. Does that sound OK to you?'

'I know what the past year has cost you and I can't tell you how grateful—'

'I don't want gratitude. I'm almost thirty years old I knew what I was doing. But we agreed. Carrie, please...'

'I can't cope with it now. My life's suddenly changed.'

'And mine hasn't?'

'But I'm not like you. You always deal with problems so much better than I can.'

'I never have a choice.' Lizzy clenched the fingers of her other hand and her jaw set rigidly as she drew a tense breath. It was a few seconds before she could speak again. 'Do you think I want to be the gritty, tough one? Am I supposed to be the fall guy every time?'

'You're amazing. I don't know anybody else who'd put her own dream on hold to help me find mine, but it's more difficult than I thought.'

'Can't Jack help you? It was his dream too.'

'He's stressed about something, work probably, and he won't talk about it.'

'This isn't the time for a man to shrink into his shell because his job's stressful. This is ridiculous.'

'Don't push me, Lizzy.'

'I don't mean to push you, but it's vital I stick to the plan.'

'Give it a bit longer and we'll see.'

'I haven't got any more time. Can't you make a bit more effort?'

'Gotta go, Lizzy!'

'No, Carrie, don't do this. Don't hang up, I need you—Carrie!' Out of the corner of her eye she saw a small child about to run across her path. She swiftly stepped aside but lost her balance and stumbled towards a huge, billowing palm plant. A gasp fled from her lungs. It was happening very quickly but she seemed to have time to realise how embarrassing it was going to be to plunge into the leafy branches. Then, as if a pause button had been pressed, something stopped her. She stared at the greenery. The air had been pushed out of her lungs, but, to her complete surprise, she remained upright.

A sonorous voice filtered through her hair and into her ear. 'It's all right. I've got you.' It sounded so intimate, so personal, as if the voice was sharing a secret with her.

She glanced down to the light grey, finely woven sleeve of his sweater, the gold watch on his forearm firm across her diaphragm. Her nostrils became aware of a trace of aftershave that was so subtle it would only be detected from close proximity. This was a stranger. She should be pushing him away by now and wafting away the embarrassment, but in those few intimate seconds she felt so at home, as if his arm was right where it should be and she should be leaning back against him, listening to oh-so-private suggestions. She had no idea what he looked like but he had wonderful hands, a deep, seductive voice and he smelled delicious.

'OK now?' he said as he released her.

Shaken and bereft of her ten perfect seconds of existence, she turned to face him. 'Fine—thank you.'

'That must have been quite a phone-call. You almost ended up in that plant.' He seemed very concerned. 'I grabbed you rather quickly I hope I didn't hurt you?'

For a moment Lizzy dallied in the glow of his charisma that was so tangible she could almost feel its pulse. He wasn't handsome, as in Prince Charming, but most certainly attractive, with the kind of hair that made a girl want to thread her fingers through it, dark brown, glossy and just long enough to fall into a parting. He was rather serious, but had the most wonderful expressive eyes; pale green irises that reflected his concern.

Well done, she chastised herself; you got so wrapped up in your phone call you couldn't even walk straight. Now you look a complete idiot. Why couldn't he have been less... gorgeous?

A swift but futile search for an intelligent response left her muttering, 'No... I'm not... no, you didn't hurt me.'

He suddenly drew a swift breath and looked at her as if he had discovered something startling, but he didn't speak.

Lizzy tilted her head and tweaked her brow. 'What?'

Several more seconds of silence passed before he said, 'Sorry, for a moment you reminded me of somebody.'

Lizzy began to feel her cheeks heating up. She willed herself not to blush. Crashing into the decorative greenery was bad enough without turning pink. A lame comment was all she could manage. 'Somebody nice I hope.'

'Yes,' he said with a faint flicker of a smile, 'somebody very special.'

The way he looked at her almost made her wish she really was the other person. For a few moments this man, his strength and positive aura, made her feel like her old self. The way she was before the upheaval of last year.

'Well you're certainly my hero for the day. Thanks for catching me. You saved me from looking ridiculous and clumsy.'

'I don't think you could look clumsy, you have wonderful co-ordination.' He faltered a little as if he'd spoken out of turn. 'You needed it to dodge that child.'

'Just ridiculous then.'

'Nor that,' he said decisively. He smiled and offered his hand. 'I'm Tony.'

'Lizzy.'

'You're local?'

'I relocated my business a few weeks ago.' She took his hand, felt his fingers clasping around hers and shivered as a tide of sensual chemistry ran through her making her insides quake and her heart race as if she'd been running. She had never experienced a reaction like it.

'You like Merevale?' Tony asked releasing her hand.

'Oh yes. I've moved into the Lakeside Centre.'

His brow lifted. 'Ah, the wedding boutique, I've seen it. It looks very beautiful—congratulations. I'm sure you'll be successful.' It seemed to take a few beats for him to continue the conversation. 'You still look shaken. Perhaps you'd like to rest awhile. I have a private lounge here. In fact, I'm on my way to have some coffee. Why don't you join me?'

Lizzy's insides lurched again and her throat dried. This was such a thrilling temptation but she needed man-trouble like she needed a broken leg. 'Thanks but I have to dash. I'm here for the book auction.'

'You like books?'

As he'd embarked on small talk, she could cope with that. 'I'm after a particular volume in the sale schedule. I've searched hard and long for it and I'm desperate to own it again.'

'Again?'

'Afraid so. It's a rare volume. My father bought me a copy when I first went to Art College. He even inscribed it. I feel terrible about it.'

'So what happened to it?'

'I…' Her frivolous and pleasurable encounter with this guy, Tony, suddenly crashed into her past emotional baggage. 'I kind of lost it.'

'*Kind* of…?'

'Left it… somewhere.' She cringed inwardly, mentally appealing to him. Please don't ask me where I left it. Don't ask for any more details. I can't think quickly enough to make something up and you really don't want to know all that. She sidestepped saying, 'Most of my things have been in storage so I've only just realised it was missing.'

'So is the book in the sale yours or another copy?'

Lizzy raised her palms towards him and frowned. 'I haven't looked closely. I don't want to know.'

'Why is that?'

'What if the bidding goes over my limit and I don't get it? There can't be many people who'd want a book about the history of braids and laces, but if it's mine I'd be mortified to lose it a second time.' She began to back away from him. 'Thanks again. I'd better go.'

'But it's early yet. And the coffee here is excellent—trust me.'

Trust? She had done that once, even accepted a proposal, but her faith had only served to increase the shock when she saw her fiancé's true colours. She broke off her engagement and deemed it a lucky escape, but she never stopped to think what she might have left in his house. It seemed to her that men were a lottery and she didn't want another ticket.

She flicked her long, chestnut hair behind her shoulders and smiled. 'I don't mind being early. I can scribble a few notes while I'm waiting.'

Dragging herself from the most compelling temptation she had ever experienced, she dashed off through the reception lounge towards the large function room.

Tony Franklyn stood and watched her, somewhat surprised at this unique experience of being lower in the pecking order than a few scribbled notes. This was a first. The momentary experience of holding her was still sending his blood coursing through his veins. And that little tweak of her brow and the tilt of her head was somewhere between adorable and downright seductive, and all the more so because she didn't know it. Neither did she know what she had done for him over the last few weeks, how important she had become in dragging him back onto his feet and recognising that life goes on.

The first time he saw her it was just an ordinary May morning, yet it held one of those moments in time that fate plants in a person's day; like a tiny seed destined to grow into a new beginning.

Reluctant to spend yet another night thrashing about in search of sleep he had remained on the sitting room sofa, restlessly dozing through a mishmash of night viewing. By six forty five a severe backache induced him to get up and make coffee. As it gasped and wheezed into the jug, he sauntered barefoot across the light-oak floor of his enormous kitchen and looked out of the window. A mantle of mist had formed over the lake and only the treetops and the church spire on the other side were visible above it. Something caught his bleary, sleep-starved eyes. It drew him closer to the window. Ghost-like and defying the eerie stillness at the water's edge there was a hint of animated colour. Gradually it took shape. Then he saw her, as she emerged fresh and lissom. Her feet hugged the lake's edge as she jogged, putting his early morning lethargy to shame. His mouth twitched into a faint smile; something that hadn't happened in weeks. A hint of warmth began to flicker inside him and it eased the chilling grief. His eyes followed for the few seconds it took her to reach the footpath into the woodland. Then she was gone. He saw her again the next day and the next and the next after that. Like an enthralling clock she paced out beats of time with the tread of her feet, while every swish of her long, chestnut hair and each swing of her angled arms, kept strict time as she ran. She was tenacious, determined, motivated.

There were few things denied Tony Franklin, design engineer, wealthy businessman and patriarchal pillar of the community, but recently he had a barbed pain inside him that even his fortune couldn't ease. Yet this enigmatic, human timepiece had blotted out his pain for just a short while each day like a ghost come to pull him from the debilitating grip of his loss.

With his heartache under control and unruly, long hair that, according to his mother, would look more fitting on an opera singer, he boarded his private jet, sank into his seat and called his London office.

'Irena, I'm on my way. Will you arrange a development meeting for this afternoon? I need an up-date on the new machine-tool trials. See if James is free for dinner. He can fill me in on the final stage of the US hand over. Reserve a table at Sanccella's. Oh... and book me in for a haircut will you?'

'Welcome back, Mr Franklyn.'

Tony snapped out of his reverie. Now he had seen her beautiful eyes with honey-coloured irises and gold, fox-like flecks. She was no longer an enigmatic athlete but a very attractive woman called Lizzy—his new tenant.

He strode to the reception area and spoke to the girl behind the desk. 'Did you see that woman going into the sale?'

'Yes, Mr Franklyn, it's Lizzy Yardley—lovely hair, don't you think? They say she's very gifted. Her wedding dresses are often in the County Magazine. You wouldn't know it, would you, seeing her in simple clothes? Mind you, I wish I looked like that in jeans...'

'I've seen her lovely hair and I've seen the jeans,' Tony interjected. 'I want you to do something for me. She's going to bid for a book. It's very special to her, something about braids and lace. Find somebody to cover for you, get a number in my name and wait for the lot to come up. If she has to drop out carry on bidding until you get it. And for goodness sake, don't let her suspect what you're doing.'

'How much shall I bid?'

He scowled. 'Whatever it takes. Just keep going.' He fixed his eyes on her with the full thrust of his authority. 'I'll be very annoyed if somebody else gets that book from her.'

Lizzy stepped back several paces, and looked at the wedding gown displayed in her window. 'You did it, Lizzy,' she told herself out loud. 'You're on your own now and you've got a shedload of collateral damage to sort out. But... hey girl... you're back!'

The Lakeside Centre was perfect, picturesque, white, purpose-built retail outlets. They stood, with the lake as a backdrop, in a pleasing arc around a paved forecourt, with flower planters bursting with coloured blooms.

Lizzy ran her eyes along the four shop windows, the art gallery, florist, jewellery designer and her new boutique. She was in immaculate company. This new start had to work—it had to.

When she returned to the boutique, Jenny, the florist came in carrying a large bunch of red roses. She thrust them into Lizzy's arms. 'Here, babe, for your showroom. Put them in water now and they'll be fabulous for the big day.'

'Jenny, you can't, they're so expensive.'

'You've slogged for this. I've seen your light burning way into the night.'

'Yours must have been burning too.'

'You deserve something nice. Besides, blushing brides in your shop might even walk along the parade to mine—get it?'

Lizzy held the blooms close to her face, closed her eyes and savoured the fresh scent. She was comforted by Jenny's gesture. In the few weeks she had been at the centre they had progressed from being newly acquainted to telling each other absolutely everything. 'So lovely,' she whispered. 'Thank you.'

Jenny shrugged her shoulders. 'You'd do the same for me.' She strolled along one of the dress rails and sighed at the range of cute little bridesmaid's dresses. 'Party frocks for little princesses. They make me feel broody.'

'Really?'

'I'm like a hen pining for my little chicks. But I have to wait for next year.'

'Then come away and stop winding your body clock. They're just there to fill the shop with something until I can get commissions.'

'They're going to fly off the rail. Hey, why don't you take some time off now? I'm going to be on my own later. Fancy coming round for a girly evening? I've got a bottle of wine and a chick flick?'

'I'm off romance.'

'Sci-fi?'

'Sounds great but I'm going to see my parents off, and collect the rest of my things. They've found a tenant already.'

'Wow, six months touring Europe. You'll miss them.'

'Yes, but it's their dream trip.' She walked through the archway and into her studio area and laid the flowers on her cutting table. 'I'll get a vase.'

'By the way,' Jenny said, 'did you get your book this morning?'

Lizzy grimaced. 'No. I had to drop out. I'm so disappointed.'

'Ah, bad luck. Please tell me you treated yourself to a cup of coffee and a big, sinful, scrummy cake to compensate?'

'Who needs comfort food when you meet a big, scrummy guy, and your reactions are much more sinful than cake.'

Jenny gasped and widened her eyes. 'Details,' she demanded. 'Everything—don't dare leave anything out.'

Lizzy laughed and fixed her eyes on her friend's expectant face. 'Charming, charismatic, strong and a sexy voice that runs down your neck... like silk.'

'And...?'

'Fabulous clothes and a watch that would pay my rent for a couple of years. A bit serious, though... just a bit. There was something in his eyes, a kind of sadness.'

'What's his name?'

'Tony.' She smiled. 'He was very gallant, stopped me falling into a plant pot when a toddler almost ran into me.'

'Good move—very effective.'

'He said I reminded him of somebody.'

'That's not very original is it?'

'He didn't seem to need chat up lines. He just invited me to have coffee—in his private lounge, if you please.'

'I'm pretty sure you've just met our globe-trotting, landlord.'

'Really?'

Jenny chortled. 'His sex appeal can chase a girl around the room before she even sees him.'

'That's true.'

'Fit, isn't he? He owns the hotel as well as the centre. That's his house on the other side of the lake.'

Lizzy caught her breath. 'You're kidding me! I've been virtually running through his back garden for days. Was I trespassing?'

'No, he lets people walk round it. I'm glad to hear he's out and about again. He's been a bit of a hermit lately.'

'Why?'

'Couldn't deal with losing his girlfriend. It was all a big surprise because he wasn't known for being the commitment type.'

'Is she local?'

'No, he never dates women from round here.'

'She must have been very special to put him in such a bad way.'

Jenny's face became grave and her eyes dulled. 'It wasn't just bad, he was gutted. Came into my shop to order some flowers, gave me an address—no name, just an address. When I offered him a card to write he waved it away and told me to leave it blank. Said there were no words to describe how he felt. He couldn't have written on it anyway his hands were trembling. I've seen sadness in my shop, people missing loved ones, but I've never seen a man like that. Honest to God, Lizzy, I could have just stood there and cried.'

'But they might meet up again. Surely they can work it out. He's rather gorgeous, isn't he? She might come back to him.'

'No, Lizzy, she's dead. Killed—in Paris.'

Chapter Two

Lizzy, I'm sure this book will inspire you. You've worked so hard to reach for your dream, always moving forwards, undaunted by what lay ahead. I know you'll make it.
All my love, darling girl. Dad X.

Tony felt a pang in his chest as he read the inscription. He was deeply moved to see evidence of a father's love declared so boldly and proudly in much the same way as his own father did. It made him feel guilty for the way he kept his grief to himself instead of seeking comfort from his family, but he had never before been brought to his knees that way. He ran his fingers over the frontispiece and felt good about securing the book for Lizzy. Now he understood why it was so important to her. His brow puckered as he read another inscription scrawled in pencil. The words were as bitter as the others were sweet.

Dream on, Lizzy! I heard about your boutique taking a nosedive. It's judgement on you. I told you one day you'd pay for what you did. I hope it was all worth it—Patrick.

What could she have done to deserve this? The person, who had blocked out his grief each morning and inspired him to deal with his pain, surely couldn't have done anything so bad. He closed the book reverently, and placed it on the bookcase to await the right opportunity to give it back to her.

'Have you seen what's happening?' Stella, his housekeeper, burst into the sitting room, bringing alarm and noise to his moment of peace and quiet. She pointed at the window, her breath jerked at her lungs as she spoke. 'Have you seen it?'

'What? Seen what?'

'Across the lake. Haven't you noticed it yet?'

'For goodness sake, Stella, what is it?'

'Blue, flashing lights—Police.'

'Good God!' Tony strode briskly along the forecourt at the Lakeside Centre. The daylight was beginning to fade, but it was very clear why the police had been called.

'Stand back, sir,' the policeman called to him, 'it isn't safe.'

'I'm Tony Franklyn. This is my property.' He looked around in disbelief. 'What the hell happened here?'

'It's too early to say, Mr Franklyn, but the tyre tracks indicate that somebody left the road, and crashed into the shop window. They obviously panicked and made off again.'

'It must have been a complete fluke to have hit it head on like this.' Tony's eyes scanned the small group of onlookers as a terrible grip of fear hit his stomach. 'My tenant… Lizzy Yardley, was she in the building?'

'No sir, she's not here.'

Jenny approached. 'Lizzy's gone to see her parents, Tony, she won't know about this yet. I'm waiting until she gets back.'

'We should head her off at the car park. Try and stop her seeing it.'

Jenny shook her head. 'We can't protect her. She won't hide from it. She'll face it head on.'

The muscle in the hollow of Tony's jaw twitched as his eyes darted about the scene. Then he caught sight of Lizzy. 'It's too late now anyway,' he said gravely, 'she's here.'

Lizzy was carrying a large bag in her hand and another one slung over her shoulder. They both slid from her rigid body and fell at her feet as she stared in disbelief. She moved slowly towards the tape barrier. This was a cruel nightmare; the kind you try to end by waking yourself up, but you can't. You find yourself screaming inside your head, *Wake up! Wake up and it'll all go away. You'll be in bed with a new day ahead and your new beginning intact.*

Dazed by the sight, she weaved through the group of onlookers lingering by the barrier. Her eyes fixed on the fractured, distorted timber of the window frame, the shards of glass strewn around where the car tyres had vandalised the paving stones, like ugly, black graffiti smeared on the forecourt. The beautiful wedding gown she'd designed especially to dress the window was now hauled over the debris. The shredded lace fluttered as it lay like an injured swan. Yet the beads that she had diligently sewn on the bodice, sparkled defiantly like tiny, blue beacons, as they reflected the flashing lights from the police car, every glint echoed an agonising pulse in her temples.

Still the voice screamed in her head, *wake up!* But there was no waking from this nightmare. She stood, like a ghost; her lungs could hardly draw breath.

'Lizzy, you don't want to see this,' Jenny said, almost weeping. 'Don't look. Please, Babe, come away.'

In a trance-like daze, Lizzy peered past her, as the early evening breeze sent silk flowers and ribbons waltzing around the forecourt.

'There's nothing you can do, Lizzy,' Tony said, resting his hand on her shoulder. 'The police will sort it out.'

She turned her pale face up to him, her eyes burned for the want of tears to cool them. 'Sort it out?' Her voice squeezed through her throat. 'Put it all back together by Saturday morning? Give me my time back?' She turned and grasped the tape. Tony's arm swiftly slid about her waist and restrained her.

'I have to get the dress,' she said.

Tony clamped both his arms around her. She felt her back against his solid frame as his voice spoke through her hair for the second time that day. 'Don't! It's full of glass. You'll cut your fingers.'

'I can't leave it there.'

'The police won't allow you near it. It's a crime scene.'

'Oh God!' she sighed.

'Nobody's hurt, but the driver took off.'

The policeman approached them. 'There's nothing you can do tonight, Miss Yardley. Is there anywhere you can stay?'

'Can't I go to my own place?'

'Not tonight, Miss.'

'But I could go round the back.'

'Sorry, Miss Yardley, we'll know more when we've looked at the CCTV. You need to get away from this now and let us do our job.'

'Come away, Lizzy,' Tony urged gently. He guided her back to where she had dropped her bags. Jenny followed.

'Can I stay with you, Jen?' Lizzy asked. 'A sofa will do.'

'That's not a good idea, Lizzy; you don't want to see all this through the window. Best if you get away from it for now.'

'I can drive you somewhere,' Tony said. 'Do you have family you could go to?'

'My parents are going away,' Lizzy told him, 'and they've let their house. I can go to the hotel.'

'It's full I'm afraid, they have a big wedding party this week. But I'm sure I can find—'

'The pub then.'

'I wouldn't advise that. You really shouldn't be alone. You can stay at Larchwood.'

Lizzy looked at him vaguely, 'Larchwood?'

'My home. It's a big house so you don't have to be concerned about your reputation, and you're in no fit state to argue. My housekeeper will take care of you.' He turned to Jenny as he scooped up Lizzy's bags. 'Would you call and tell Stella what's happening?'

Lizzy was in a daze when she followed Tony to his car, yet she was still aware that she had once again experienced the perfection of being close to him, his voice weaving through her hair. He held the door for her and she sat in the front seat. It smelled new. Sitting there made the situation even more unreal. They only met this morning, yet he behaved as if he had known her for much longer than that. Was that because she reminded him of his tragically lost love?

As he drove, his eyes were fixed firmly on the winding road. She could see that his jaw was tight, save for a small twitching muscle. He was angry. She could tell. Was that what happened to the love of his life? If it was a car crash then that horrendous sight, back there, would have been an agonising reminder. When he pulled her away from the danger, was he really pulling *her* from it? They left behind the streetlights and the road ahead looked darker.

Lizzy made an attempt to sound composed. 'That's your house by the lake?' she asked.

'Yes.'

'It seems a long way approached by the road.'

'It winds round the neighbouring farm before it leads to Larchwood. Are you all right?'

'I don't know. It still feels like a nightmare.'

They reached the wrought iron gates of the house. It was a long, winding drive. In the fading light she could just make out the parkland on either side. Everything seemed to be happening around her but she wasn't part of it. In an attempt to feel a sense of reality again she asked, 'Is this a family home, Mr Franklyn?'

'Tony,' he corrected. 'It came down from my Grandfather.'

'So you were raised here?'

'Not really. My father was. But he was the younger son, so my uncle inherited it. As a child I spent a lot of happy times here. Christmas was always at Larchwood. And I'd spend part of my school holidays here, along with two of my cousins.'

'Were you close to them?'

'Yes, we were boarders at the same school so that brought us closer together. They're on my mother's side—she has two brothers. We don't share the same name. They were known as the Gallier boys.'

'Sounds like a notorious gang.'

'Certainly does. We looked out for each other. We still do.'

The outside light of the house made it look white and the inside lighting glowed through the tall, rectangular, Georgian windows. 'It's beautiful,' Lizzy uttered.

'My uncle neglected it. Unlike my father, he wasn't a strong man. He gambled, drank, and then mortgaged the place far beyond his diminishing means. As soon as I was able, I paid off his debts and bought him out.'

'Like Heathcliff,' Lizzy commented flatly, amazed that her brain still functioned when her body felt so chilled and numb.

'Not quite as gothic or callous as he was. My uncle is very happy, living in a beautiful villa in France. I was glad to be able to get the restoration work done before it was too late.'

'So now Larchwood will be there for *your* children.'

Tony's hands momentarily clenched the steering wheel. 'I don't think about that.'

Lizzy knew she had touched a nerve and wished she had kept her questions to herself. It had been hard enough to make polite conversation. She vowed to watch her tongue in future. He was obviously still very raw from his grief. 'I'm sorry it's none of my business.'

'Not at all, it was a fair assumption. But it isn't that kind of property any longer. I'm not bound by traditions of heritage. I just couldn't see it gradually crumble into the ground.'

The car approached the main entrance and stopped sedately. A man, built like a bodyguard, greeted them on the gravelled forecourt. Tony addressed him as Joe, and asked him to put the car away.

Lizzy stood in the entrance hall and looked up at the white, bulbous balusters that skirted the curve of the landing around the hall. Through the haze of her shock, the shape pleased her. Her eyes climbed the blue-carpeted rise and tread of the sweeping staircase and then down the polished bannister to the patterns on the tiled floor.

A woman approached, slender and nimble as she walked. Her silver hair was pulled neatly into a knot at the back of her head.

'This is Stella,' Tony said, 'she'll show you to your suite. Perhaps you should see a doctor.'

'No, I'll be fine, thank you.'

'Then you must try and rest.'

'Please don't go to any trouble,' Lizzy protested politely.

'It's no trouble,' Stella said. 'It's all ready for you. Just follow me up the stairs.'

'I'll take your bags up,' Tony said. He climbed swiftly to the top, put them in the guest suite and met Lizzy by the door. 'I can't tell you how sorry I am that this has happened to you. If there's anything I can do, just ask.'

'Thank you.' She turned and followed Stella into the room. She gasped unashamedly at the sight of it.

'Yes,' Stella said. 'It's a lovely room isn't it? This suite's only just been done. You're the first to stay in it.' She made for the door. 'Make yourself at home. I'll bring up some tea.'

Lizzy looked around. The wardrobes and dressing tables, the colour of rich cream, stood in contrast to the sumptuous, gold curtains on the two windows. She crept across the luxurious carpet and ran her hands over the fabric of the drapes. She drew them to her face to inhale the wonderful scent of new, expensive silk. She checked out the bathroom, the size of her living room, it echoed the colour tones. The bath was huge, square and with two steps around it. The shower was in the opposite corner. She returned to the bedroom, lay on the biggest bed she had ever seen, and absent-mindedly caressed the quilted contours of the silk counterpane as her eyes traced the patterns on the pale, subtle wallpaper. She felt so alone. Her parents would be at the airport by now, and Carrie—goodness knows what Carrie was doing. Strangely enough the only person she really missed at that moment was somewhere in this enormous mansion with his heart breaking. And so was hers, but it was only a loss of time, energy and money. Eventually she could recover the loss. He would never be able to replace what he lost in Paris.

Chapter Three

Stella brought morning coffee into the sitting room where Tony was talking to DCI Brent, a middle-aged man, small, sharp witted and alert in contrast to his tired clothes. A younger woman, tall and smart with her blonde hair pinned up in a neat knot, accompanied him.

'Thanks, Stella,' Tony said steadily. 'I expect Lizzy had a bad night, and she really won't want to do this but would you go and call her? We need her here.'

'She was up early,' Stella answered. 'Out running at seven o'clock she was. Said she runs round the lake when she's angry and frustrated. It helps her focus on what she's got to do. She's being very brave, trying not to let it get to her.' She looked at DCI Brent. 'She's in the kitchen having some coffee. She knows you're here. She won't be long.'

Tony jumped to his feet when Lizzy walked in. She stood, quietly composed. He could see that she was putting up a fight, that her calm exterior was just a veneer to hide the turmoil that raged inside. He made eye contact with her and said, 'Was that wise?'

'What?'

'I'm sure you know what I'm getting at, Lizzy,' he said curtly. 'I expect you've been to take another look. Don't you realise how dangerous it is?' He was then sorry for his outburst, having failed to show the control she seemed to have. But he felt so angry on her behalf. 'Forgive me,' he said, 'that was uncalled for. I was just thinking of your safety.'

Although she had attempted to take control of her situation, Lizzy felt anger replacing the numbness of yesterday evening. For weeks her business recovery had been like a mountain ahead of her, challenging her to climb it alone. But, at least it had footholds and she could see around her. Now it was a huge, uncompromising brick wall and all she could see was chaos. She stood and stared at Tony, irritated by his comment. 'I jogged to the centre, walked past, had a good look, and then went straight to get my car. I didn't go in. I'm stubborn, not stupid.'

'I really am sorry, Lizzy,' Tony said, 'I didn't mean to insult you. This is a dreadful thing. I'm concerned about you.'

Lizzy raised her chin a notch. 'It's a mess. I expected the dresses to be lost, but my textile stock will be lost too, glass and dust all over everything.' She dragged in a breath, 'Probably some mindless idiot on his mobile instead of looking at the road.'

'Miss Yardley,' DCI Brent held up his ID and introduced himself. 'And this is DC Grant. We need to ask you a few questions.'

Lizzy scowled. 'I don't mind but I wasn't there to witness the accident.'

'I'm afraid it wasn't an accident.'

A bolt of shock hit Lizzy's insides. She swayed a little and saw Tony take a step towards her. 'It's OK, I'm fine.'

'Perhaps you should sit down,' Tony said.

'No thanks. I'm more comfortable standing; fight and flight and all that.'

DCI Brent nodded. 'Last night's incident was a deliberate ram-raid. An SUV smashed through your window, backed out and then made off the way it came.'

Lizzy stared at the detective. 'Why would anybody…?'

'I was hoping you could tell me, Miss Yardley.'

'Me? Why should I know?'

'Do you know anybody who might bear a grudge?'

Lizzy's brow knitted and she shook her head.

'No strange phone calls?' DCI Brent prompted. 'No letters or notes through the door?'

'No.'

'How about boyfriends?'

'I don't have one.'

'Ex-boyfriends?'

'A broken engagement but that was a year ago.'

'Have you had an affair with somebody else's partner or husband, somebody who might want to teach you a lesson?'

Lizzy's eyes almost popped. 'Certainly not!'

Then Tony spoke up and delivered a bolt from the blue. 'This ex-fiancé,' he said cautiously, 'was it Patrick?'

Lizzy couldn't believe it. Tony Franklyn seemed to have inside knowledge about her, but from where? She felt invaded. Her brow creased. 'Patrick? What do you know about Patrick?'

'Nothing.' He strode over to the shelves and retrieved her book. 'Except for his comments.'

'You bought it? Was that you who kept bidding against me?'

'Absolutely not,' Tony returned sharply. 'My bids were made after you dropped out. It seemed a pity for you to lose it again. Your father's inscription confirmed that it was yours, but obviously Patrick—whoever he is—felt compelled to add his comments before parting with it. Rather childish really as you might never have seen it.'

'Why would Patrick write in it?'

Tony spoke steadily in contrast to Lizzy's rising angst. 'I don't know, Lizzy, but he seemed angry enough to scribble a very bitter message. You have to consider the implications of this.'

'Implications?'

'Can I see that, Mr Franklyn?' DCI Brent interjected. He opened the book and scanned his eyes down the two messages. 'Why did you break up?'

'What does that have to do with all this?'

'We have to consider every angle.'

'He issued an ultimatum.' Lizzy was becoming increasingly annoyed by the two men and their theories. 'You know the kind of attitude. Either you see things my way, or it's over. I didn't see his point of view, so I walked out of the relationship. That's how I lost the book.'

'An ultimatum? About what?'

Lizzy drew a sharp breath. If this detective dug any deeper he'd find out. She couldn't bear that. She felt fidgety and her heart raced making it difficult to breathe steadily. 'Why does that matter?'

DCI Brent then read the message aloud.

Lizzy's throat tightened. She was lost for words. How could she stand there and tell them what Patrick was talking about? She looked at Tony. He was still very serious and seemed uneasy. How would he look if she told them the truth? What if he shared Patrick's warped opinion? It shouldn't matter, but it did. Much to her confusion, it mattered a great deal.

DCI Brent then asked, 'What did he mean by, *I told you one day you'd pay for what you did?*'

'I...' Patrick's words resounded in Lizzy's head. They were at his house, one rainy weekend last year. She had made a momentous decision and wanted to tell him. She was happy about it, but her heart sank when she saw the bitter twist in his face.

'You can't be serious,' he said arrogantly as he peered over his book.

'Of course I'm serious. That's why I'm telling you about it.'

'Without consulting me first?'

Lizzy was astounded. 'Consulting? It's not your decision it's mine. I don't need your permission. It won't affect you at all.'

'Of course it affects me and if you go through with this ridiculous idea...'

'Go on, Patrick, tell me.'

'It'll finish us because what you're planning is...' he struggled for a word, not normally a problem for him. 'It's just not right.'

'Don't talk nonsense, Patrick. I've made up my mind. It's going to happen whatever you think.'

'I can't allow it.'

'Excuse me?'

'For goodness sake Lizzy, don't be such a pushover.'

'I'm not being a pushover, it was *my* idea. It's the right thing to do.'

'The idea's bad enough, but when will you find the time? What about your business?'

'I'll do whatever it takes.' She stared at him, suddenly seeing him in a clear light. 'Well, Patrick,' she said coldly, 'if that's your best shot at moral support, I'll do without it.'

'Miss Yardley?' DCI Brent interrupted her thoughts.

'I'm sorry? What did you say?'

'What was it that rattled Patrick's cage?'

'It might have been because I called him a misogynistic, bigoted nerd, as I walked out of his life.'

A chuckle escaped DC Grant's throat. DCI Brent swiftly turned on her. 'There's no need to giggle every time somebody chalks *one-up-for-the-girls.*'

'Sorry, sir.'

DCI Brent was like a terrier, digging and sniffing out clues. 'Do you know where he lives now?'

Suddenly his question hit her like a flash of lightning. He was bent on questioning Patrick. They would ask him what the message meant, and his bitter opinion would gush from his mouth like water from a gargoyle in a rainstorm. She felt cornered. What was hers to know and keep to herself would be bandied about and seen totally out of context.

Tony spoke up. 'Lizzy, I realise that this is upsetting for you but it's important to get to the bottom of it. Somebody wants to hurt you.'

'Not Patrick, for goodness sake.' She laughed nervously at the idea. 'He wouldn't go near an SUV, he thinks they're a drain on resources. I've known him since college. If he wanted to hurt me he'd send a virus to my computer or something.'

'Did you live with him for long?' Tony asked.

'I didn't live with him at all.'

'Then you might not know him as well as you think. A man can act out of character when a woman walks out on him,' Tony reasoned. 'You'd be surprised.'

Lizzy's shock and disappointment turned to anger. She glared at Tony, and then at the detective. 'Oh, so you think he's been stewing in all this anger for a year and now he's decided that SUVs aren't going to ruin the planet after all, so he might as well drive one through my window? This situation is bad enough for me without being interrogated like this.'

'Lizzy, you're not being—'

Lizzy cut off Tony's attempts to calm the situation. 'My God, I'm glad I haven't committed an offence. I can't imagine what would happen if I did.'

Tony moved to her side and rested a hand on her shoulder. 'For goodness sake, you're the victim of a very serious crime.'

'Victim? I've no intention of being a victim. And I can't afford the time to stand here discussing the ridiculous idea that Patrick did it. You're mistaken.'

'That's for us to decide,' DCI Brent returned gravely.

Lizzy fixed her eyes on Tony. 'Do you have an iPad?'

'Sure,' Tony answered quietly, and located the tablet on the occasional table.

Lizzy ran her fingers briskly over the screen, and then showed it to DCI Brent. 'I'll show you how scary Patrick is. This is his website. He sells envelopes, pens, note pads, paperclips and packaging.' She lowered her voice to a theatrical whisper. 'And the really dodgy product—refilled ink cartridges. So when you need a new notepad, he's your man.' She thrust the iPad back at Tony. 'Go get him before he clubs somebody over the head with a packet of envelopes. Can I go now? I promise not to leave town.'

DCI Brent didn't comment further, he just nodded and said, 'Thank you for your time, Miss Yardley.' It was almost as if he felt that he'd solved the case already.

Lizzy left the room.

Tony followed her out. He spoke quietly and decisively. 'I need to talk to you.'

'You've got what you wanted—a suspect. What more do you want? If you need me I'll be staying at the pub.'

'No, Lizzy,' Tony protested, taking her hands in his. 'This man has to be stopped.'

'Patrick, you mean?'

'Whoever did it might not be finished. We don't know what else they're capable of or when they'll strike again. I want you to be safe. I have staff here and security people. This is the safest place for you.'

Lizzy felt overpowered by his strength and his resolve to protect her. She wanted to hold on to her anger, it was her only comfort, but his hands gripped hers draining her of her will to face this alone. She was silent for a moment and then she said, 'I just want to get on with my work.'

'You need to recover first.'

'I've got six months to rescue my business—no—I *had* six months. Now I have five. By the time I re-stock I'll have three. Three months to do what was already impossible with six.'

Tony smiled and squeezed her fingers. 'Give me half an hour to finish up with our visitors, and I'll show you around. We can talk and come up with a plan. There's room for you to work here.'

'It's not your problem, Mr Franklyn.'

'It's Tony, and it *is* my problem. I'm your landlord. We'll work something out. You're doing brilliantly. Many women would be a total wreck.'

A tear escaped down Lizzy's face. 'God knows I'm trying not to be.'

Tony watched her walk away and wondered what he could do to make this go away for her. She had blotted out his pain, but he didn't know how he could do the same for her. Money? Money's easy; it's the heartsickness from the deferred hope that's difficult.

He returned to the sitting room. 'She's being extremely brave,' he said to the detectives.

'She's a feisty one, that's for sure,' DCI Brent said.

'She shouldn't be put under any more pressure. She's got enough to worry about.'

'But she's hiding something.'

'Why do you say that?'

'Just a gut feeling, Mr Franklyn. She didn't want to discuss the real reason for the breakup?'

'Because it's private, sir,' DC Grant spoke up. 'In the same situation I wouldn't have told you either.'

'Nobody's driven an SUV through your front door, have they DC Grant?'

'I *still* wouldn't have told you, sir.'

DCI Brent made for the door. 'She's probably defending him. She's hiding something, I know it.'

Chapter Four

A vintage hat, bought at the recent auction, delivered Lizzy from the jaws of gloom over that first weekend. Stella had bought it to wear on her day out, thinking that it would measure up to the parade of hats at the races. However, it emerged from its box like a sad old movie star in great need of a face lift. Stella was crestfallen when she showed Lizzy. As nothing galvanised Lizzy more than a troubled person who needed comfort she immediately offered to restore it.

'I can't take up your time,' Stella insisted. 'I'll look for another one.'

'But you've obviously set your heart on this one,' Lizzy said.

'Yes, but…' she shrugged and put the hat on the kitchen table.

'I've nothing else to do, Stella. Today was going to be my grand opening. This would help keep my mind off it.'

****

On Monday morning Tony dashed off somewhere with a great sense of urgency, not stopping to explain. Lizzy assumed that he was going to his work—somewhere in the business world. She felt bereft as she watched him from one of the kitchen windows. He strode across the lawn to a waiting helicopter. It rose like a noisy dragonfly into the June sky. As far as Lizzy was concerned it was a definite *goodbye.* It wasn't easy, in fact it hurt, but she was determined to get over this ridiculous crush before she saw him again. It had been a new experience for her. Until now any talk of powerful, physical attraction or chemistry, left her wondering what all the fuss was about.

'Well thank goodness for that,' Stella sighed. 'He's starting to get back to normal.'

'Going to work in a helicopter is normal?' Lizzy asked.

'Sometimes, if he's in a hurry, he hires one just to take him to the airfield where he keeps his plane.'

'I can't imagine hiring a helicopter let alone owning a plane.'

'He's a lovely man, like his father, but his life isn't like ours, Lizzy. People like us work close to home and we can't imagine his responsibilities, the pressure or the distance he travels.'

'Do you think he's getting over his bereavement now?'

'He's mending. His work should help but it'll crop up again. Grief does that, and usually when you least expect it. You might find a cinema ticket in your pocket or a photo in a drawer, and back it comes.'

Lizzy sensed that Stella knew what she was talking about and decided to change the subject. 'Can I use the kitchen table while Tony's away? I'd like to do some new sketches. I'm going to need something to put on the shelves—help me catch up.'

'Course you can.' She smiled. 'Tony loves that table. Sixteen feet of elm and it's been standing there since the nineteenth century. The refurbishments were done around it.'

Lizzy smiled at the thought of it being a busy workstation for a number of mob-capped kitchen maids, beating batters, kneading dough, gossiping about the members of the household. Now it would serve as her temporary studio.

'Spread yourself out,' Stella said, 'Tony's gone for the rest of the week.'

Working on the hat had unlocked a tidal wave of inspiration as if to cock a snook at Lizzy's dilemma. New ideas tumbled onto her sketching paper like silky petals through the air. It seemed that all the responsibility of making stock to fill the shelves and rails in the boutique, was lifted and her natural creativity breathed once again. A whole new range of fabulous lingerie, a sensational array of underwear in a rainbow of colours, filled her mind. She dreamed up delicious, delicate things to tempt women who wanted to look special, for their husbands, lovers or simply just because they loved beautiful underwear. She could see the products in her mind's eye, enveloped in soft, pastel coloured tissue paper and packaged in fine gift boxes or carriers; maybe even carried home on Saint Valentine's Day, anniversaries, birthdays. She had no idea why this host of alluring products had suddenly come into her head, but it charged her enthusiasm for getting back to work and by Wednesday, she even felt that she was cured of her infatuation.

****

'Lizzy.' Stella stood in the kitchen, holding up two outfits on hangers—one in each hand. 'Which one will go with the hat?'

Lizzy looked up from her sea of sketch paper. 'The blue, I think, but it might be too hot.'

Stella sighed, her shoulders dropped. 'You're being very polite, come on, be honest.'

Lizzy bit her lip and then admitted that neither of them was suitable.

'The hat's so lovely. It deserves a new outfit,' Stella said, 'but I haven't got time to go to Bowbury. It's Wednesday already. I've only got a couple more days.'

'Can't you go now?'

'I've got to get the jam strawberries. Bryn said that if I don't deal with them soon they'll be over.'

'Bryn?'

'The gardener.'

'I can do that.'

'I like to go to the gardens and collect them. Then I have to prepare them.'

'I wouldn't attempt to make the jam but I could collect the strawberries and prepare them. They won't perish in the fridge.'

'But you're a guest.' She frowned and shook her head. 'No, no, Tony won't like it.'

'Tony's not here, is he? By the time he comes home it'll all be over. For goodness sake let me do something to earn my keep.'

Stella's eyes lit up. 'I suppose I could do the jam this evening. There's only the two of us for dinner and it would be nice to get something new. I'm sure all my friends have, they've talked about this trip for so long.'

Lizzy laughed. 'Well you've got to keep up appearances. Go! Get yourself a fabulous outfit.'

'If you're sure. Joe's on duty if you need him. Tony's asked him to take care of you.'

Lizzy smiled. 'Well, thank God for Mr Darcy, on his big white horse.'

'You've got a wicked tongue on you, Lizzy Yardley,' Stella laughed.

'I know it. Everybody reminds me.'

'I feel wicked, too,' Stella said, 'going off shopping like this. My daybook is by the phone. There's a list of numbers. And I keep that answer machine switched on in case Tony rings. I'm a bit of a Luddite, I know, but I prefer my old answer machine to voice mail. I'll see you later then.'

Lizzy waved her off and then walked round to the gardens where she was presented with a huge, old fashioned shopping basket full of strawberries—small ones.

'Likes them like that for jam,' Bryn told her.

'They're wonderful.'

Bryn narrowed his eyes. 'Don't you go eating them, I've counted them.'

Lizzy smiled at his dry wit. 'I'm sure you have.'

'I heard about that fracas with your shop. Sorry about that—nasty thing to do.'

'Thank you.' She looked around and then back at Bryn. 'It's lovely here, isn't it?'

'You like it?'

'Oh yes. I like it very much.'

Bryn touched his cap. 'I'll get on then.'

Lizzy felt like *Little Red Riding Hood,* going to Grandma's house, as she strolled back. She crossed the old, cobbled yard leading to the back entrance hall. As she pushed open the heavy, studded door she heard a faint, haunting sound… music. A woman's voice drifted illusively through the air and along the echoing passages of below-stairs. Each step moved Lizzy closer to the sound, affording her more clarity and the recognition of the aria that her grandmother used to play in the hope that her granddaughter might learn to appreciate opera as much as she did.

At the kitchen doorway the full impact of the famous soprano hit her senses, but when she peered round the door she almost dropped the basket. Her heart pounded. Her lungs fluttered.

Tony stood, barefoot and jaw-droppingly gorgeous, even though he was dressed-down in jeans and a well-worn sweatshirt. His hair fell casually over his forehead. Eyes closed, his hands rested on the light oak worktop, his chest rose and fell slowly as he breathed in the sensuous caresses of the voice. This was so private, so utterly for *his* soul only. Was he recalling a special moment at the opera—in Paris perhaps—when he sat with the love of his life and watched her tears rolling down her cheeks? Did his heart swell at the sight of her emotion? Was he thinking of her now?

Lizzy quickly stepped back out of the kitchen and leaned against the wall, breathless and shaken to have intruded on his precious memory. A pang of jealousy made her realise that her expectation of being free of his magnetism was futile.

When the aria ended, there was a silence so tangible that it ran down Lizzy's back like a cool breeze.

The soprano didn't sing again. The only music to be heard was from the metronomic sounds of steam hissing and spitting into the coffee cone.

She was reluctant to go in because the kitchen was a kind of bolthole for Tony, and when he was home he spent much of his time there. A throwback from his childhood visits, he had told her, when the stone fireplace burned huge logs on cold, winter days and made him feel safe and warm.

She tiptoed a few more paces back along the corridor.

Tony sensed that somebody was approaching. When he looked up he saw Lizzy in the doorway. 'There you are.'

'I didn't know you were home. I thought you were staying on until the end of the week.'

'Change of plan,' he said casually, 'got in late last night—well morning really.' His eyes lingered on her, standing there with a huge basket of strawberries hanging from the crook of her arm, her face flushed, her hair falling over her shoulders. Each day that passed, his self-control became more challenged. He no longer saw his mythical guardian angel by the lake, he saw a woman who heated his blood until his body burned to hold her, and it burned all the more knowing that he shouldn't flirt with her. Other women had never given him cause for concern. He dated them, bought them expensive gifts, had fun, then they parted company. Lizzy wasn't other women—she was different.

He gave his over active imagination a cold shower. You're her landlord, for God's sake. You can't just play with her, and then pack her off back to her boutique. 'Clearly it's the jam season,' he said with a cool veneer over his heated thoughts.

'I look ridiculous don't I? I'm making myself useful.'

A frown fixed on Tony's brow. 'You don't have to do anything in the house. You're a guest.'

'Stella needed to go shopping so I said I'd help.'

'Stella can go shopping whenever she likes. You don't have to pick up the slack.' He took the basket from her and put it on the worktop. 'I need to talk to you. Shall we sit down?'

Lizzy, mindful of the fact that she was a guest, decided to co-operate. She made for the table. 'I'll move my stuff.'

'No need. We'll sit in the window seat. I talked to Stella on the phone yesterday,' he said. 'She told me about the hat.'

'You sound like my maths teacher complaining about my homework. What's wrong with the hat?'

'Nothing, she's delighted with it.'

Lizzy sat down. '*You* don't sound too pleased though.'

'It's not my place to be pleased or otherwise.' Tony sat down, stared at her a moment and then added, 'But you shouldn't do these things as a favour.'

'Why not? I enjoyed doing it. It helped me fill my day.'

'It should have helped you fill your pockets.'

'I can't take money from Stella,' Lizzy protested.

'Stella doesn't work for nothing. Why should you?'

Lizzy was quiet for a moment. He seemed so close, even though he was at the other end of the seat. She became distracted by the low neckline of his sweatshirt that afforded her a view of the tantalising hollow where his collarbones met, and allowed her to see how his throat moved when he spoke. She was caught between her displeasure in his attitude and her intoxicating attraction. But she dragged her eyes from him and said, 'It was good to have some work in my hands.'

'You have tenacity for your work, Lizzy, but you have little regard for your business?'

Lizzy was astounded. Guest or no guest, she wasn't going to be treated like a fool. 'You're being very pushy. None of this was my fault. Where are you going with this?'

'Your ex described your business as *taking a nosedive*, and—'

'I know what he wrote,' Lizzy snapped. Her insides twisted. Until a few days ago Patrick was just a memory, now the very thought of him made her anxious. 'Why is it that a man who never attracted anybody's attention in his life, is suddenly villain of the month? I thought you wanted to discuss something relevant, not Patrick's bit of juvenile scribble.'

'It *is* relevant,' Tony insisted. 'How long were you in business?'

'Three years.'

'Then it doesn't make sense. The footfall, in Bowbury, was good last year.'

'And…?'

'So what happened?' The muscle in his jaw twitched. 'You need to analyse it so that it doesn't happen to you again.'

'There's no mystery. It wasn't the public footfall that was wanting—it was mine.'

'Please don't be offended.' Tony's voice softened and he reached his hand to where hers rested on the seat. 'I'm not criticising you, but this recovery might not be as easy as you think. Your parents are miles away. You said your sister's away, too. It's important that you don't feel you have to face all this alone.'

Lizzy was uneasy. She wanted to get right away from this subject, but the sound of Tony's voice and the touch of his hand began to weaken her willpower. He was wise and protective; he could take away this anxiety about the past. All she had to do was tell him. Seize the moment and the secret would be out in the open instead of burning inside her. He was silent, as if he was giving her time to speak, but his eyes seemed to draw the words from her.

'I… I had…' She faltered.

Tony's fingers tightened around her hand.

Lizzy drew a steadying breath. Get out of this one, she told herself. Carrie believes you're strong so where's that strength now? She looked straight at him and managed to steady her voice. 'I had a deal with my sister. She's older than me, but she needed my help and support. I know it was a long time to give her—a whole year, but I couldn't... The bottom line is that I couldn't stand her pain.'

'I'm sorry I shouldn't have pressed you on that.'

'It's over now. She's fine. But it was supposed to be my turn, she was going to help me, but now she's off the radar.' She was desperate to rest her head on that powerful shoulder and tell him all about it, the anguish, the tears, and the stress. How her loyalty should have been celebrated, but Patrick had broken her heart by making it seem ugly. She couldn't have this man who sat with her now; she knew that. She didn't belong here in his world, she was only visiting. He would never arrive home, desperate to find her so he could hold her and kiss her. She would never know the pleasure of being in his arms through the night. But that didn't change how she felt and if he saw it all in the same distorted way as Patrick, when his eyes had chilled her to the core, made her feel tainted, it would be agony. She mentally shook herself, realising that Tony was like a beautiful Trojan horse, stealing through her defences to conquer her secrecy.

She retrieved her will power. Spoke swiftly and positively. 'I was taking too much time off. I decided to close it down until I was free to get back to it. It was a reckless move, but it was mine to make. It's as simple as that.'

'Simple?' Tony challenged. 'You can't keep making major sacrifices and doing freebies.' He gestured to her sketches spread over the table. 'You've started to work again. I don't know about designing clothes but I know about designing in other areas of manufacture. *That* is a lot of excellent work, but you abandoned it to fetch a basket of bloody strawberries. If you continue this way the numbers just won't crunch in your favour.'

Lizzy felt cornered, and flew at him with the first thing that entered her head. 'Are you afraid I won't make the rent?'

'Don't be ridiculous. I don't care about the damned rent and *you* know it. That comment was insulting to *you* as well as me.'

'All I did was put my work on hold for half an hour to help Stella.'

'But you put your business on hold for a whole year to help your sister. You'll be chasing your dream around in circles for the rest of your life.'

Lizzy was stunned for a moment then she glared at him. 'I slogged all day and well into the night to stock that boutique. You understand how to build things so let me put this into nuts and bolts terms. I processed over a hundred metres of silk, eighty metres of satin, five hundred of lace, four hundred glass beads, thirty five zip fasteners, numerous reels of cotton and thread. So tell me, Tony,' she challenged, her eyes burning angrily into his, 'where, in the Boston Matrix, does it say that some mindless vandal is going to trash your dream and drag it across the ground?' Suddenly all her composure, her tolerance snapped. She sprang to her feet and moved away from him. 'When are you going to realise that it's my shop that needs fixing—not me?'

'I'm not trying to fix you or change your misplaced generosity.'

'And what about *your* generosity?'

'I can afford mine.'

'Then do me a favour and billet me at the hotel.'

'There won't be any room for weeks. It's booked up with weddings and conferences.'

'Well if you think I'm going to settle for this grace and favour thing, you can think again.'

'Don't be such a damned snob, Lizzy. You don't just need somewhere to live; you need to work. You've demonstrated that clearly enough. I'm your landlord. I'm supposed to provide you with that.'

'Don't bind yourself in honour on my account. I'll stay at the pub. I just want to work.'

'And you think you can process all those raw materials at the pub, with the noise coming through the mediaeval floorboards? You think you can lock up your problems inside you and forge ahead?'

'Oh, and I suppose you talk about your troubles all the time.' She stopped suddenly, closed her eyes and said, 'Oh God! Please tell me I didn't say that. I'm so sorry…'

There was a silence for a few moments and then suddenly Lizzy was breathing against his shoulder, drinking in the scent of him; not the way it was when he broke her fall in the hotel; the new clothes and expensive aftershave. This was the intoxicating scent of his flesh. It heated her blood and sent it coursing through her veins. Tony's arms were firmly locked around her shoulders. Her face touched his jaw and she expelled a shuddering gasp against his cheek.

'Hold on, Lizzy,' Tony breathed against her hair. 'You'll make it, just hold on.'

She shivered sensually, from her head down to her toes, when she realised that his fabulous neck was within reach of her mouth. She ached to press her lips to it. The world seemed to stop as their mouths hovered tantalizing close and the puckish chemistry danced about them, urging them to kiss. It seemed that they would, but Tony released her. The chemistry continued to burn fiercely inside her, like a raging crucible, and for the first time she knew the excitement and longing of being aroused by a powerful lover.

'That was brutal of me,' Tony said softly. 'Forgive me, I didn't mean to upset you.'

'When I get stressed I'm prone to feisty outbursts and my mouth argues by itself.'

'I've noticed, but no harm done. If you'll excuse me I must get changed. I have meetings at the hotel.'

'I'm seeing Jenny there this afternoon. Wednesday's our tea and cake day. But if it's as busy as you say perhaps we won't get a table.'

'Of course you will. Ask for Daniel. Excuse me.'

Now Lizzy knew that the sweet guerdon of love-play really did exist. And she wanted it—she wanted it with him.

****

Jenny ceremoniously sunk her fork into her chocolate fudge cake. 'He does,' she said firmly.

'Rubbish!'

'Lizzy, he fancies you,' Jenny insisted. 'I saw him that night when—well, you know.'

'Yes I know,' Lizzy said steadily. 'He was just being protective.'

'So were the police,' Jenny argued, 'but they didn't hold you like he did. Arms wrapped round you, pulling you up against him, his cheek against your head. A man doesn't hold a woman like that if he's just being protective.'

'Maybe he does—if she reminds him of somebody.'

'Who?' Jenny's eyes rounded in surprise. 'The mystery lover?'

'If it's her then there can't be many similarities between us. I only ever had one serious boyfriend. He sells envelopes and he never went to work in a helicopter. Whether I want him or not, I'm nowhere near Tony's league.'

'Yea right! He wouldn't fancy a designer with a to-die-for body, gorgeous legs and sumptuous hair?'

'I'm not someone you date in Paris. I'm a small-town girl with a small-town business.'

'Do you want him?'

'I wish I could deny it but I can't. We had a really heated discussion this morning. I got upset and he gave me a hug. I wanted more. I wanted him to kiss me. To tell you the truth I thought he was going to. But it didn't happen.'

'You must've been gutted,' Jenny said. 'You should've helped it along a bit. He made the first move. Invited you for coffee the first time you met.'

'I almost fell into a jardinière. He was being polite.'

'Yea—right.'

'It was just a moment in time. I would have been completely out of my depth. You grow up believing that sighing, erotic nights between the sheets are romantic or even fun, but I can't actually say that I ever experienced any of those things.' She looked down for a moment and remembered how easily she sank into Tony's arms when he was comforting her, the intensity of her attraction toward him, the feel of that old sweatshirt against her face as she leaned against his chest. Her hands began to tremble. She put down her fork and leaned across the table. 'This morning,' she whispered, 'something woke up inside me and it all seemed possible.'

'Now you're wondering what he's like in bed.'

'All that energy and strength—those shoulders...' She stopped for a moment and then diverted her line of thought, 'For goodness sake, I'm being so naive.'

'So you want him to carry you off to bed, what's wrong with that?'

'The thought of being with such a successful man, somebody so genuinely strong and...' She sighed, 'I can't even cope with it in conversation. Besides, I have a mission in life and it doesn't involve spontaneous flings with every eligible hunk I bump into. I'm very attracted to him. Who wouldn't be? But I'll get over it. It's all going to stop right here and now.' She frowned. 'Don't look at me like that. Everybody has a life plan.'

'Yes,' Jenny agreed, 'but yours was carved in stone and brought down, from Mount Sinai, on your tenth birthday.' She dealt with her last chunk of cake and then said, 'Haven't you ever experienced these feelings before?'

'No—not like that.'

'Wow! Watch this space. You made a huge leap from Postman Pat and his envelopes to the handsome squire in the big house.' She leaned closer to Lizzy. 'What's the matter? Why are you so afraid of being attracted to Tony?'

Lizzy shrugged. 'Maybe at another time I'd risk getting my heart broken, but at the moment I can't. My business has got to come first.'

'But everybody takes that chance.'

'With my baggage there's a greater risk.'

'Nobody tells their secrets unless they have to. You can spend time with a guy, enjoy his company, flirt, kiss or even sleep with him without telling him about your skeletons. You only need to fess up if it gets serious. Besides he wouldn't care about that stuff you call baggage.'

'Patrick couldn't deal with it. He made me feel demoralised. What if Tony did that?'

'Then get over it, because you'll know he doesn't love you enough. I mean, look at me. I'm blunt and sometimes downright insulting, but Will loves me. A man who really loves you will accept who you are—baggage an' all.'

'You make it sound so straight-forward.'

'No, Lizzy, it's a minefield but we all go through it. I've been blown to pieces a couple of times, but sooner or later you make it to the other side.'

'I'll remember that in the future. We'd better get back. You've got flowers to arrange, and I've got to find somewhere else to work. Tony's home and I can't design underwear with *him* looking over my shoulder.'

'You design underwear?'

'I do now.'

Jenny sighed. 'Designer lingerie…'

'I'll make some for you as soon as I'm up and running again.' She raised a hand to the waiter for the bill.

'It's taken care of, Miss Yardley,' he said discreetly.

'What do you mean?'

'Mr Franklyn dealt with it.'

Jenny groaned. 'And here's me drinking tea. We should have had wine.'

Lizzy wasn't so pleased about Tony seizing her prerogative to pick up the tab. She was almost broke, ruined even, but she could buy a cup of tea and a cake.

When they arrived at Lizzy's car, there was a note behind the windscreen wiper. Lizzy snatched it out. 'It's probably a flyer or something.'

'I expect the scouts have got a jumble sale.'

Lizzy read it out loud. '*Forty plus and rising. Find him Lizzy Yardley and tell him to sort it.*'

'What on earth does that mean?'

'It's a prank,' Lizzy said. She felt very nervous about it. It was an invasion of her privacy at the very least. She didn't want to trouble Jenny, so she slipped it in her bag. 'It's just some kids playing *the wag* and messing about.'

Jenny looked around the car park. 'Nobody else has got one. And it's got your name on it.'

'So has my car. That's probably why they picked it out.'
'Oh yes, course—kids.'

Chapter Five

The next morning Lizzy woke and looked out of her window. The lake looked so beautiful in the early morning light. She could see that it was going to be a scorching day. The garden was urging her to forget sketching. To be out there among nature's superior designs—fabulous colours, shapes and textures.

She showered and dressed in jeans and a simple top, and with her camera slung around her neck, she went out into the garden.

The sounds of summer dawdled in the balmy stillness; birds, bees and the distant droning of a lone tractor. The sky was a brilliant blue, save for a few feckless wisps of white cloud. She joined the butterflies and insects, as they visited the flowers and shrubs, oblivious of time.

When she passed by the swimming pool the glass, sliding doors had been pulled aside, exposing one side of it to the open air. The sun was still fairly low in the sky. It painted the tiles, turning the pale, sandy tint into a rich gold. The water was still. She smiled at the parody right there before her eyes. 'Hockney,' she said to herself, and moved closer to capture it.

As she lined up the shot, Tony came out from the adjoining gym. A pair of sweat pants clung perilously low to his hips; not enough to reveal anything intimate but enough to suggest they might. He was naked right down to his taut abdomen as he raised a bottle of water to his lips.

Lizzy aimed the camera and zoomed in and before she could question the morality of invading his privacy this way, she had captured the image; the beads of perspiration that rolled down his temples onto his jaw and then down his fabulous neck as he raised his chin to drink the water, allowing drops of it to merge with the sweat. A fine patch of chest-hair between his wet, tanned pectoral muscles glistened in the amber light. This was so unlike Tony, the ruggedness, the dishevelled hair and the careless way he was dressed—half dressed. The aristocratic bearing and the sophistication had all been cast away to reveal a tantalisingly raw male, untouched by the disciplines and restraints of his self-imposed rules and boundaries.

Lizzy had never seen him so primitive. She tried to look away, knowing that he would be uncomfortable if he thought he could be seen. But she was riveted. Seeing with the eye of an artist yet feeling with the body of a lover—one feasted while the other hungered. Her erogenous zones throbbed fiercely, taunting, mocking her belief that she was in control of her physical reactions, while the real master of her body stood by the pool, oblivious of his seduction. She felt the grip of reality; what then could he do if he really tried?

She lingered, a fly on an invisible wall, totally captivated as he stretched his arms above his head, shook them down by his sides and then turned about. The muscles on his back flexed, taunting her as if they knew she couldn't touch them.

But one person—his lost lover—would have felt free to gaze, call out, go to him and hold him close, feel those powerful arms around her and breathe in the scent of his flesh. Lizzy wasn't his lover, she was just a host to bring him faint, comforting echoes of nostalgia because she reminded him of her.

Lizzy retreated behind the shrubs and looked at the picture on her camera screen. It thrilled her to see it, not only because of Tony, but it was a fabulous photograph. She sighed, fighting the decision to delete it, knowing that she shouldn't have taken it. He thought he was alone; it's an intrusion. But then she reasoned that if she waited for him to leave, that incredible light would be gone and the pool would be just a pool and not an echo of a work of art.

She glanced back at him. He had discarded his sweat pants and stood like a supreme athlete, in ancient Greece, dressed in little more than a mantel of golden light. He was so beautiful. He was the masterpiece. As he dived into the water, Lizzy's vow to resist him deserted her like a fickle companion. It was no longer a matter of prevention but a definite case of cure. She wanted him but told herself that she couldn't have him. You can't afford a broken heart.

****

Tony had spent a gruelling morning trying to get one step ahead of a day that had begun badly. Being a practical, successful man, he was shocked to find that such a simple thing as seeing a memento in his bedside drawer would cause the grief to return and grip his insides like a clawed vice. He reasoned that vigorous, physical activity was the answer, but working out in his gym and swimming until he could hardly breathe had debunked his theory. When he tried to lose himself in work he was bad tempered with people on the 'phone.

Eventually he gave up trying and took his battle-weary soul to the kitchen. He was half way through a cup of coffee when he realised that Stella had been talking to him.

'Sorry, what was that?'

'The decorators have finished in the reading room. They want you to check it.'

'I'll go along in a minute.' He glanced around. 'I thought Lizzy had taken to working at this table.'

'Only when you're not here.'

'Why's that?'

'She's designing a new range of underwear.'

'And?'

'She feels a bit self-conscious about it when you're here.'

Tony scowled. 'The consumer world doesn't hide underwear from anybody, neither will Lizzy when she stocks her boutique with it. I can't imagine why she's afraid of me seeing what she's doing. Do you think she'd like to work in the reading room instead?'

'I'm sure she would. She could do her sketches but she couldn't actually make anything in there.'

'What does she need for that?'

'Whatever she had at the shop. Cutting table, sewing table, storage, good lighting…'

'That must have been quite a big investment for her.'

'She can claim for most of it. It's the lost time that's hit her hardest.'

'She won't have any figures yet, to claim loss of earnings either. No wonder she's anxious to get on.' He moved from the table. 'I'll go and take a look at the decorators' handy work. If she turns up in the next few minutes, would you ask her to come and find me? We'll sort something out.'

The idea of helping Lizzy solve her problems was a more effective antidote to his state of mind. Although he was still smarting, his stride was positive as he walked to the reading room—Grandma Franklyn's holy of holies.

It seemed that Uncle had retained some respect for his mother and had resisted the temptation to sell the figurines that stood on the mantelpiece over the little white fireplace and the fine, delicate watercolours that she loved.

The room, now freshly painted with sanded floorboards and new rugs, took him by surprise. He had expected the familiar redolence of the old days. The smell of the books, the lingering tang of floor polish that, layer upon layer, had been worked into the wood for generations.

Grandma often allowed him to sit in one of the winged chairs, by the fireside, as long as he read a book. Or he could stretch out on the floor with his chin resting on his folded arms, the comforting scent of the old rug in his nostrils. When he was older he would read to her—her favourite poems or passages from a much-loved book. He leaned to smell the yellow roses on the desk. That, at least, hadn't changed.

'Tony?' Lizzy called softly from the open doorway.

As he turned, his blood burst through his veins. A surge of erotic intensity clashed head-on with the anger that had tormented him all morning. He stretched his frame to its full height and drew a long breath. 'Lizzy, I was hoping you'd find me.'

Lizzy hesitated. Considering that he hoped she'd turn up he looked very surprised to see her. She was reluctant to break his moment of nostalgia particularly as this was the second time today she had intruded on his privacy. 'Am I interrupting?'

'No, of course not. Come on in.'

'Stella said you were looking for me.' She went to the flowers and smelled them. 'Lovely! They bring life into a room, don't you think?'

'They certainly do.'

Lizzy tilted her head and her brow tweaked momentarily. 'Are you all right?'

He hesitated a moment then smiled. 'Yes, I'm fine.'

Lizzy couldn't help thinking that he was putting on a brave face, but she nodded and said no more about it—except to herself.

How much longer will he suffer? Will he never get over this tragedy? Why does *my* heart ache just because *he* hurts? Whoever you are, you must have been an incredible woman to bring him to his knees this way.

She was anxious to find something to prompt more small talk and her eyes scanned the bookcase on the end wall and then the French window that led to a small, paved garden.

'This room...' she sighed.

'You like it?'

'It's so lovely.'

'It was Grandma's den. Grandpa had a powerful and consuming love for her and didn't care who knew it. Always made sure there were fresh flowers on the desk.'

'That's so special.'

'My father's the same with my mother—a king among men until she goes away or she's unwell, and then he's hopeless until it's all over.'

'A Franklyn trait?' Lizzy said, but wished she could have taken back her words. Yet the slight tension in his mood and the sadness behind his eyes backed up her comment. All three Franklin men had become hopelessly in love.

'So what have you been up to?' Tony asked.

'I took some photographs in the garden.'

'Get some good shots?'

Her heart suddenly bumped. She could hardly tell him about snapping a fabulous shot of him standing there, beautiful, erotic and overwhelmingly sexy. 'Oh yes, just flowers, you know.' Her conscience cringed at her deception so she moved off the subject quickly saying, 'Stella told me about the tapestry in the banqueting room. I thought I might take a look at it.'

Tony scowled and shook his head. 'Pitiful.'

'What?'

'Nobody wants to renovate it. It's of no historical significance and there's a gaping hole where a knight's head should be. So it clings to the wall for dear life. The last relics of the Franklyn estate are all in the banqueting room, obviously too big or too ugly to be sold. Otherwise Uncle would have fed them to his demons long ago.' He shrugged his shoulders. 'Well who wants ten foot pictures of dead pheasants and hares anymore?'

'Obviously you don't, so why do you keep them?'

'I suppose there's a lingering pressure to take care of them—such as they are.'

'From your family?'

Tony surprised her by a sudden tongue-in-cheek expression and an alluring twinkle that filled his eye. He lowered his voice as if someone was listening at the door. 'No, from the ancestors.'

She chuckled. 'You have ghosts?'

'No, but their cracked, old faces around the wall peer down at me as if to say, "I passed this on to you so you must take care of it and then pass it on to your son and then on to his son and his son after that…"'

Lizzy's chuckle became a laugh. 'Heaven forbid it should go to the daughters.'

'I can leave it to the cat's home if I wish because perpetuity doesn't rule here anymore, just the lingering history.'

'Paranoia isn't your style. Deep down you must really want to keep all those dead pheasants and cracked faces.'

'Let's just say that the jury's still out.'

'Or maybe… just maybe you want to prove that you're a better man than your uncle.'

Tony raised one of his brows. 'To whom?'

'Yourself. Why don't you forget your macho pride, put the ancestors in storage and fill the banqueting room with wonderful works of art?' She lifted her brow. 'You can afford it.'

Tony regarded her good-humouredly. 'You're a tonic, Lizzy Yardley,' he said. 'I woke up in a bad mood this morning, but you've made me feel better.'

'I knew I was put on this earth for something.' She laughed and was glad to see the light in his eyes. 'So why were you looking for me? Was there something else, other than my healing charms?'

'To ask if you'd like to use this room. I know it can't be easy for you, but I want you to feel at home.'

'I'd love to use Grandma's den.'

'Call it yours while you're here—Lizzy's den. That has a ring to it.'

Lizzy was touched by his warmth and consideration. 'I'll treat it with the greatest respect.'

'It isn't a shrine. You must do what you wish. Grandma won't come back and slap you if you bring your lap top in here.'

Stella arrived, a little out of puff. She knocked on the open door. 'The police detectives are back. Lizzy, they want to talk to you.'

Lizzy wrinkled her nose. 'Oh no. What now?'

'Don't rush, dear, I'll make them some tea. By the way, do you want some help with those portfolios you put in the utility room?'

'No thanks, Stella, they're full of brick dust and there might even be bits of glass hiding in them too. I'll sort them out later.'

'OK. I'll go and make that tea then.'

Tony looked puzzled. 'Bits of glass? What are you talking about?'

'I went to pick them up earlier. They need cleaning.'

Tony stared in disbelief. 'On your own?'

Lizzy's heart sank to see the harmony between them disintegrate, but she defended her actions. 'The builders said it was OK to quickly collect some things.'

'For God's sake, Lizzy.'

'It didn't take long. I needed them. I only had what I brought from my parents' house.'

'You should have gone with a chauffeur. What's the point in my putting safety procedures in place if you're going to completely ignore them?'

Lizzy was astounded. 'Why do I feel like a teenager who just broke curfew?'

'Because you're behaving like one. What on earth possessed you?'

Lizzy's irises pierced his stare, driving home the fact that she didn't need to be challenged. 'Seeing months of slog coming to nothing—that's what possessed me. This is my problem. Do you think I'm going to come running to you because you can fix every—'

'I can't!' Tony snapped. He paused for several seconds, his jaw rigid, and then he spoke quietly. 'I can't fix everything... it took a terrible personal tragedy to point that out to me.'

Lizzy's eyes widened to hear him speak of it. Her breath stuttered, but she said nothing.

'I've shocked you,' Tony said curtly. 'I'm sorry. I assumed that somebody in this community would have told you about it by now.'

Lizzy didn't know how to react. Even though she intended to avoid any romantic ideas about Tony, it was a painful experience to feel so attracted to a man who yearned for another woman. She spoke quietly. 'Jenny told me, just a little about it.'

'That's all anybody knows—just a little.' The muscle in his jaw quivered. 'It annoys my friends and family intensely,' he said, 'but I'm not prepared to share this with them.' He turned and looked out of the French window.

Lizzy knew it was to hide his feelings because he would never turn his back on a woman that way. 'You're entitled to deal with your pain any way you choose.'

His shoulders dropped and the strength seemed to drain from his body for several seconds, then he braced himself and stood tall again, lifting his head high. 'Nothing prepares you does it?'

'No.'

'There's no alarm bell. Fate doesn't leave a presentiment hanging in the air to warn you.'

'A warning wouldn't protect you from the pain.'

'But it would give me a chance to prevent it. Despite my money and power I failed to protect my... a very vulnerable person.'

Lizzy's heart ached for him. 'People in your position still encounter road accidents, Tony. Fate will have its own way. We can all look back and think *if only.*'

Tony turned and fixed his eyes on her. A look of determination replaced the pain. 'There's a strong possibility that you're still in danger. I consider that to be a warning and I'm damned if I'll fail a second time. So, like it or not, I'm going to protect you.'

'I'm not your responsibility. We don't even know why it happened—why they...'

'Had you been in that shop window you could have been killed—at the very least, disabled. You might have been totally dependent on your family for the rest of your life.'

Lizzy snatched a breath and her face paled.

'You didn't think of that, did you?'

Although Lizzy had balked at Tony's words he was right, she could have been behind that window when it burst into a myriad of wounding shards. She was so caught up in trying to recover her losses she hadn't stopped to dwell on the, *what if*. Now it sent a chill through her. They stood in the numb aftermath of conflict, silent, save for the sound of the clock on the mantelpiece, ticking away the seconds of agonising stress in the room.

Lizzy spoke softly. 'So how would you...?' She gulped at the tension in her throat. 'So how would you like your money and power to protect me?'

Tony's response was quiet but sharp. 'That's rather a cynical comment, but I suppose it's the closest I'll get to cooperation.'

'It's not easy for me to accept help.'

'I've noticed.'

'You should be able to understand that.'

He nodded and then said, 'I'll assign a man to drive you wherever you want to go. His name's Joe. He's big and he can handle himself. He'll take care of you. I understand how you feel, but just go along with it until we can learn more. These measures aren't to take away your self-empowerment, Lizzy, but to help you maintain it.'

Lizzy nodded then turned from him. 'I'd better go and see what the police want. More questions leading nowhere.'

'Let me know how you get on.'

****

Lizzy burst from the sitting room and dashed towards the entrance hall.

'Lizzy?' Tony called after her as she ran up the stairs. 'Lizzy, what's the problem.'

'Me,' she called back over her shoulder. 'I'm the problem.'

'What the hell does that mean?'

'Didn't you know? Apparently it's all my own fault.'

Tony strode up two steps at a time and headed her off. He braced his hand on the bannister to bar her way. 'That's ridiculous.'

'It's the favourite theory now. Let me pass, Tony, I need to be alone.'

'I'm not moving until you tell me what's going on here.'

'I'll tell you later.'

'No. Sit down and we'll talk.'

'Sit down?'

'Trust me. It's the best seat in the house.'

They sat on the top stair. Lizzy sighed and leaned her folded arms on her knees. 'What's so special about this seat?'

'It's elevated. It makes you feel tall.'

'You *are* tall.'

'But I don't always feel it.' He put his arm across her shoulders. 'What did Brent say to upset you like this?'

'I suspect that he was disappointed because Patrick's out of the frame.'

'They checked him out?'

'Somebody's house sitting for him. He's been out of the country for several weeks—backpacking. He's not due back until next month.'

'Obviously that isn't what upset you.'

'DCI Brent has decided that I must have hooked up with some other aggressive boyfriend.' She looked at him. 'I haven't, Tony, truly I haven't. I've done nothing to bring this on—nothing.'

'It's OK you don't have to convince me.'

'He questioned me about my boutique in Bowbury. Wanted to know why I closed it and suggested it was financial difficulty. I argued but I could see in his face that he didn't really believe me. It didn't take a genius to work out where his mind was going; he was fishing around for evidence that I'd actually arranged it myself.'

'An insurance scam?'

Lizzy nodded.

'That's not feasible,' Tony told her. 'Once you'd paid somebody to do that there wouldn't be anything left.' He tightened his arm round her shoulder. 'I'll go and talk to them. This is insulting.'

'No, don't do that. It doesn't matter.'

'Of course it matters.'

Lizzy shook her head wearily. 'I don't care what they think any more. It's over.'

'What is?'

'I'm giving up this futile fight to save it all.'

'Futile? You can't take a quantum leap from determined to giving up, all in one morning.'

'You can if you've only ever been half a beat ahead of it. Bouncing back is all very well but sooner or later the last straw is going to land on the camel and end it all.'

'Come on, Lizzy, you're just upset and angry. You have every right to be, but you can't throw away what you've already achieved.'

'My achievements have boiled down to a couple of portfolios covered in debris, and whatever's lying in shreds at Lakeside. I've been kidding myself that I could do it all again.'

'You can.'

She shook her head. 'I'm no good at business, you discovered that very quickly. It's all very well being pig headed and burning up with ambition, but to quote your expression, the numbers won't crunch for me. I'll get a job, retrain or something.'

Tony turned her to face him. 'Look at me, Lizzy,' he said firmly. When she looked up he fixed his eyes on hers and said, 'I didn't build the Lakeside Centre for profit. I did it for people like you; talented artists who create products with their own hands and not with complex machinery, like I do. Take as long as you wish, Lizzy, but don't give up.'

'But whoever heard of trying to start half way up?'

'You're more than half way, Lizzy. You just need time and I can give you that.'

'I'm not some teenage protégé.' Lizzy couldn't see the light ahead that Tony was so sure about. This was the end of her carefully structured life plan. Apart from his role as landlord, Tony hadn't been written into it. He had appeared from nowhere, but now she had to say *goodbye* to him as well as her dream. This thought stabbed through her heart like a splintered stake. 'You've been amazing. I'll never forget what you did for me, but I have to re-think my next move.' Then, before she could throw herself into his comforting arms she jumped to her feet and stepped onto the landing.

Tony seized her hand as she tried to move towards her room. 'Lizzy, please…'

'There's nothing more to say. I've lost my foothold now. I can't do it all again. I just can't. Let me go, Tony.' She felt Tony grasp her fingers tightly then he released them and allowed her to move on.

Chapter Six

Tony looked up from the newspaper that was spread on the kitchen table, and spoke to the huge figure that filled the doorway. 'Good morning, Joe.'

Joe ducked his head under the doorframe as he approached. 'Morning Boss.'

Tony preferred to be on first name terms but Joe wasn't comfortable with that. At first it made Tony feel like a gangster but after several weeks he stopped noticing. He got up in response to the final gasp coming from the coffee machine. 'Self-service today,' he said. 'Stella's at the races.'

'Good day for it,' Joe commented.

'Have you talked to Lizzy yet? I haven't seen her since yesterday afternoon.' His brow puckered above the bridge of his nose. 'I'm afraid she's avoiding me.'

'She came to see me this morning. She's agreed to some safety procedures.'

'That's good.'

Joe reached into his pocket and took out a piece of paper. 'She showed me this. Doesn't know what it means. Thought it might be a prank.'

Tony scowled as he read it. His insides tensed at the possibility that it was linked to the ram-raid. 'Did it come in the mail?'

'No, it was left on her windscreen a couple of days ago. Thought it was kids playing the wag—messing about in the hotel car park. I don't know about you, Boss, but I think the police should have it.'

Tony handed back the note. 'I daresay we've contaminated any forensics they could have gleaned from it, but you're right.'

'I'll see to it.'

'Maybe you should take a copy of it.'

Joe nodded. 'Will do.' He turned to leave, then stopped and looked back. 'I'll take care of her, Boss, no worries.'

'I know you will, Joe.' He watched the gentle giant walk away and then he took his coffee to the table and looked at his newspaper. But the facts and figures of high finance seemed to glance off his brain as his usual single-minded concentration was challenged by other thoughts. His life was hectic, exhausting, high-powered but always contained within his careful management; and that included his emotions. He once believed that he made his own luck with a combination of hard work and making good decisions, but in recent months he had learned otherwise. He stared at the tinted pages. You won't find the answers here, he told himself. Success can't bring back what was lost—who was lost.

Lizzy came in and drew a glass of chilled water from the fridge.

'You sound out of breath,' Tony said, his eyes still trying to align the figures.

'I've been for a run.'

Tony turned swiftly. 'What?'

'In the gym. I don't need Joe for that do I? It normally helps me over my frustration but it didn't work.'

'I could have told you that,' Tony said, remembering his own fruitless efforts. 'I tried to shake off a bad mood that way.'

Lizzy walked over to the window and looked out at the lake. 'It's not the same as running out there. You can't hear the birds or smell the trees and the lake. Instead you hear the heating system and smell the chlorine in the pool.'

'Joe's got a motorbike, he could go with you.'

'What kind of a job is that for a man like Joe? I'm not going to turn into a spoilt princess because I've got a minder.' She stared out of the window. 'I'm disappointed; I was hoping a solution would fly into my head.'

Tony approached and stood by her. He spoke quietly but directly. 'You can complain about having a minder, Lizzy, but you've got to shake off this negative attitude towards your business.'

'I'm not being negative I'm trying to be realistic.'

Tony was becoming frustrated. 'You have a great deal of potential, Lizzy. Why do you think the Trust agreed to your tenancy?'

'Trust?'

'The custodians of the property. A tenant at Lakeside is an asset to this community.'

'What do you mean?'

'You know that you can put a great restaurant on a bomb-site or as far off the beaten track as you like, but people will find it. This is the thinking behind the whole project. All the tenants are outstanding in their field. You know that. You had to prove that your product was among the very best of its kind. That's not snobbery, Lizzy. My mission wasn't just to build a fancy block of shops; Lakeside is a centre of excellence for the betterment of the whole area. Once established the reputation of the tenants draws people to Merevale. That's good for trade throughout the community.' The muscle in Tony's jaw twitched as his exasperation simmered. 'This isn't Franklyn charity it's part of the Lakeside Centre ethos. Your pride is standing in the way of a far bigger picture than the one you're looking at. You could stay on board a great project and get your sights back on your dream, but it seems you'd much rather live in a bedsit and get a job in a sweatshop.' He looked at Lizzy's face. She was stunned into silence. He'd hurt her, even insulted her. He could see that in her eyes, but his frustration made his blood boil. He had to walk out.

After the row with Tony, Lizzy went to the reading room. If it worked for Grandma Franklyn, she assumed it could work for her, give her some peace from the stresses of living at Larchwood. She spent several hours there. Browsed through books, smelled the flowers, sat at the desk and sketched lingerie. She should have been totally content, but the nagging questions still bombarded her brain. How will you survive? Take a market stall? Sell on line? She sighed to herself; can you sell fancy underwear at a craft fair?

She was startled by a knock on the door.

'Can I come in?' Tony asked, seemingly respecting the protocol originally laid down by his grandparents.

'Of course you can.'

Tony looked serious as he quietly closed the door behind him. 'I owe you an apology for my outburst earlier, it was out of order, and I'm sorry.'

The formality of his approach gave Lizzy reason to think she wasn't really forgiven for being stubborn.

'These things happen at stressful times,' she said softly. Although she didn't admit it to him, she knew that his offer made sense. He could back her business and not feel a thing but it would keep Lakeside running smoothly.

The apology allowed them to bury the hatchet for the time being, but there was an underlying issue still to be settled.

'My sister's here,' Tony said. 'We're going to sit on the terrace. Will you join us? Grace is looking forward to meeting you. She knows your work; she has friends who were your clients in Bowbury.'

Lizzy nodded. 'Happy times,' she said.

Tony smiled. 'Your fame goes before you, Lizzy Yardley, whatever you believe.'

His comment seemed loaded, another finger pointing at her negativity. She wouldn't go so far as to think he would bear a grudge, but she was a business cog that was out of sync. It would trouble him until it was fixed.

There was no conversation as they walked through the empty drawing room, only the sound of their footfall on the wooden floor. Nothing remained of the old days, no trappings of the gentile tradition, followed by decades of Franklyn ladies, who withdrew to it after dinner, thus escaping the cigar smoking, port-passing world of risqué anecdotes and political debates.

Lizzy hated the chilly silence but made no attempt to break it.

At last Tony's sonorous voice brought ease to the tension. 'The drawing room,' he said. 'It needs a new name but I haven't decided what to do with it yet.'

'It's so light and airy,' Lizzy said, looking along the wall at the four huge windows where the summer sunshine streamed in.

She scanned the ornate ceiling and the polished, wooden floor, 'Even empty it's very beautiful.'

'You like it?'

She couldn't help but sigh out her answer. 'Oh yes.'

'It's been renovated, but I don't want to fill it full of furniture just for the sake of it. How many sitting rooms can one man need? I'd really like it to be functional in some way. Be of some use. Then at least we can give it a more appropriate name.'

'When you decide what to do with it, can I come and see it?'

Tony looked ahead saying, 'You can come to Larchwood any time you wish.'

The comment warmed Lizzy's heart for it was genuine. 'Was Stella here during your uncle's time?'

'No.' His brow puckered momentarily. 'She came to Larchwood when she was very young, in my grandparents' time, but she couldn't bear to see what was happening after they'd gone. Besides she probably wouldn't have been paid. I was glad she was available to come back.'

The French windows at the end of the room were already open wide. They walked onto the terrace, a semi-circular structure with a balustrade and steps leading down to the neatly mown lawns.

'I found Lizzy,' Tony called to his sister, and he instantly looked more relaxed.

'You make her sound like a lost spaniel.'

Lizzy could see that Grace was a Franklyn, tall, slender and very attractive. Her hair, dark brown like Tony's, was cut short and very stylish.

'Come and sit down, Lizzy,' she said. 'I've made some tea.'

The table was shaded by an umbrella. They sat, evenly spaced, around it and Grace set about pouring the tea.

'Grace and Charlie are both doctors,' Tony said. 'They're getting married in the spring and then they're off to work in Africa for a year.'

'That's amazing,' Lizzy said. 'It must be so good to be able to make a difference to people.'

'Come on now, Lizzy,' Tony chided playfully, 'you said you wound up your business to help your sister. Didn't that make a difference?'

Alarm bells rang in Lizzy's head and a hint of fear ran through her as Tony stepped into forbidden territory. It would have been so simple to be more open about last year but the more time she spent with him, the less she wanted him to know about it. She hesitated a moment and then spoke positively. 'But that's family, not Africa.'

Grace stopped pouring tea. 'All the same, that was a huge sacrifice. Was your sister ill?'

'Not exactly. But she was extremely unhappy.'

'And now life has given you a shedload of lemons for your trouble.'

'I guess all I need to do now is find the sugar.' She then expected Tony to make some kind of comment about it, but he didn't.

Grace passed her a cup of tea. 'I was going to come to you for my wedding dress, but that's not possible now.' She shrugged her shoulders.

'Were you really?'

'It's not waffle, designed to make you feel better, Lizzy, it's the truth. People with your talent normally go to big cities to get onto the rag-trade ladder. But, fortunately for us, you chose to stay in this county.'

Lizzy's heart suddenly quickened. Grace's comment was like a light shining through the dark reaches of her doubts. Just a glimmer but it rekindled her self-belief. She saw Tony smiling as if he'd perceived the impact of Grace's words. He wasn't gloating; his eyes were warm and expressive.

'I'm sure I can still take it on,' she said. 'I don't have any commissions yet.'

Tony turned to Lizzy. 'Grace has talked about her dream wedding since she was in the sixth form.'

'Yes but I'm not a teenager doing A levels now. It isn't appropriate anymore.'

'What's suddenly changed?' Tony asked. His brow furrowed.

'I'm older now—a doctor with responsibilities. I can't go floating about in a cloud of net and lace.'

'I'm sure Lizzy has designed dozens of stunning gowns for women of your age.'

'And much more,' Lizzy added. 'Designs are based on your wishes, around you—who you are.'

Grace set down her cup, drew a long breath and said, 'That's not really what I meant. The truth is…'

Tony fixed a suspicious eye on his sister as the light-hearted aura fell flat. 'What's wrong?'

'Nothing's *wrong*. Just a change of plan, is all.' She became quiet again, as if to search for the right words to continue.

'Gracie…?' Tony prompted.

She sighed and then looked him in the eye. 'There won't be a wedding in the spring. That's what I came to talk to you about.'

Tony looked shocked. 'I'm sorry, Gracie, I just assumed you'd been sent here to check on my state of health.'

'That's one of the reasons, but I needed to tell you about the change of plan.'

'You and Charlie haven't—'

'No—good heavens no.' She waved away his question with a flick of her hand. 'Charlie and me are glued together for all eternity. It's just that we have to bring the wedding forward.'

'Forward?'

'Quite a bit actually.'

'How much?'

'Six weeks.'

'So now you're looking at a Christmas wedding instead?'

'No. It's in six weeks' time.'

'What?'

'There won't be a dress or a marquee—just a quiet, family do.' She paused a moment and then added, 'In Bowbury Register Office.'

Tony stared at her. 'You're going to break Mum's heart.'

'I can't help it. Africa's been brought forward. We want to be married before we go. It's always been our plan.'

'So has the beautiful dress, Charlie's nieces looking like little princesses. Charlie was sold on it as much as you.'

'Our work is more important than a big wedding. Don't make it more difficult for me, Tony. I need you on my side.'

'Gracie, I'm *always* on your side, but there must be a better way to send you guys off to this enormous change in your lives.'

Tony's cell phone rang. He scowled and took it from his pocket. 'Yes Joe.' He listened a moment and then looked at Grace. 'Are you expecting Holly Parker?'

'Holly?' Grace echoed. 'I told her she didn't need to come.'

'OK, you can let her through,' Tony said to Joe. 'Tell her we're on the terrace. I'm sure she can remember how to find it.' He put his phone down. 'I'm surprised you've involved her. You must have closer friends than Holly.'

'Yes but… well we made a pact when we parted company to go to Uni. We'd be each other's chief bridesmaid.'

'But you're both thirty three years old now. You've hardly set eyes on her since.'

'Lately she's made an effort to renew the friendship,' Grace explained.

'Why?'

'I've no idea. She's started gatecrashing family dos. Mum and Dad invite the Parkers for dinner and Holly turns up too. Her profile has suddenly risen dramatically. She reminded me of our teenage vow—in front of her parents, and Mum and Dad. I had to honour it out of respect for them. They're still close friends. Come on, Tony, if one of your schoolmates turned up with an old score, you'd settle it honourably. She's OK, a bit selfish and indulged but we've always known that.'

'Well, with a bit of luck she might have matured.'

'Don't hold your breath,' Grace said. 'Anyway, that's the way it is.'

The sound of Holly's heels, thudding through the empty drawing room, heralded her arrival. Lizzy noted that she didn't so much arrive as make an entrance, like some minor movie star building up her image. She certainly looked the part: tall, leggy, very attractive and with a good body and long, blonde hair way past her shoulders.

'I was stopped at your gate,' she complained. Then made straight for Tony, and kissed his cheek. He seemed surprised, but didn't comment. 'What's that all about?' She dropped her huge, expensive handbag on a vacant chair and then took the seat next to Tony.

'Nothing,' Tony said casually, 'just security.'

Once in the shade, Holly took off her sunglasses. Her makeup was immaculate. 'Why have you got such a small table out here? Don't you entertain?'

'Not here.'

She turned from Tony and looked at Lizzy, who sensed that she was being weighed up. 'I don't think we've met.'

The way she owned the moment, as if her arrival was of primary importance, got right up Lizzy's nose. Conscious of being a guest, she swallowed the urge to be curt. She smiled and said. 'No we haven't met, I'm Lizzy Yardley.'

'I've heard that name somewhere,' Holly said, in much the same way as she would comment on the weather.

Lizzy still had to bite her tongue but she said, 'My boutique was ram-raided recently. There was a small piece about it in the local paper; perhaps you read my name there.'

'No, but I saw it on the way into Merevale. What a mess. Drunken driver I suppose.'

'He might well have been drunk,' Tony said, 'but it was deliberate. That's why I've tightened up security. At least until we find out more about it.'

'You must be devastated,' Holly responded, once again with the same emotion as talking about the climate.

'Lizzy isn't beaten yet,' Tony said, and reached for her hand across the table. He gently squeezed her fingers. His attentive gesture might have been more enjoyable had Lizzy not noticed Holly's nostrils twitching. It made her wonder if the elegant and obviously wealthy Miss Parker had her sights set on establishing a pecking order. Was she pulling rank? Pointing out that she was a family friend long before Lizzy came on the scene to be comforted across her line of sight?

'You must have rattled somebody's cage,' Holly drawled.

Still mindful of her situation, Lizzy took it as a joke. 'I must have done. I do that all the time.'

'You didn't have to come, Holly,' Grace said.

Holly flashed a smile. 'I'm your matron of honour. I came to give you some moral support.'

A quizzical expression filled Grace's face. 'I don't need backup to talk to Tony. He's my rock.'

'Charlie's supposed to be your rock.'

Grace chortled. 'No, Charlie's my blankie.'

'So,' Holly said, 'you've spilled the beans about the wedding?'

'Of course I have, that's why I came.'

Holly turned to Tony. 'Tell her that she should have a proper wedding when she gets back.'

'I'm not a child, Holly. My mind's made up about this.' She turned to Lizzy. 'You've had a lot of experience with weddings. A bigger wedding can't be done in six weeks can it?'

Lizzy was torn between politely staying out of this family debate and trying to prevent Grace from throwing away her chance of a lovely day. 'Well I doubt you'd get a last minute date in Church, but once you've come to terms with that, you can get married anywhere.'

Everybody looked at her.

She felt a little uneasy but she pressed on. 'Tony's right about the Registry office, in Bowbury. It's historical, I grant you, but it's dark and dull—all those panels and tiny little crooked windows. The floorboards creak and break the mood every time somebody moves. And you'll be lucky if you can get all your family in there. You can find somewhere more interesting than that.'

'A hot air balloon for instance,' Holly said.

'I didn't mean that,' Lizzy returned. This woman was beginning to push her towards one of her feisty outbursts but she held on. 'I meant that you can marry in hotels, castles, beaches, all sorts of lovely places.'

'But it's the timescale,' Holly argued. 'You're talking about a lot of organising and research with a very short deadline. Surely it's better to wait and take more time over it. Do it properly.'

'Research is no problem,' Tony said, with a ring of authority in his voice. 'I've got secretaries, PAs, administrators, lawyers… This can be done, Gracie. Don't you think it'll be less disappointing for Mum and Dad to see their only daughter married somewhere special?'

'Course it would. I've slogged myself senseless for the past few years, and my wedding was something I looked forward to—some kind of reward for all that grafting. But life makes you compromise sometimes. It sounds lovely, but what's going to be available at this short notice?'

'People cancel,' Lizzy said. 'Why not search for a vacancy somewhere—a villa perhaps?'

A light came into Grace's eyes as she seemed to teeter on the brink of hope. Then she shook her head. 'No, this is crazy.'

'No it isn't,' Tony insisted. 'Lizzy wouldn't have raised your hopes if it was a bad idea. We can do this.'

'It's worth a few hours research,' Lizzy said. 'I'm not doing anything today. We can get on the Internet. I'll try and contact some of my previous clients. Get some advice. I've even got some venue brochures in my portfolio.'

'Good place to start,' Tony said, nodding positively.

Lizzy and Grace looked at the portfolio, taking down details in between Grace's sighs and gasps at the dresses. Tony went to his study to use his business phone, with a view to tapping the brains of Irena, his genius PA in his London office. She arranged all the hospitality and conferences. Holly did nothing in particular except sigh now and then to remind Grace how she felt about it. Grace didn't seem to notice. It was as if she had known Holly so long, her spoilt behaviour didn't register.

Tony returned and said, 'That's the strangest thing. I just didn't see it.'

'What are you talking about?' Holly said.

'My PA pointed out that my corporate villa could be utilised to accommodate the wedding.'

Lizzy looked up from her notepad. 'You actually forgot you had a villa?'

'No, it's not a holiday venue per se it's a place for conferences and business hospitality. I only ever go there to work, that's why it never occurred to me. But Irena didn't see any problem. She said we could meet the deadline.'

'Where is it?'

'Tuscany.'

Holly gasped. 'You're kidding me.' Suddenly she seemed enthusiastic. 'A villa in Tuscany?'

'Florence to be exact,' Tony said. 'What's the point in holding conferences in a boring place? Even workaholics like to stop sometimes.' He looked at the surprised faces. 'So what do you think?'

'It sounds perfect,' Grace said, 'but I wouldn't know where to start.'

'You don't have to do anything. Irena manages all the events there. It's part of her job. She said this would just be the same as a convention… only with flowers. She'll keep in touch with you about the details. You know… if you want a marquee or use the gardens. Things like that.'

'Florence…' Grace sighed. 'I don't care if it's in a bloody tent. Can you cost it and let us know?'

'That might prove to be fiddly, winkling out what's business and what isn't. Call it a wedding present, but you'll have to explain to Dad. He started your wedding fund when you were toddling about, putting bandages on your teddy.'

A look of doubt crossed Grace's face. 'Now it feels scary. It's all so quick.'

'We're working to your timescale, Gracie,' Tony said. 'What are you afraid of?'

'I can't make much of a contribution. I've got so much to do to finish work and prepare for Africa.'

'Irena will do everything. She leaves nothing to chance, covers every angle. You won't have to give it a thought. She'll even liaise with Mum about the guest list. And you don't have to search a thousand miles to find a dress designer.' He fixed his eyes on Lizzy.

Lizzy smiled and said, 'This is a good time for me.'

Grace thought a moment. 'But can you do it in time?'

'Course I can.'

'OK. Let's do it.'

'Why don't we go to my study and look at Villa Firenze on the bigger screen?' Tony said.

'Villa Firenze,' Grace sighed as she lunged at her brother and hugged him.

Lizzy smiled as she watched them go into the house, thick as thieves, as they might have been as children with an exciting game afoot. Their laughter and chatter rang through the drawing room as they went.

Holly snatched up her bag and pulled out her iPhone. 'Of course you won't have time for the bridesmaids,' she said, 'I'll get myself something.'

'No need,' Lizzy said lightly, having very quickly learnt that Holly would keep on wheedling and sighing until she got her own way. But she was back on her professional feet now and wasn't going let the chief bridesmaid call the shots. 'We'll do whatever Grace wanted for the spring wedding. You mustn't worry. You've got quite enough to do.'

'Like what, for instance?' Holly said as she flicked her thumb across the screen of her iPhone.

'Organising a nice, tasteful, hen night in Tuscany.'

'To include you?'

'Heavens no, I'll be far too busy.'

Lizzy wondered about Holly's recent move to rekindle her friendship with Grace. Was it genuine? Had she suddenly felt that too much time had passed since they were regular companions? Or did she have another motive for gatecrashing family events? Was it possible that she hoped Tony would be there? And what about all the sour looks, as if she had set her sights on her friend's brother?

Holly seemed to be able to hold two conversations at once—one physical and one electronic. Her thumbs moved swiftly. 'Are you and Tony seeing each other?'

'No.'

'Don't you fancy him?'

'He's a generous, protective and charming man with the body of an athlete, so who wouldn't fancy him?'

'He seems to like you. It wouldn't take too much effort on your part. And it's all very cosy here... just the two of you.'

'I've only just met him.'

'Maybe so, but this is the twenty first century. A girl doesn't need a proper introduction and two turns round the pump room to kick-start a fling. She can make all the moves.'

'I'm not about to make a move on a man who's in love with another woman.'

'In love, Tony? Not his style.'

'She was obviously very special, it hit him hard.'

'Oh her, the one who was killed in the car crash. But she's out of the picture now isn't she? Life goes on and all that.'

Lizzy was shocked at Holly's lack of compassion. Tony's emotions were still raw and painful, yet she could discuss it and text somebody at the same time. 'Not at all, she'll always be the love of his life. He'll never remember times when she was difficult or insensitive. She's pure—a perfect angel.'

'She might well be, but Tony's not. He's alive and well, and I wouldn't mind betting he's as hot-blooded as ever. While his heart's bleeding for his pure Madonna, his body's probably crying out for somebody a bit more... *sinful,* don't you think?'

Holly's hint that she had experienced Tony's hot-blooded lovemaking was a shock to Lizzy. It was true that she felt her own blood heating in his presence, even though she was trying to avoid it, but the vivid image of him in a heated encounter with another woman, spiked her heart. His ghost had no image so that was tolerable, but Holly was larger than life and had known him for a long time. 'That's none of my business.'

Tony had talked of fate placing a presentiment in the air to tell you of trouble ahead, and there it was, a warning that whatever Lizzy thought, said or did, Holly would perceive her as a competitor. The casual questions were clearly to check out her rival. It seemed that not only was she about to re-kindle her friendship with Grace, but she was also intent on a second chance with Tony. And to that end, any mischief she did would be calculated, subtly executed and very damaging.

Chapter Seven

'Lizzy!' Grace called over the hullaballoo of Charlie's twin nieces, Ruth Franklyn's attempts to calm them down and Holly's Skype chatter. 'Do you need help with those?'

Lizzy looked up from her cutting table where she was packing the small bridesmaid's dresses; swathing them in reams of tissue paper. She loved the gentle rustle of it as she packed a finished item, but at that moment she was hardly able to hear it. 'I've done the small dresses and accessories but I thought I'd leave the other two until tomorrow evening.'

'Shall I come back and give you a hand?'

'Yes please, it'll be much easier to get them packed neatly if we work together.'

'It's amazing how you've done it all, Lizzy.'

'Only an idiot would fail in here. I mean, look at it. I asked for a place to work and I got a fabulous salon.'

It was Tony's idea to use the drawing room. As it was for Grace's wedding, Lizzy couldn't argue. Far too big for Lizzy's needs, it was divided into two; the work area was at one end where there was a small adjoining room to store textiles, trimmings and haberdashery. The other part was arranged with sumptuous, lounge furniture, but the windows were left bare to allow in as much daylight as possible.

'Are you coming, Mum?'

'What's that, Grace?' Ruth called back.

'Tomorrow evening, packing the dresses ready for off, do you want to come?'

'Oh yes. But does it really need three of us?'

'Who cares?' Grace said laughing. 'It's fun.' She was radiant; her happiness touched everybody around her.

Ruth caught hold of one of the twins who was galloping about, waving scrap pieces of silk. 'Sarah, calm down; you're getting too excited.'

'We're being flying horses.'

'If you're flying you don't need to thump your feet quite so hard, do you?' Ruth reasoned. 'Can't you be butterflies or fairies instead? This is Lizzy's studio. I'm sure she can't hear herself think.' She ushered them towards the occasional table close to one of the sofas. 'Do something quiet for a while. You've got your books. Lizzy gave you that big sketchpad. You could draw something.'

'Can we go out on the terrace?'

'No.' Ruth stared at them until they sat down. 'If we let you out you could be down by the lake in no time.'

Lizzy laughed. 'That sounds like experience talking, Ruth.'

'It most certainly is. I know all the places, at Larchwood, where one might find a small child in a lot of trouble.'

Grace laughed. 'Even more trouble when we got back here.'

'Don't think, for a minute,' Ruth warned, 'that your children ever stop being a worry to you, no matter how successful they become or how old they get.'

'At least you're getting one of us married off at last.'

'That's true; mind you I've long since given up on seeing my one and only son walking up the aisle.'

'You've done an amazing job, Ruth,' Lizzy said. 'You had so much to organise in such a short time.'

'I only emailed the information. Tony's PA did the rest. She's a wizard at admin, but I don't know what's happening about anything else. Got it all under control, she said, so we have to have faith I suppose.'

'I can hardly expect everything to be perfect, Mum. We'll have to make allowances under the circumstances. Charlie's sorting out the last minute transport details with Tony and Dad. Everybody's done their best.'

'Yes,' Ruth agreed, subtly shaking her head at Holly, who was anchored in one of the easy chairs still talking to her iPhone, 'almost everybody.'

Lizzy had kept her dignity during the past weeks. She stepped around the petty obstructions and challenges that Holly threw in her path; the most troublesome being cancelled fittings. It didn't take long to work out that the cancellations came when Tony was working away and re-scheduled when he was home.

'Grace,' don't forget Lizzy's advice,' Ruth said. 'You mustn't lose any weight over the next few days.'

'Not much chance of that,' Grace chortled. 'But I'll make sure I don't.'

'And you, Holly,' Ruth added.

Holly looked up, 'What's that?'

'Don't lose any weight before the wedding.'

'I might, I lose weight easily.'

'You're the matron of honour it's your responsibility to make sure you don't.'

'But what if I do?'

'Eat something or your dress will droop and Lizzy won't be there to help you.'

'Not coming, Lizzy?' Holly asked. Although her voice was casual, Lizzy could see a glint of satisfaction in her eyes.

'No. It all sounds lovely but I can't—must press on.'

'I wish you were,' Grace sighed, 'but I understand where you're coming from. I almost gave my wedding up for my ambition.'

Lizzy hated turning down the invitation. A few days in Florence with Tony's family sounded wonderful. No looking over her shoulder for danger. But she had to stick to her guns and claim that she wanted to press on with her work. If Holly's renewed interest in the family was a prelude to re-kindling what she once shared with the *hot-blooded* Tony, then Lizzy wasn't going to witness it. Neither of them had invited a wedding partner; Grace had commented on that. So would they emerge together, purring like two contented cats, at breakfast time? The thought made Lizzy's whole body and soul ache—let alone her heart. One thing was certain she wasn't going to be there to see Holly gloating. And just in case the lovers returned to Larchwood together, she wasn't going to be there to greet them either. Threat or no, somehow she had to get back to Lakeside.

There was a solid knock at the door. When it opened, a tall man with a thick mop of fair hair, stood with his eyes closed tightly. 'Is it all right to come in now?'

'Come on in, Charlie,' Grace chuckled, 'it's all out of sight.'

Lizzy loved how they were together. Charlie's uncomplicated, good-humoured persona made people feel secure. Their relationship was a happy blend of love, friendship and respect.

He crossed the room reaching his arms to Grace. He embraced her and then said, 'We've sorted out the travel plans. We'll arrive four days before the wedding. The family can have a little holiday. When they've all gone home we can stay on for a few more days.'

'I can't believe we've pulled this off.'

'Teamwork,' Charlie said proudly. He smiled and kissed her. 'A four-day wedding and a bespoke frock, you're a spoilt brat, Gracie Franklyn. I'll soon put a stop to that when I drag you off to Africa.'

'You're not dragging me anywhere, I can't wait. We're actually going, after all this time talking about it.'

'Yes, I was afraid the years would go by and we'd never do it.' He looked around. 'Anything I can do here?'

'Can you take the girls home—please? They're getting a bit hyper. I'm just going to run through the check list with Lizzy and Mum; then we're going to have a nice cup of tea on the terrace.'

'No problem.' He turned and called out, 'Come on girls, let's get you home to Mummy.'

'Tell her they've been really good,' Grace urged.

'Do I have to cross my fingers behind my back when I do?'

'No, they behaved well. They're just a bit excited about being flower girls.'

The twins ran towards the door just as Tony entered the room. He was carrying Lizzy's book under his arm.

'Uncle Tony!' Sarah called out. 'We've got princess dresses and they're—'

'Shh!' He put his finger to his lips. Then he smiled and dropped to one knee to talk to them. 'Uncle Charlie isn't supposed to know about the dresses.'

'Why?'

'Because they have to be a surprise.'

'Why?'

'Why? Well... I... Uncle Charlie will tell you.'

'Pass the buck, why don't you?' Charlie said with a quizzical expression on his face. 'Thanks a bunch... *Bro*.'

'Any time,' Tony said with a chuckle. He stood up again and watched the two flying horses gallop off.

The room became silent. Lizzy felt she could hear her heart thumping. This wasn't supposed to happen. Neither was the dry throat, nor the nervous fluttering in her stomach. She was positive that by now her wilful emotions would be under control. That she would no longer be prey to nature's chemical trickery.

She had a foolproof plan to prevent it. Had isolated herself as much as possible, using the wedding dresses as an excuse so she wouldn't have to spend any time with Tony.

As he approached her, the *out of sight out of mind* proverb was well and truly debunked. She had carefully re-educated her mind to deny him, but her body had clearly not been paying attention.

Tony put the book on the end of the cutting table. 'It's time you took possession of this.'

Lizzy clenched her hands to hide the trembling. 'Yes, I can pay you back now.'

'I don't want to hear all that. It belongs with you, no matter who bought it. Don't you think you've earned it these past few weeks?'

'You paid me.'

'Not enough. I've seen these lights burning well into the night. You must be exhausted.'

'I'm fine. It's how I work. I do it all the time.'

'And this is what I do—*all the time*. I buy gifts. It's yours, and there's an end to it.'

Lizzy ran her hand over the battered leather binding.

'Your hand's trembling,' Tony said. 'It just shows how much you wanted it back.'

Lizzy nodded. 'Thank you,' she said softly. 'And thank you for bidding for it. I wouldn't have found this copy again.'

Tony's mouth twitched a brief smile. 'Excuse me I need to talk to Grace.'

Lizzy watched him with his mother and sister. He told them what had been planned. Grace, Charlie, bridesmaids, witnesses and parents would all go in his plane, four days early, to ensure that all the main people were there. Then the plane could be used to collect other close friends and family nearer the day.

Lizzy turned as if to make an exit from a scene that no longer concerned her. Her job was done. She tried to tell herself not to panic about her emotions. It was just a glitch, caused by the endearing way he talked to the children. That's exactly what it was—a glitch.

Armed with her theory, she went into the storeroom and began to tidy the fabric on the shelves, getting back into the security of her own world.

The sound of Holly's voice made it clear that she had joined the family group in their happy conversation.

'So it begins,' Lizzy whispered to the rolls of silk and satin. 'The reunion is afoot.' She focused on tidying up the textiles.

'There you are,' Tony's voice surprised her and she gasped. Her hands froze where they rested on a bolt of fabric.

'Hiding yourself away again. I've hardly set eyes on you these past weeks.'

'I'm not hiding.'

'Don't be touchy,' Tony scolded gently, 'I'm only joking.'

As he spoke he rested his hand on her back. The warmth of it permeated the silky smoothness of her top. It seemed as though his fingers were directly touching her skin. Erotic shivers, rippled down her spine, and goose bumps pinpricked her flesh. All the powerful hankerings returned as strong as ever, along with an almost overwhelming urge to seize this gorgeous man and kiss him breathless.

'Are you avoiding me?' he said quietly, as if to keep the conversation strictly in the storeroom.

Lizzy was still wondering how he could actually touch her, quite innocently, and yet stimulate reactions far removed from innocence.

'Hmm?' he prompted gently.

Two choices hovered in her mind; she could lie or admit it, neither option appealed to her. She braced herself and turned. 'Why would I do that?'

'I don't know. That's why I asked you. You seem tense.'

'My mind's turning somersaults. A few weeks ago I was about to give up but now I'm back on track. It's happened so quickly and it's a bit scary.'

'You're still not alone.'

'It seems such a long time since I finished an actual commission instead of just making stock.'

Tony's eyes were soft and mellow. 'I missed you. I'd sit in the plane thinking how nice it would be to chat and enjoy a glass of wine on the terrace when I got home. But there you were, locked away with your head bowed over your work.'

'It was necessary.'

'Come with us,' he urged.

A breath staggered through her lungs as all the images of Holly and Tony rushed back into her head. 'I... I can't. This has been a great opportunity, but I mustn't take too much time off.'

Tony scowled sending away the softness in his eyes. 'You can't possibly be thinking of going back yet.'

Lizzy willed herself to keep focused. 'The repairs are almost finished. There's no reason to stay here.'

'There's every reason.'

'I can't spend any more time running away from, God knows who, waiting for the police to come up with something other than imaginary ex-lovers.'

'You think it's all over because it's gone quiet? I suppose you've convinced yourself that the ram-raid was an accident and the note was a prank. What if this guy's a stalker?'

'But a stalker wouldn't damage... I mean he wouldn't behave like this, would he?'

'Who knows what the crazy thug will do? When you're here, you're on private land so he probably wouldn't show up. And the sight of Joe will keep him at bay when you're out. But he could be biding his time until he finds you alone? And you're going to walk right into it.' He was quiet for a moment and then he said, 'If you won't come away with us then maybe you should contact your parents—'

'No!' Lizzy interjected. 'I'm not a child in boarding school, don't you dare try and contact them. They've waited all their married life to go on this tour and I'm not going to ruin it for them.' She rubbed her fingers across her forehead, not knowing what to say next. 'God, I've never needed this much support. I'm normally totally independent.'

'Lizzy, you worry about the most insignificant things.'

His comment annoyed her intensely. She glared at him, 'My independence is insignificant? What right have you to say that?'

'In the light of what's happened to you it isn't the main issue. It's a matter of priorities.'

He was irritated; she could see that but still his insistence on being in control of her plan offended her. 'My priorities are my own, to deal with as I wish. Believe it or not, Tony, I actually managed without you before I came here.'

'For God's sake, Lizzy, your safety is more important than a bloody shop?'

Lizzy was affronted. Her irises burned into his face. 'You're a successful man and I don't grudge you one minute of your globe-trotting, whistle-stopping success. But that *bloody shop* you refer to—'

Tony held up his hands as a gesture of peace. 'I didn't mean it to insult—'

'You can't ride rough-shod over my plans because they don't yield a fortune like yours. I've slogged for years but to you, my bit of rag-trading is worth no more than a bag of tiddly-winks.'

'That's not true.'

'Is that your mantra? Trample down the little guys and put something *big* in their place?'

Tony's shoulders sank and his breath gushed from him. 'Jesus Christ, Lizzy, where did you get such a notion?'

'It's how I perceive it.'

'I've never trampled on anybody in my life.' He met her glare, his eyes challenged her. 'There's no shame in being successful—on your level or mine.'

Lizzy was silent. She hadn't meant one word of it. It was her predicament speaking, her fear of a broken heart. Yet this thumping organ inside her chest was already creaking painfully. Now it hurt more because she had offended Tony. She couldn't remember ever being in such a mess. Oh to just lean against his chest and hear him say she was forgiven. His breath pulled at his lungs just as hers did. Was he so angry?

Tony spoke first. He was quiet and his face had paled a little. 'Lizzy... do you really see me as an invasive, callous man who tramples over everybody in his path?'

She looked at him, his eyes had softened and she wished that his haunting irises would stop talking to her soul without her permission. She turned away and rested her hands back on the bolt of silk. This was what she knew, these rolls of silk and satin and wonderful pieces of lace. They spoke their own language to her hands and she understood. 'No,' she said softly. 'I know you're not. I'm so sorry. I didn't mean any of it. I just hit one of my...'

'Feisty outbursts?'

Lizzy nodded. 'I'm not in denial, Tony. I really do feel afraid. And I'm even more scared that this strange exile will never end. Why me? What did I do to cause all this?' Her voice trembled as she spoke. 'I don't mind a challenging situation as long as I know what I'm up against. I'm so tired of this mystery.'

Tony rested his hands on her shoulders and turned her towards him. He spoke softly but positively. 'Lizzy, look at me.' He waited until she looked up at his face. 'I keep reminding you that you're not alone. This concerns me as well as you. I deal with things the only way I know how. Forgive me if I'm not very subtle with it. But I have to do something. And if you go back to Lakeside, alone, then I will have done nothing.' He gripped her shoulders and pulled her closer to him. 'Come to Tuscany... Please...,' he whispered.

Lizzy stared up at him. The magnetism between them seemed to emerge, powerful, taunting and relentless, like a supernatural influence beyond their control. Lizzy knew that pressing their lips together in a heated kiss and pulling their bodies together in sighing, consuming pleasure, could be just a second away. It would only take a word or a snatching of breath to ignite it.

Tony's head leaned forward and his mouth hovered in her hair. Then she felt his breath on her forehead, her temple, her cheek, her jaw and then the corner of her mouth. It was as if he had but one kiss, in his whole life, to give her and he wouldn't squander it.

A quivering sound rippled through Lizzy's throat when she knew that this precious kiss was going to be on her lips. Her whole being wanted that long-awaited touch of his mouth. Denial had its chance but now it was banished by her longing. She would be taking one more step towards heartbreak but she would have this kiss. She reached her face to his.

'Who's Patrick?' Holly's voice, loud and deliberate, came from the doorway.

The kiss, the mellifluous moment of sweet promise, died, unfulfilled.

Lizzy could almost hear Holly's cry of victory, but she wouldn't allow it to last. She was angry inside, but cool on the outside. 'What?'

'Patrick,' Holly shrugged. 'Who is he?'

'Why the hell do you need to know that?' Tony said, disbelief ringing in his voice.

'He's my ex,' Lizzy said casually, as if it was of no importance.

'Ex what?'

Lizzy shrugged, taking the impact out of Holly's challenge. 'Fiancé—why?' She waited for another question but Holly, seemingly out of ammunition for the moment, turned and left the room.

Although Lizzy had ruined Holly's brief triumph, she felt cheated and angry—angry with Patrick for encroaching on her valuable moment with Tony. She likened Holly to Patrick; two bitter, selfish beings who couldn't put themselves second to a single person on this planet. Lizzy wanted that kiss, but now they had invaded it. 'I have to go,' she said, 'I'm meeting Jenny at the hotel.'

'Your weekly tea and cake soirée,' Tony said with a smile. 'I was just about to suggest we take a drive somewhere, find a tea shop and have a quiet chat that doesn't include business or stalkers.'

'I'm sorry it's the only time Jenny can get away during the week.'

'Well that might have scuppered plan A,' Tony said, 'but there's always a plan B.' He mischievously paused, leaving Lizzy to wonder. His eyes sparkled.

'Plan B?' Lizzy fell for it.

'Great food, wonderful Champagne, and uncomplicated conversation.' He looked straight into her eyes and said, 'Tonight—Sanccella's.' He touched his finger to her lips. 'And no protests.'

'I don't know Sanccella's? Where is it?'

'London, I'll arrange a flight plan.'

Lizzy's insides went crazy. She had often dined with Tony, but it was here at Larchwood, and cooked by Stella, because they had to eat. A feeling, rising from the depths of her soul, urged her to accept. But, if she couldn't control her reactions in the store cupboard, how would she manage on a private jet with Champagne and conversation that didn't include harsh realities? She could almost feel herself sitting in the restaurant, dressed up to the nines, hungry, not for food but for him. She felt as though she had been swung around in a whirlwind, but she took a breath and said, 'I'd like that.'

'That's the right answer,' Tony told her. Then he smiled. 'Enjoy your tea. Don't eat too much cake, you need to be hungry this evening. I'll see you later.' He brushed her cheek with the back of his fingers and returned to the studio.

Lizzy followed shortly afterwards.

Holly hovered by the cutting table. 'So what on earth did you do to your ex?'

'I walked out on him, is all.'

'All? It seems much more... *involved* than that. She read from the book, '*I told you one day you'd pay...*'

'If you're interested in Patrick Smith, he has a website. He sells stationery on line. Why don't you look him up yourself?' She took the book and put it in a drawer. Then she picked up her bag and the gift carrier she was taking to Jenny.

'Lizzy!' Tony called to her as she was leaving.

She stopped and turned.

'You'll go with Joe—yes?'

She smiled. 'Yes.'

****

'Lizzy, they're delicious.' Jenny took the gift bag and sighed with joy as she eased out a cellophane package.

'They won't break,' Lizzy told her.

Jenny held the package to her chest as if she was hugging a small child. 'My very own designer lingerie.'

Lizzy laughed. 'Show everybody in the restaurant, why don't you?'

Jenny put the bag under the table and returned to her characteristic routine of savouring a wedge of chocolate gateau. Holding her fork like a pencil she ploughed furrows along the glossy, brown frosting. 'I love tea and cake day,' she sighed. 'It's so mellow and chummy with lots of…'

'Chocolate cake.'

'Not just that… well you know how I love to talk… chick stuff.' As she raised her fork to her mouth, somebody caught her eye. 'Heads up! There's a guy over there, a businessman I think, very smart. Got some papers and he's reading them.'

Lizzy glanced at the man seated at the table by the wall. 'Wow! Reading you say? Then he must be very smart.'

'You might mock, but he keeps looking at you.'

'Ridiculous!'

'He does,' Jenny insisted. 'He read for a while and then looked up—twice.'

'How do you know he's looking at me and not you?'

'Because I'm the one stuffing my face with chocolate cake, and you're the ladylike one with the lemon drizzle—and you're not even eating that.'

'I'm not supposed to eat much,' Lizzy said.

'Why not? You sure as hell don't need to watch your figure. And your stomach's as tight as drum.'

Lizzy sighed nervously and leaned towards Jenny. 'You've no idea what I've done.'

'No, I'm a florist not a psychic. So what have you done—crashed Facebook?'

'I'm going out to dinner, with Tony.'

Jenny's fork dropped on to her plate with a clatter. 'Tell me! Tell me everything,' she demanded. 'When?'

'Tonight, but before you make my wedding bouquet, it's not really a date, he just wants to… you know, thank me.'

'Yea right! If he wanted to thank you, he could have asked me to make up a bouquet. He sends flowers all the time.'

'Oh God, Jen, what have I done? I'm trying to keep my distance. I don't know what made me agree.'

'I can't think,' Jenny teased. 'It must be awful going out to dinner with a fit, eligible multi-millionaire.' She raised her brow. 'Mind you, it'll make the locals talk.'

'We're not coming here. We're going to a place called Sanccella's, it's in London.'

'Long drive.'

'Short flight.'

'You're kidding me,' Jenny cried out and then looked around sheepishly before lowering her voice. 'Out to dinner in a private jet? That's awesome! I only ever saw that in a movie.'

'Sanccella's sounds Italian, doesn't it? What do you think I should wear? I don't want to be seductive or anything but I want to look attractive.'

'You're a dress designer you're hardly going to look like a hick.'

'I don't want to give him the wrong… What are you doing?'

Jenny had fished out her phone and was searching the internet. 'Is that two c's?'

'I don't know.'

'Got it…! Oooh… yes. Candlelight, grand piano, pianist in a DJ, quiet little tables…'

'Do they serve food, or should I eat my cake?'

'Don't be cynical. You're scared and you're trying to cover it up.'

'What scares me most is that it's difficult to hide it. My hands are shaking already. It's a good job I'm not going to Tuscany. I'd never be able to keep still.'

'You should go.'

'I would have done if only to dress the girls, but six days watching Holly, draped all over Tony—no thank you. She can be a complete bitch all day and still sleep at night. I've got virtual bruises from dodging her tactics.'

'What's her problem?'

'Me! Every time Tony speaks to me she closes in, like a *she* leopard, as if I'm in her territory. When she thinks I'm scoring points by getting Tony's attention, she has to get even. It's like some crazy game of man-ping-pong. Anyway that's all over now. She's officially out of my life. Any other contact will be purely coincidental.'

'I wish I could go,' Jenny sighed, 'Florence is amazing. Have you ever been?'

Lizzy shook her head and sipped her tea.

'You'd love it, the architecture, the atmosphere, the whole Michael Angelo thing.'

Lizzy grimaced. '*Whole Michael Angelo thing?* You make it sound like a tribute concert.'

'You know what I mean.' Jenny lowered her voice. 'Mind you, I wouldn't go sightseeing with Tony if I were you.'

'I wasn't planning to, but why wouldn't I?'

'I went on a sixth form trip, and I fancied the art teacher rotten. I can still remember it—so embarrassing.'

'What was?'

'The statues, David, Hercules, Neptune, etcetera.'

'I think it's time to talk about something else.'

'See, you're blushing already.'

'I just don't want to talk about naked men, whether they're made of green copper, white marble or golden tanned flesh…'

Jenny froze and stared, her eyes rounded like huge, shiny buttons. 'Golden… tanned… flesh? You haven't…?'

'No I haven't,' Lizzy interjected sharply. 'I think about it though. But I don't belong in Tony's high profile life; I don't fit the mould.'

Jenny screwed up her nose. 'What mould?'

'Tall, blonde, long legs—that kind of mould.'

'Since when have you been afraid of a challenge?' She narrowed her eyes. 'It's not really all about ghosts and women with long limbs, is it? The bottom line is the bullshit that Patrick Smith fed you. You think Tony's going to break your heart with the same stupid attitude.'

Lizzy drew a long breath and then released it through pursed lips. 'I don't think he would but I don't have the courage to risk it. It would hurt too much.'

'But you're hurting already, Lizzy, and you haven't even started yet.'

'I've never known feelings like this. I don't know what to do with them. It's so difficult.'

'None of it's easy, Babe, but we do it anyway. All the good stuff comes with *some* pain. What would life be without peaks and troughs? Take a chance. Hold your head high. Spend the rest of the day making yourself beautiful and sexy. Then go to London, drink Champagne, listen to the piano, and share anecdotes over the candlelight. Then come home a bit tipsy, in a private jet. If you can't have it for ever then at least have a blast.' She glanced at her watch, snatched up her package and said, 'Sorry, Babe, got to go early today. Big order, you know how it is?'

Lizzy always felt good after her time with Jenny. She watched her dash off carrying her gift bag and calling another *thank you* over her shoulder.

The reception area was busy, groups of people stood around talking. Lizzy approached Joe, who was waiting in reception, but her phone rang.

A faint voice called out, 'Lizzy?'

'Carrie? Where are you? I've been trying to get hold of you.'

'We needed to get away.'

'But it's been weeks. What's going on?'

'Have you heard from Mum and Dad?'

'Yes… postcards mostly. Carrie what do you think you're doing?'

'I told you we needed to get away for a bit.'

'Hold on! You're fading.' She weaved through the people then signalled to Joe that she was going out to take the call. She stepped outside, 'Can you hear…?'

A crashing jolt shook her body as somebody seized her and dragged her off her feet. Shock and fear paralysed her mind and she couldn't react; even breathing seemed impossible. She tried to think what was happening but all she knew was that a man had his arms clamped around her and was dragging her. Above her gasps for breath she heard a car screech to a halt close by. It triggered an urge to fight and her legs kicked furiously. The man's arms tightened so much that her frantic calls for Joe were muffled against his chest. Intense fear weakened her muscles as she realised that she was going to be thrust into the car. A momentary slip of the man's arm enabled her to scream for Joe, and she could hear him calling back, his voice tight and rasping. But where was he? Her legs thrashed about, striking the man's shins, causing him to grunt and growl. Her body writhed and twisted but her efforts only served to tighten the vice-like grip on her body. In desperation she clawed at his cuffs, her fingernails gouged his knuckles. He gasped angrily, 'Bloody bitch!' and trapped her neck even tighter in the crook of his arm. The open door of the car loomed and she knew that in seconds she would be inside it. Her eyes began to blur as her gasps for breath caused her to hyperventilate. The waves of darkness impaired her vision even more as she came closer to that yawning, black doorway to an unknown hell. Who were they? Where were they taking her? What would they do? Joe, where was Joe? She screamed for him, but she didn't know if the sound was coming out of her mouth or whether it only sounded in her head. She felt herself sinking into darkness and knew she had lost the battle and could fight no more. Her last fading thoughts reached out to Tony. Oh God, Tony.

Chapter Eight

Tony stood in the entrance hall. No amount of comfort from his family gave him ease. They told him there was no more he could have done. But there was always more a man could do, so why didn't he? Why didn't he call in a private detective instead of trusting it to the police and trying to play it by the book?

He climbed the stairs, trying to suppress the rage that knotted his insides, and walked along the landing to Lizzy's room. His hands braced on the doorframe as some kind of reptilian instinct forged through his integrity and urged him to track down and beat the living daylights out of the man who had grabbed her so brutally. Never in his life had he raised a hand to anybody but that feeling tore at him. The compulsion to open the door was strong but a man bursting with vengeance was no use to her now so he quietly strolled back along the landing and sat down on top of the stairs to wait. His eyes traced around the patterns of the tiles on the floor as if there might be an answer there.

Grace's voice broke his troubled thoughts as she sat by his side. 'This is a blast from the past, seeing you sitting here with your troubles.'

'How is she? Can I talk to her?'

'Yes but give it a couple of minutes to gather yourself, calm down a bit. She's got enough to cope with without seeing you in a state.'

'Whatever you say, Doc.'

'We haven't done this for a long time.'

'Sitting here you mean?'

'All those family Christmases when we came to stay. Sitting here in our pyjamas and dressing gowns.'

'Presents under the tree, tormenting us.'

'Wishing we could join the fun downstairs with all the grownups. They laughed a lot didn't they?'

They smiled and instinctively leaned towards each other.

'We never got old enough to stay downstairs, did we?' Grace said.

'Uncle wasn't interested in family. He didn't want to continue the tradition.'

Grace linked her arm through his. 'When I get back from Africa, can I come to yours, for Christmas, so we can stay downstairs and be grownups having all the fun?'

'Sure, we'll start a new tradition. When you've got kids, they can stay downstairs with us instead of sitting up here in their dressing gowns. And if they want to prod all the presents, they can, open them even—what the hell, we'll get some more.'

'I'd like that. You've done an amazing job on this house. Dad's so proud of you for saving it.'

'Dad was never going to inherit, and he was estranged from Uncle so I grew up presuming we'd have to walk away from it one day. But when I found out what had happened to the old place, I couldn't let it go.' He turned his head and looked back along the landing. 'You've been a long time in there.'

'We talked.'

'About the attack?'

'No—something else.'

'Then what?'

'Just things.'

'You mean about her business? She told me she gave it up to help her sister.'

'And so she did—big time. She's an amazing woman, Tony. I can't tell you more than that.'

Tony smiled. 'Will you have to shoot me if you do?'

Grace chuckled. 'Doctors just give you a lethal injection.'

Tony's control, over his anger, lapsed for a moment and his jaw set rigidly. 'I've got to do something, Gracie. I can't stand by and watch Lizzy go through any more of this.'

'Be patient, the police have more to go on now.'

'All this is a far cry from a nice quiet dinner at Sanccella's.'

Grace was silent for a moment and then she asked, 'Does that mean you two are dating?'

'I don't know.' Tony turned to her. 'Does it worry you?'

'It's none of my business.'

'But something concerns you. Come on,' he prompted, 'what is it?'

'Women have never been a problem for you, have they?'

Tony shrugged. 'I've had my fair share of killer heels shied at me, but I always managed to dodge them without getting hurt.'

'Exactly.' Grace looked him in the eye. 'You've actually dumped some of the most beautiful women in the world.'

Tony scowled. 'That's a terrible expression.'

'On the contrary, it's a very good one. It fits perfectly. That's exactly how it feels to have given yourself, body and soul, to a person who doesn't want you—dumped.'

'You think I'm a love rat?'

'You might well be and I daresay the sports cars, sparkly bracelets and other expensive parting gifts softened the blow for them. Probably eased your conscience at the same time but that's not what I'm getting at.'

'Where's this going, Gracie? Are you telling me to back off? You think I'm going to hurt Lizzy?'

'No, you idiot, I'm afraid she might hurt *you*.'

Tony's brow lifted and he sat up in surprise. 'What... what are you talking—?'

'You see, you're shocked. It never even crossed your mind that Lizzy might be the one to do the *dumping.* You thought you'd never be on the other end of the old *it's not you it's me* speech. Do you think Lizzy's pithy parting shots are only for *bigoted nerds?*'

'Gracie, there's nothing going on...'

'Of course there is. There's so much brewing between you two and we can all see it. You want her but you're the one out of your comfort zone.'

'I know that.'

'Lizzy's different. When you're with her *you're* different, and she isn't making it easy for you.'

'I know that, too. Why don't you stop worrying and let me work it out?'

'Look, Tony, you told us nothing when your girlfriend was killed in that crash. We know you suffered. We had to stay at a distance and watch you in your agony. You didn't talk to us about it.'

'I know. I'm sorry. I didn't know how to deal with it.'

'That's what I'm getting at. When you were only dodging shoes it was OK, but we'd never seen you really hurt before. If it ever comes to that with Lizzy, and you get hurt, for God's sake, talk to us.'

'All right, I'll talk to you.'

'Promise.'

'I promise. Now, why don't you concentrate on your own love life and enjoy your wedding.'

Grace smiled. 'Oh, don't worry I'm going to. I can't wait. It's all going to be fabulous. Look at me, thirty-three years old, a doctor who's about to face some harsh realities in Africa, but inside I'm bubbling like a teenager.' She nudged his arm playfully. 'Charlie's right, I'm a spoilt brat. Not just my wedding but I've got a great family, and I'm marrying the best man on the planet.'

'Charlie's a great guy, but a lucky one.'

'You'd better go and see Lizzy now. I've given her a sedative. She wasn't very keen but she took it. I'll come back, in the morning, to check on her but call me if there's a problem. It's a pity she's not coming to Florence with us. She could do with a few days lounging by the pool.'

'I'll come up with something. I'm not leaving her here.'

Lizzy was sitting in the window seat with her back resting on the shutters. She was dressed in pyjama bottoms and a sleeveless top. Her knees were raised and her arms linked around them.

Tony's lungs tightened. Just how many more knocks was she supposed to take?

She looked at him and smiled.

He smiled back and said, 'What are you doing out of bed, you're supposed to be sedated?'

'I *am* sedated, can't you tell?'

'Yes, you look very calm for somebody who's been in the police station all afternoon.'

'At least I've stopped trembling. I wanted to sit here and look at the lake for a while.'

'It isn't going to disappear overnight, no matter what you're going through.'

'I know. That's what's so great about it.' She turned to the window. 'No matter how many times you look, it's always there. Never lets you down—does it?'

'No.' Tony sat on the opposite end of the window seat and faced her. 'Sometimes it holds amazing surprises.'

'Like what?'

'You should get to bed. If you stay there any longer you'll fall over.'

'Will you catch me?'

'Always,' he said softly, as if he was making a new vow that nobody would hurt her again.

'Joe caught me today.'

'Yes, thank God.'

'Will you talk to him?' she said languidly. 'He's really beating himself up. But it was my own fault. I broke the safety rules. Joe's always supposed to leave first. I'm really sorry. Will you tell him?'

'Yes, I'll tell him.'

She raised her chin and turned her head. 'Am I going to get a bruise on my neck?'

Tony's brow puckered for a moment to see the red marks that would turn blue and show up for some days. 'Afraid so.'

Lizzy's brow wrinkled. 'He called me a bitch—no—a bloody bitch. What an attitude. It was OK to man-handle me but hurting him was way out of order.' She paused a moment and then said, 'He ruined my evening.' She turned her head and spoke softly to the window. 'I was so looking forward to it.'

'Mr Sanccella's restaurant is like the lake, it's always there. We can go another time.'

'But… it would have been so much nicer to be woozy after drinking Champagne and listening to piano music instead of being sedated.' Her eyes closed but she opened them again. 'Am I talking rubbish?'

'Not yet,' he said gently.

'I can hear myself talking, but I don't really know what I'm saying. Will you tell me if I talk rubbish?'

'Reluctantly,' Tony said smiling at her. 'I'm rather enjoying this, new you.'

'You think I'm easier to manage when I'm sedated?'

'It's good to see you so relaxed.'

Her eyes closed again. 'Can I ask you something?' She wavered and gripped the windowsill.

Tony jumped to his feet and scooped her up. 'You can ask me whatever you like when you're safely in bed.'

Lizzy put her arms around his neck and expelled a gentle laugh against his ear. 'I feel like a frail heroine in a novel. Cathy taking one last look at the moors.'

'That's the second time you've likened me to that gothic tyrant.'

'You're not Heathcliff,' she assured him. 'He was cruel and bitter and cold.' She rested her forehead against his neck. 'You're none of those things. You're warm and protective... and...'

'And?'

'A bit bossy sometimes.'

'Is that right?' He lowered her gently and covered her up. 'Come on now—stop fighting it—sleep.'

'Don't go yet,' she whispered. Her hand waved in the air searching for his.

Tony clasped her fingers and perched on the side of the bed.

Lizzy laughed softly. 'Now I'm Camille. We should sing an aria. You like opera don't you?'

'Yes.'

'I wanted to ask you something,' Lizzy said, fighting to keep her eyes open.

'Sure. Ask away.'

'What... what was her name?'

Tony swallowed. He knew what she meant. He also knew that the sedative was responsible. She would never have mentioned it otherwise. 'Louisa.'

'Do I... remind you of her?'

'Not in the least.'

'But that first day we met I reminded you of *somebody*.'

'You're pretty unique, Lizzy. I don't know anybody like you.'

'Then who did you think I was?'

'Somebody that…' Tony began and then hesitated. 'She was one of those surprises that come from the lake.'

'Who was she?'

'An angel that came to help me through a dark time.'

Lizzy's eyes closed. 'And I thought I was the one talking rubbish.'

'Go to sleep.'

'I have to pack dresses tomorrow.'

'Grace will be here, and my mother.'

'I love your family… such a comfort… while mine… mine are… away.'

'Then come to Florence. Grace would love you to be there… Lizzy?'

'Mmm?'

'Was that a yes?'

As her head rolled to one side she uttered, 'Yes,' and fell asleep.

Tony raised her limp hand gently to his lips. 'That's the right answer, sweetheart.'

Chapter Nine

'Oh—my—God. I'm so excited for you.' Jenny dashed across Lizzy's bedroom, at her Lakeside apartment, and pulled open the wardrobe door. 'Right! Let's pack.'

'Thanks for coming to help me, Jen. I know you're busy.'

'I wouldn't miss this for the world. You're actually going. Tomorrow you'll be in Florence. What changed your mind?'

'Tony caught me at a weak moment.'

'What?'

'He asked me while I was sedated and I agreed—apparently. When Grace came back yesterday morning she was so thrilled, I couldn't go back on my word, even if I didn't remember it. We had fun yesterday evening, packing the dresses. Ruth was so sweet. Treated me like a daughter.' She opened a drawer and began to search through the contents. It was strange to see her apartment again. She could hear the decorators below, working on the boutique. It would be ready soon but she began to wonder if she would be constantly looking for unfamiliar vehicles. Her throat tightened and she drew hard on her lungs to breathe. Her life was such a tangle. The goodness and the hope entwined with dark, barbed threads. It wasn't just the attack that had shaken her that afternoon it was the harrowing time at the police station, it seemed like hours.

DCI Brent's interview was more like a grilling. 'Sorry about the forensic procedure, Miss Yardley, but it's vital. This is the first real lead we've had.'

'Bloody thugs!' DC Grant muttered.

It didn't go unnoticed, and DCI Brent scowled at her. 'Your bent for women's rights is very commendable—but personal. Keep it professional, will you, and leave your banner at home?'

'You weren't meant to hear it, sir.'

'I can hear your spare rib rattling a mile off. Of course I heard it.'

'Sorry, sir, I have a problem with bullies.'

'Lucky you've got a chance to get some of them banged up then, isn't it?' He turned back to Lizzy. 'I'll keep this as brief as possible, Miss Yardley.'

Lizzy was in a daze. All she could say was, 'I wish you'd call me Lizzy.'

He nodded and then said, 'We've already gathered information from your chauffeur, Joe, is it?'

Lizzy nodded.

'Your friend had gone and was well out of the way when it happened but there are plenty of witnesses at the hotel, can you remember anything that might help?'

'Anything, Lizzy,' DC Grant said, 'anything at all. Even if you think it won't be relevant. This guy who grabbed you, did you notice him in the restaurant?'

'Jenny said he was looking at me. I thought she was just joking.'

'Joking?' DCI Brent queried. 'In what way?'

'He was very smart, seriously good-looking, and glanced up at me from time to time. She commented on it.'

'Do you know him?'

Lizzy was taken aback with his suggestion. 'No.'

'Are you sure? I mean, he could have been an old acquaintance, somebody you knew a long time ago—somebody who might bear a grudge.'

An indignant look broke through Lizzy's confusion and shock. 'If I knew him I wouldn't joke about him over tea and cake. He was a total stranger.'

'But you're not a stranger to *him*. We're not dealing with a case of mistaken identity. You were his target and we've got to find out why. So we need to turn all the stones over and see who crawls out—OK?'

Lizzy nodded. She wished she could think of something—anything so that he would leave her alone. Her brow puckered as she tried to take her mind back to a place it didn't want to go. Then she recalled something. 'A new shirt,' she said suddenly. 'He was wearing a new shirt.'

'What made you think that?'

'When he had his arm round my neck, my face was pushed into his chest.' She snatched a shivering breath, and then continued. 'I could smell the new fabric.'

'Of course you work with textiles. You'd know that.'

'Yes.' She looked at the detective. 'It's not new now, my lipstick's all over it. I hope his wife finds it and gives him hell.'

'Can you let us have the lipstick, Lizzy?' DC Grant asked.

'It's in my bag but I don't know what happened to it.'

'Forensics have got it. You might have to do without it for a while though.'

Lizzy nodded.

'What made you think he was married?' DCI Brent asked.

'He was wearing a very substantial wedding ring. I noticed it when I dug my nails into his knuckles.'

DC Grant cleared her throat.

DCI Brent pulled rank with a swift look in her direction.

'I never said a word, sir,' she protested.

'No, but you're grunting volumes.' He turned back to Lizzy. 'Do you gamble?'

'Gamble? I wouldn't know where to start.'

'TV, Internet, they make it very easy to throw your money away these days. You don't even have to get out of bed.'

'I don't gamble.'

'How about finances? Have you ever borrowed money, privately that is?'

'No—never. You think I've brought this on myself, don't you? I don't have a jealous lover so I must be in debt.'

'I'm just trying to find a reason for it. Your meeting with your friend, was it a special occasion? Had you planned it for some time? Did you talk about it to other people perhaps? Somewhere where you might be overheard?'

'We get together once a week.'

'*Every* week?'

'Yes.'

'Same time—same place?'

'Yes... Oh no!' she sighed.

'No wonder they were able to plan it so carefully. They knew exactly where to find you, and when. Maybe you even sit at the same table.'

'So I brought this on myself after all.'

'Don't take the blame for being attacked, Lizzy,' DC Grant admonished. 'It shouldn't happen wherever you are. Remember that. And well done you. We've got forensics now. These guys are bound to be in the system. And you won't be their only target. They do this all the time, to somebody somewhere. We just don't know why they've done it to you.'

'Wow!' A loud cry, from Jenny, broke Lizzy's thoughts. 'Look at this.'

'What?'

Jenny hauled a large, suitcase onto the bed. 'This is quality luggage. It looks new.'

'It's sort of new. It hasn't been anywhere further than my wardrobe. I bought it for my honeymoon. We were planning a trip to Greece. A compromise between his tastes and mine. Art for me and ancient history for him.'

Jenny laughed. 'Now *he's* ancient history.'

'I was being very romantic about getting married. I designed clothes, put things away for the big day.' She tossed a bathing costume onto the bed. 'I'll take this. I've got another one, at Larchwood, so I'll have a spare.'

'Lizzy,' Jenny complained, waving the swimming costume in the air, 'this old cozzie?'

'It isn't old, I bought it last year. It's very nice.'

'It's *very nice* for the public swimming baths.' She dashed it back onto the bed and opened the case. 'What's in here?'

'It's just stuff. Tip it out. I don't need it.'

'It's all vacuum-packed.' Jenny twisted the cap on one of the bags. It made a hissing sound as it breathed, making the plastic crackle and crunch. As the bags widened so did her eyes. 'Look at all these fabulous things.'

'Don't, Jenny, just leave them. I don't want to keep Tony waiting.'

'You said he was doing courtesy visits at the other shops.' She shrugged. 'He takes ages over that.' She unpacked the case, placing the clothes on the bed. 'Wow! These are to-die-for; bikinis… sarongs… Is this a maxi dress?'

'Can we just deal with the essentials?'

'Look at these.'

'I'll take those scarves. I can cover up this bruise.'

'What's this?' Jenny leapt to her feet and began to waltz around with a wraparound dress held in front of her. 'I tell you what, Lizzy; if this was mine I wouldn't hide it in a case.'

'You can have it.'

'Don't be daft. How far would it wrap around me? What a collection. Did you design it all?'

'Yes, for my honeymoon. The fabrics cost me a fortune. I was making some money back then. Come on, I haven't got time to wander down *might-have-been-lane.*' She began to search through her wardrobe. 'I need something cool to wear during the day.'

'Clothes don't come any more cool that these. You'll look a million dollars in this… *stuff*, as you so casually call it.'

Lizzy turned to her. 'I don't need to look a million dollars.'

'Why not?' There was a sudden sharpness in Jenny's challenge. She raised her brows and waited for Lizzy to respond.

'I was going to be with my new husband wasn't I? But this is just a short break to get out of danger for a while. They're not the kind of things I feel like wearing at the moment. They belong to a time when I thought I was special, valued and respected.'

'But you are, Lizzy. Tony certainly respects you. Can't you tell?'

'I'm too busy trying to look normal when he's around. Every time he walks in the room I have to bluff my way through the first few seconds. It's not easy to talk to a man when you're a dithering lump of jelly. It's ridiculous at my age. I thought I'd get over it but it just isn't happening.'

'Why should you? It's obvious he's attracted to you. He asked you out to dinner.'

'That was by way of a thank you.'

'He waited for you at the police station yesterday. For goodness sake the man came here to protect you while you pack.'

Jenny shook her head. 'Have a bit of faith. There's no way Tony's going to judge you the way Patrick did.'

'But I don't want to find out—not yet.' She took Jenny's hand. 'Come here, I want to show you something.' They went to the window. 'Look across the lake. What do you see?'

'Tony's house.'

'Well just imagine that it belonged to your Will. And imagine that you both fell in love. But you lost him because he thought what you'd done was ugly? He found somebody with no past, no baggage, and they lived in that house. You watched from your window as he walked with her, played with his children, enjoyed a family picnic maybe. You'd have two choices; live with it or walk away from this place and everything you've done to build it up.'

'Oh, don't!'

'I never experienced these feelings with Patrick. But Tony… I could fall into that man's arms so deeply that I'd leave my heart right there inside him.' Hot tears began to slip from her eyes. 'On an even playing field I'd risk that pain but at the moment there's just too much going on and I can't handle it all at once. I can't divide myself up into segments so I can deal with my sister, my business, the danger, the police, and still have enough left to face a broken romance.'

'Oh Lizzy.'

Lizzy shook herself and pushed the tears aside. 'Don't. I'm good with this. I'll work it out. Now come and help me pack.'

'OK, but you must remember that you're the designer of the bride's dress. You'll discredit your work if you don't look the part. You can pack what you like, Babe, but these,' she said, returning to the honeymoon clothes, 'are going in. So what else have you got tucked away? You need a dress for the wedding.'

'I salvaged some things before I closed my other place. Evening-do stuff, one or two prom dresses. Some of them should fit me. Can you see if there's anything suitable in that trunk over there?'

Jenny knelt and opened it up. 'The great thing is that you already know what Holly's wearing.'

'She'll wear the bridesmaid's dress for the wedding but she's sure to have something stunning for the evening.'

'Then you must do the same. Oooh, I like this one. You'll suit a halter neck.'

Lizzy reached up to the shelf in the wardrobe and took down a shoebox. She reverently placed it on the bed.

Jenny looked at her. 'What's that?'

'My souvenir box. It's Tony's birthday the day after tomorrow. I thought I'd take a gift for him.'

'From your souvenir box?' Jenny peered into it and wrinkled her nose. 'What are you going to give him, your brownie badges?'

'I've got a rare theatre programme that my Nan gave me years ago. It's from Covent Garden. He likes opera. It's just a token. I mean, what could I give him that he couldn't get for himself, many times over?'

Jenny held up a beautiful, pale blue chiffon, knee-length dress. A broad band of beadwork encircled the top of the bodice and continued over the thin, shoulder straps. 'How about an up-close and personal dance in this little kiss-ass number?'

'It isn't finished.'

'What does it need?'

'About four hours of beadwork, I've only finished the front bit. I suppose I can do it when I get there. I should be able to finish it in time.'

Ignoring Lizzy's protests, Jenny squeezed in several dresses from the trunk, and when the case was full she pushed home the latches with a loud click. 'These honeymoon clothes say a lot about you, and I'm not talking about how good you are with a needle and cotton?'

'What do you mean?'

She stared at Lizzy. 'Patrick was weak, insensitive and selfish; he drained you out. So you forgot how to feel attractive and sexy, how to send out the signals, flirt even. These clothes were to help you feel good about yourself again. To try and turn a nerdy frog into a half-way decent prince; you wanted your man to be crazy for you.'

'How do you know that's what I wanted?'

'It's what we all want.'

'That's an awful lot of tough love you're doling out, Jenny.'

'Comes a time when a friend has to do it.'

Lizzy smiled. 'I do dream of being special to a man; loved, needed, wanted like crazy, but I can't deal with everything at once. I'm just not brave enough to seize the day.'

'Then try and grab part of it. At least have a taste of what you want.'

Tony called from the living room, 'Everything OK, Lizzy?'

Lizzy drew a steadying breath and called back, 'Yes, all packed now.'

'I'll take it down for you.'

Jenny slapped her palm on the lid of the case. 'You've got some powerful ammunition in here,' she said quietly. 'So all you need to do, girl, is nudge Holly out of the picture, light the fuse and have yourself a blast.'

Chapter Ten

Lizzy looked around. Everybody was seated except for Tony, he was chatting to Charlie. She did the maths; one passenger standing, one seat left—the one next to her. There was no time to prepare, nowhere to run. Where could she run to in a private plane? Normality seemed to be lingering in the doldrums of cuckoo-land, and the great healer out to lunch. It was pointless to see it as an infatuation any longer, to blame the chemistry or the magnetism of a powerful attraction. She was perilously close to the real thing, and that was the plain truth. She could no longer see Tony as a gorgeous hunk breaking her fall by the palm plant or the beautiful athlete by the pool at Larchwood. It was the true colours of the man that she saw now; the character that lay beneath the trappings of his wealth and the power at his fingertips.

Tony sat down by her side as if it was as natural as Charlie sitting by Grace. He was so relaxed, laughing and joking with his parents, across the aisle.

He fastened his seatbelt then turned to Lizzy and smiled. 'Well, the gang's all here,' he said, 'some of it.'

'I hope you didn't put anybody off to give me a seat.'

'Of course not. I've always counted you in on this flight. All the other guests are coming nearer the day. Some are travelling independently.'

'Even when I said I wasn't coming with you?'

'I hoped you'd change your mind. I'm very glad you did. Now you can relax for a few days. Nobody's going to hurt you now. We could spend some time together; do some sightseeing in Florence, perhaps. What do you think?'

Lizzy recalled Jenny's advice about avoiding *the whole Michael Angelo thing* with a guy you fancy like hell. 'Sightseeing?'

'Yes, lots of art and architecture to see. Shall we do that?'

Lizzy made a clumsy attempt at evasive action. 'I'd love to go to the flea market,' she blurted, then regretted it. Oh no! What did that sound like? He's offering you culture and you're going to drag him to the flea market.

Tony's brow lifted, causing a lock of hair to drop over his forehead. 'Really?'

Lizzy's focus became fixed on this lock of hair and sensible thought left her high and dry. 'I heard about it and...' She gave herself a mental kick. Sort yourself out girl. Make this sound good or you're going to look a complete fool. She cleared her throat and then spoke as boldly as she could. 'I like to look for antique braids, buttons, lace, and...' Her voice ground to a halt. The case of Michael Angelo versus the flea market was weakening. Tony continued to look at her, waiting for her to speak again. '...Beads, you know, bits of glass... I mean glass decoration that you sew onto fabric.'

The plane began to move.

'Right, that's decided,' Tony said as if he was concluding a board meeting. 'Is your belt fastened?'

Lizzy sighed inwardly. On reflection, the naked statues, as seen from the point of view of Jenny, would have been far less embarrassing than dragging a multi-millionaire round the flea market. 'Sorry... What was that?'

Tony's brow puckered. 'Your seatbelt, is it fastened?'

'Oh, yes.'

'Something wrong? You seem really agitated.'

'No.'

He clearly wasn't convinced. 'And you're trembling.'

Whilst Lizzy's mind groped about for an excuse, Tony threw her a lifeline.

'Afraid of flying?'

'Yes,' she returned swiftly. 'I suppose I am—just a little bit.' Her reply teetered on the fragile borderline of truth and fiction. 'I haven't done much travelling,' she told him. At least that was true.

Tony reached his hand to clasp her fidgety fingers where they rested on her lap. 'We're not expecting any bad conditions. It promises to be a smooth flight. You'll be fine.' He smiled. 'Besides, I promised to catch you didn't I?'

'When?'

'A couple of days ago, when you were sedated and almost fell off the window seat, I promised to catch you.'

'Did I fall?'

'No, I carried you to bed.'

Lizzy's eyes widened.

'Don't worry, you conducted yourself very well. And just to put your mind at rest, so did I.'

Tony was surprised to see her so apprehensive about flying. He knew she wasn't normally daunted by life. She always faced everything with a positive attitude. This made him realise that he knew so little about her. Their time had been spent, either worrying about her safety or organising the wedding. He knew nothing of the simple things in her every-day life. Would she freak out at the sight of a spider, leap onto a chair if she saw a mouse? What kind of music did she like? What kind of books? Maybe she liked opera. That would be nice. 'You say you haven't travelled much,' he said. 'Don't you enjoy new experiences, new places?'

'Of course I do. I was always too fixed on my studies or my business to travel.'

'How about family holidays, when you were a child?' It was as if he had pressed a switch and turned on a light in Lizzy's eyes. They shone like honey coloured, polished gems. It warmed his heart to have done this—hit the right button first time out.

'They were fabulous,' she said, 'but very simple. My parents are both teachers so we spent the whole of the school summer break at our cottage in Wales.'

'All of it?'

'Absolutely,' she answered. Then she smiled. 'It was perfect. Both parents spent all their time with us. During the school holidays we were their priority because they both worked during term time, you see. They seemed to wrap themselves around us, helping us enjoy it all, whatever the weather.'

Tony felt the comforting aura of her memories, like a warm blanket on a cold night. Her obvious joy in re-visiting them was infectious. 'In the mountains or by the sea?' he asked gently, afraid to break this magical, umbilical thread to her childhood.

'It isn't far from either. On hot, summer days, you won't find a better beach anywhere in the world. The water looks blue, and the sand gets hot under your feet. The waves dazzle you when you run towards them. The sea…' She stopped a moment as if she was enjoying it all over again. 'It seems to make a special sound on those days, sort of muffled and soporific.'

Tony heard the sea, followed every footprint in the hot sand, watched the dancing light in her vibrant irises as she began to relax and share her golden memories. 'What about the mountains?'

'We didn't climb up very far but we'd go walking in the lower hills and play in the streams. The water was always cold. Sometimes, after a really hot spell, when the grass was dried up and crunchy, we took a big piece of cardboard with us.'

Tony chuckled softly. 'I can't imagine what for.'

Lizzy smiled. 'To sit on so we could skid down the bridle path.'

'Like tobogganing?'

Another laugh rippled through her throat as she asked, 'Have you ever done that?'

'No, but I wish I had. I feel quite cheated. Tobogganing in the warm weather…'

'Sometimes, if there was a freak tide in the night, we helped Dad hunt for fossils on the rocky parts of the beach.'

'Now that's just showing off,' Tony said fixing his eyes on hers, for fear they would dim and the moment would be gone. He didn't want this to pass. He wanted to cling to it, hold it—keep it.

'They were just simple pleasures.'

'Aren't they the best kind?' Tony said softly, and at that moment a powerful surge of something far more gripping than chemistry, hit him hard. He knew his body hungered for her but now he had the feeling that his heart was getting involved.

'Anyway,' Lizzy said dismissively, breaking Tony's thoughts, 'you don't want to hear how I ran my parents ragged all summer.'

'Of course I do.' He chuckled. 'I'm sure you weren't that bad.'

'I think I was.' She expelled a gentle laugh. 'Especially in the evening when the day was almost over. I never wanted it to end. Carrie was always ready to go to bed, but I wished I could stay up all night. Mum would say, "Go and tire her out for goodness sake." Dad would take me up to the stream. I couldn't resist the water and invariably went home with my clothes soaking wet. "You always do this, Lizzy," Mum would say. "You always come home soaking wet." I was a terrible child—really stubborn.'

Tony smiled. 'Stubborn? Staying up all night? *That* I believe.'

'And it won't be any surprise to learn that I was outspoken.'

'Will you show me this cottage one day?'

'It can't possibly compare to your Villa Firenze.'

'Don't you believe it, with the exception of Larchwood, and my pied-a-terre in London, everything I have is attached to business. Even the villa belongs to my company. It's for corporate hospitality; conferences, jollies etcetera. This is a welcome diversion from nauseating meetings and interminable think tanks.'

'Don't you like your work?'

'I don't get much enjoyment out of it. In growing so big it lost its soul somewhere. It all happened so fast. Of course I had business plans but they weren't necessarily life plans. You followed your dream but I didn't have one. I just had motivation, became successful because I *could.* You see, I had a lucky start. While I was at university I designed a little gadget that could save fortunes in manufacturing. I made a lot of money out of it. I was fired up, ambitious and totally seduced by success.'

'So do you know what you want now?'

'I spent most of last year selling off all my American interests so I could spend more time at Larchwood. I wanted... I *needed* a new beginning. I enjoy the advantages of success. Money's great. And I'll put my hand on my heart and say I don't want to lose it all, but eventually you realise that it can't do *everything*. You can design a gadget to make you rich, but you can't come up with one to make you happy. That's a different game.' He cleared his throat as a sickening stab hit him in the stomach. He drew a long breath and continued. 'You can make plans, wonderful dreams to give your life a better purpose, but sometimes, without warning, they just come crashing down.' He stopped, knowing that he had caused the wonderful, amber light in Lizzy's eyes to fade. He was angry with himself. *What the hell did you do that for, you idiot? She took you to the haven of her childhood. She shared precious memories with you, and you wrenched her away with your own bitter ones. Do something for God's sake.*

'By the way,' he said, 'I owe you dinner to make up for missing Sanccella's. Will you come?'

Lizzy looked at him, pan-faced. It worried him for a few moments but then, a glimmer of mischief flickered in her irises. 'Will there be a grand piano?' she asked.

'Of course.'

'And a pianist in a DJ?'

'Certainly.'

'Candles?'

'Hundreds.'

'Pasta to die for?'

'Absolutely.'

'Champagne?'

'Compulsory.'

'Then I will.'

Tony's insides quickened with the way Lizzy's sense of fun instigated a fleeting but delicious flirtation.

'Uncle Tony.'

He was not yet accustomed to his new role as honorary uncle to the twin bridesmaids and their four-year-old brother, Eddy. It wasn't until the blue-eyed, fair-haired boy tapped him repeatedly on the arm and addressed him again, that Tony responded.

'Hi, Eddy. Have you come to sit with us?' He observed that the boy was a more reserved child than his excitable sisters who could be heard chatting and laughing.

Eddy thrust a sketchpad towards Tony, conveying the impression that he deemed uncles to be like fathers, they were there to help. 'Will you draw me a digger?'

It wasn't often that Tony was thrown, but Eddy's request stumped him. 'A digger?' Thinking that manufacturing one would be less challenging, he took the sketchpad from Eddy. 'Well, let's see.'

'Then I can colour it.'

'Just a line drawing then,' Tony said to nobody in particular. He handed the pad to Lizzy. 'I'm sure we can come up with something.'

'We?' Lizzy queried. 'What happened to the genius who redefined the wheel, at university?'

'He did it on a computer. I'm much more creative with a mouse than a pencil.'

'What makes you think I can do it?'

'You draw things all the time. Tell you what. I'll do the maths, and you can do the creative part.'

After that, conversation was strictly concerned with the technicalities of drawing heavy machinery. Prompted by Tony's encouragement and technical knowhow, Lizzy achieved a sketch that delighted Eddy, who went away to colour it in.

Lizzy joined the family party waiting for transport to take them to Villa Firenze.

Tony had dashed off, calling over his shoulder, 'Sorry, got to go. I'll catch you up.' It sounded like a polite, *thank you for a lovely time I'll see you around.* Lizzy was glad of the time to pull herself together. The flight was calm and uneventful; it was her own journey that had been a white-knuckle ride. Yet she had to admit that it was wonderful. The way he held her hand to comfort her, how he listened with genuine interest when she talked about her childhood. The fun they had with their efforts to draw the digger.

'So… you came after all.' Holly made her usual invasive entrance into Lizzy's privacy. Her chilled greeting seemed to slice the hot, Tuscan atmosphere. 'I thought you were sitting this one out—staying at Larchwood.' She looked a million dollars; hairdo, sunglasses, bespoke bag on her arm, high heels that were more a work of art than footwear. 'It was quite a surprise to see you boarding the plane.' She made Lizzy feel that she had violated a code of practice.

'It was a last-minute decision.'

'Have you invited a guest to follow on?'

'I'm happy to be alone.'

'You were hardly alone on the flight.'

Lizzy was accustomed to Holly's sugarcoated jibes, even her cold sarcasm, but today she wasn't dressing it up. There was a change in her approach. 'There was an empty seat so I sat in it.'

Holly took off her sunglasses, revealing her flawless eye makeup. 'Whatever will you do with yourself... all alone?'

Lizzy got the message; *keep your hands off Tony.*

'I've got some sketches to do, new designs to develop.'

'As long as you keep your designs on your pad and not on your landlord.'

Lizzy noted the gauntlet so clearly thrown down at her feet. 'My choice of canvas isn't your shout, Holly. And I don't need your permission to make an impression on it.'

Holly visually moved up into another gear. Looked Lizzy over as if to inspect her smart but simple outfit and her hair, loosely tied back. 'I'll hand it to you, Lizzy, you're a fabulous designer. I can't deny that. You make women look and feel beautiful, but you don't work your magic on yourself. Your *girl next door* image has its advantages but even on your best day, you're just not Tony's type.' She flicked her hand in a dismissive gesture. 'Oh he'll make a fuss of you at the moment, flirt with you for a bit, even buy you things, but it won't last. He obviously sees you as a homeless tenant who needs his protection. If you weren't going through such a *terribly* tragic time, he wouldn't have given you a second look.' She rolled her eyes upward and then fixed them back on Lizzy's face. 'What are men like, hmm? Absolute push-overs when they see a damsel in distress.'

Lizzy didn't need Holly to tell her this. She already knew that she wasn't really Tony's type. She recalled the pain that filled his eyes when he talked of dreams that were shattered. She knew he was thinking of Louisa, she was his future and only needed to creep into his thoughts to torment him. It was as if she lurked in the shadows of his mind to do just that. Even death hadn't parted them.

Lizzy held her head high and fixed her eyes on Holly's arrogant face. 'I'm not looking for a fight,' she told her. 'I'm not looking for a man either.'

Holly sniggered. 'You're kidding yourself. Although we're not coming from the same place, you want him as much as I do. But in the end I'll win whether you fight or not. The only difference is that you're ruled by your heart.'

'And you're not?'

'No such sentiments. Tony's my ticket out.'

'Out of what?'

'My boring life. I want a more defined role to play, some genuine status.'

'Status, but don't you already have that?'

'I have money—*new* money, that is. But I want into the *old-money* world. Tony can give me that.'

'Tony's money is as new as yours.'

'But he's a Franklyn, the pedigree is still there.'

'That's the oldest trick in the social book.'

'But I'll make it work. Not straight away, it'll take time, but eventually he'll see that a wife who can measure up to his role as a pillar of the community, a woman who can run Larchwood, the way it should be done, is exactly what he needs. In return I'd be an asset to his business life. And, of course, have the right kind of image at high profile events.'

'This isn't the 19th century, Holly. Larchwood isn't an estate, it doesn't need a lady to look over the menus and take baskets of food to the needy.'

Holly shook her head slowly and deliberately. 'You're only saying that because you don't have what it takes to put up a fight.'

'Then why do you see me as a threat? As there are no thugs hereabouts, waiting to attack me, I'm not a damsel in distress am I?'

Lizzy turned away, not wishing to be drawn any further into a cat fight over who should be the lady of Tony's house. She shuddered at the chilling thoughts running through her mind. Holly must have reached a crossroads in her apparently boring life and was bent on becoming Mrs Tony Franklyn. Oh God! What a nightmare. The idea of her strutting around the community and making a mockery of Tony's subtle approach to supporting it was horrendous. And what if she came with him on the courtesy visits?

If that happened then Lakeside would be minus one bridal boutique—that's for sure.

They both turned when they heard a car approach. Tony arrived behind the wheel of a beautiful, dark blue convertible.

'Oh good!' Holly said, taking a step forward.

Tony called out. 'Come on, Lizzy, you're travelling with me.'

The glare from the million dollar bridesmaid's eyes was piercing and cold. 'Don't despair,' Lizzy said. 'You know it's only because he feels sorry for me. You wouldn't begrudge a poor, dowdy seamstress a bit of kindness from the master of the house, would you?' Although Lizzy was playing out the scene set by Holly, she knew it wasn't just friendly rivalry. Holly meant business.

Chapter Eleven

A warm feeling of peace came over Tony, as he steered his Bentley Continental along the hot, hazy Tuscan roads, cruising past orderly ranks of lush grape vines, golden carpets of post-harvest corn stubble scorched by the hot sun, and fields of brown-faced sunflowers. He had made this journey many times, keyed up, ready for corporate battles and presentations, never heeding the incredible views and sights. Those times when his only passenger was a heavy bag containing the tools of his trade: a laptop and hard copy files. He didn't even need to pack clothes. He had all he needed at Villa Firenze, and Irena, his PA, tied up all the loose ends to allow him to go straight to the main events. He always said that he couldn't imagine how many wheels would grind to a halt if she moved on. This time the event was the wedding but the same corporate machinery, steered by Irena, had made it possible. Today, Lizzy was his passenger and he was glad.

'You're looking very smug,' Lizzy said.

'Of course I'm smug. I feel like a college graduate dating the prettiest girl at the prom.'

Lizzy laughed. 'It's a long time since my prom. I designed my own dress. My friends thought it was so cool to do that.'

'You're a talented girl, Lizzy Yardley.'

'I need to be, to redress the balance.'

'What balance?'

'My *girl-next-door* image. I stand next to Holly and we look like a before and after ad—me being the *before* of course.'

Tony suddenly laughed out loud.

'Are you laughing at me?'

'No... well perhaps... sometimes you're funny.' He cringed inwardly, realising that he was on the slippery slope into the chasm that is the gender divide. That frustrating place where a man and a woman never see eye to eye and the more you try the wider it gets. 'Lizzy, please don't be offended. It wasn't meant to hurt you.'

'Perhaps I should get a red nose and big, wobbly shoes? Maybe work in the circus then you could buy a ticket to sit and laugh at me.' She raised her voice as she was making an announcement. 'Roll up to see the amazing girl next door, turning somersaults to try and land on her feet.'

Tony pulled over on to a grass verge, turned off the ignition and looked at her. 'Nobody thinks you're a clown. You're charming, witty, great company and extremely attractive. I laughed in an endearing way, because you're *all* of those things.' He regarded her quizzical expression suspiciously. 'What does that mean?'

'It means that I should believe you, but I'm not sure if that's just another *pretty girl at the prom* comment.'

Tony ran the back of his fingers down her cheek. 'You don't trust me. You think I'm just making conversation.'

'I don't know. I've never been with a man who says nice things like that, except my dad—and yours.'

'People say I'm like my father. Does that make it more convincing?'

Lizzy smiled and nodded. 'It helps.'

'Didn't Patrick say nice things?'

Her eyes flickered a moment, her brow puckered. She didn't seem to like the question. But then she said, 'Sometimes, he'd say, "Thanks, you're a pal," when I bought him some software he couldn't afford.'

'So he really is a nerd.'

'Right through in pink, candy letters.'

Tony raised one eyebrow. 'You're mocking him.'

'Yes. Not very dignified is it? I've been away from him for some time but his holier-than-thou attitude still tries to hang around my neck. I'm sorry, that was a lot of fuss over nothing, wasn't it?'

Tony brushed back a few wisps of hair that escaped and fluttered across her face. Her eyelids flickered and she turned her head to meet his touch. The mood was fragile and he lowered his voice to meet the moment. 'Was he *very* angry when you left?'

'I suppose so.'

'He didn't want to lose you?'

'He didn't like things out of place. He was comfortable with the way things were.'

'But you took that away from him.'

'Yes but he…'

'… took something from you.' He heard her breath quiver in her lungs and knew that he had touched a nerve. 'It's obvious that he was very bitter. Those things he wrote in your book proved that.'

'I want to forget him,' Lizzy said softly. 'He's nothing to me.'

Tony hardly dared breathe. She seemed so close to unburdening herself of a painful secret. He decided to take a risk and ask outright. 'What has he done to you, Lizzy?'

She was silent for a while, seemingly on the verge of speaking. At last she said, 'It's as if he put an indelible stamp on me and I can't rub it off. Oh God! That sounds so weird.'

'Of course it doesn't.'

'As more time passes I feel that his warped opinion is going to haunt me for the rest of my life.'

'Why would it do that?'

She looked straight into his eyes. 'I'm afraid people will think the same as he does.'

'And you think I'm one of them?'

'I don't think so. But I couldn't bear it if you were.'

'You're putting me in the same frame as a fool? A *misogynistic, bigoted nerd?*'

'No.' She smiled faintly. 'I'm just playing for time. I know I should be honest with you, but I can't cope with everything at once. Please understand that.'

He pressed her hand gently to his mouth. Her eyes were moist and he felt that if he said one more word about Patrick Smith, tears would roll. But it would be cruel to try and coax the real truth from her. Why should she tell him her secret if he hadn't yet volunteered his own? She looked so vulnerable. Of all the things that had happened to her during the past weeks, she had never looked like this. 'Why do you concern yourself with one idiot, when so many other good people admire you so much? There are other men in the world, people who would treat you properly. Can't you have faith, a little trust?'

'I'd love to do that but... it's like... it's as if you can see something you really want, something so good, so special, but if you reach for it you might drop it and ruin it. So it's better to leave it where it is, where it will always remain undamaged.'

'You'd deny yourself a chance to be happy rather than risk being hurt? That's the most ridiculous thing I ever heard.' Tony put his arm around her shoulders. 'You're very special to us. To Grace and Charlie, Mum and Dad... and to me.' He drew closer to her and gently pressed a warm kiss on her cheek. He was shaken to find himself so swiftly intoxicated, engulfed with the sheer pleasure of the first touch. He kissed her face again and she turned toward him. Then a kiss, full on the mouth, sent powerful, erotic tremors through his body. He snatched his breath through his nostrils as he perceived a faint, shuddering groan that rippled from Lizzy's throat and into her lips. His mouth drank it, tasted it, savoured it until it heated his blood and fired him with a passion he didn't recognise. He mistrusted his own control and ended the kiss. When he eventually looked at Lizzy, he knew that she had been gripped by the same powerful feelings. Her pupils were like large black beads and her chest rose and fell rapidly.

He released her. 'We should move on,' he said. 'We're only a few minutes away now.'

****

Lizzy was still cocooned in the torrid heat of erotic chemistry. She had absolutely no resistance to Tony's kiss; the sensual pleasure of his mouth still cavorted mischievously through her body and her mind. Her limbs seemed detached from the rest of her as she walked with Tony through the flower gardens and across the lawns, where a wooden dance floor was being laid for the reception.

'It seems that Irena's got everything under control,' Tony said. 'She's incredible. Never misses a thing. If somebody told me she'd arranged the weather, I'd believe them.'

'It must be comforting to have that kind of support.'

'She certainly backed me up these past months.'

They strolled past the pool; kidney shaped and skirted by cream-coloured paving slabs. An arc of white steps fanned out across the recess.

'It's a bit smaller than the one at home, but it's very pleasant, don't you think?' Tony said.

Lizzy thought of the pool at Larchwood, and smiled to herself as she recalled Tony's beautiful body stretching and twisting after his workout. She looked at him, no longer the athlete with his jogging trousers clinging to his hips. Even after a journey he still looked immaculate in casual summer clothes.

'That's an enigmatic smile,' Tony said. 'What's on your mind?'

'Just thoughts.'

'Good ones by the look of you.'

'You got that right,' she said, conscious that they were walking away from the huge villa and its sweeping driveway. 'Where are we going?'

'You're the chosen one,' he teased, 'you have a choice of accommodation.'

'Why me?'

'Like I said, you're special.'

'Are you having a giggle at the prom queen again?'

'Course not. This is Grace's advice. She was adamant that you should have a place where you could be alone if you found things catching up on you. Shock is a tricky thing. It can leap out at you when you least expect it. She was being half friend, half doctor. You know Grace.'

'Please tell her not to worry. It's her wedding not my holiday.'

'Grace doesn't see this as just her wedding. It's an opportunity for them to spend some time with us before they go to Africa. She'll feel better if you're comfortable.'

They approached a small villa; Tony referred to it as the cottage. It nestled on the higher ground beyond the pool. A grassy hill rose behind it.

'I stay here when I come to work. Some business people have endless capacity for sitting around, drinking and talking well into the night. So I like to get away.'

A cobbled footpath took them through a shrubbery and into a terraced garden. Lizzy looked up at the picturesque villa. 'It's lovely.' She moved swiftly, keen to see more. The door was approached via a flight of stone steps that seemed narrow because the flowers billowed over them. 'OK if I go in?'

'Sure.'

Whereas the outside was typical of the red-roofed local architecture, inside it was new, pristine and very spacious. It comprised a kitchen, dining area and utility. Through an archway there was a sitting room with a huge window overlooking the gardens and the pool.

'Tony, it's beautiful,' Lizzy said, 'but it's yours. You should stay here, like you usually do.'

'Stop worrying, I'll be fine. I'm going to be surrounded by family, not businessmen. Would you like to see the other villa before you decide?'

'No, I love it. I'm very honoured.'

'Don't say that. You've earned a break.' He strolled towards the wooden staircase set against the wall. 'The master bedroom is for you. There's a small room where I keep my things so I can travel light. I'll call in later and collect what I need.' They climbed the stairs. Tony opened a door to a beautiful bathroom with a large, white, square bath and a separate shower.

'Fabulous!' Lizzy said on a sigh. 'I just love to wallow in a hot, aromatic, frothy, candlelit bath.' She grimaced. 'Sorry, was that too much information?'

Tony smiled, his eyes mellow and seductive. 'Not at all. That's the kind of thought that keeps a guy warm on a cold night.'

'Can I see the bedroom?'

The sight of the enormous bed put ideas into her head and sensations into her body. The pale, lawn curtains were twisting and turning in frenzied spirals as the breeze blew in through open

French windows. On closer inspection she saw that there was a balcony and beyond that, a breath-taking view of the Tuscan landscape. In the distance, a row of cypress trees stood, like sentinels, by a stout villa with a terracotta roof. Its windows were like dark eyes looking across the golden fields. In contrast, the textured tapestry of hills rose behind it. Lizzy felt that she could reach out and touch it.

'Oh,' she sighed, 'look at that!' She dashed through the French windows. 'Look, Tony. Acres and acres of sunflowers, and look at—'

'No!' Tony's voice rang with panic. 'Get back! Get away from there.'

The sudden volume of his voice halted her. 'What? What's the matter?'

'Come away from that damned balcony, will you?'

'What's wrong?' Lizzy returned to the bedroom. 'Is it damaged?'

'No, of course not.' He seemed to be shocked. His chest rose and fell rapidly, as if he'd been running.

'I don't understand. What did I do?'

'Just leave it, Lizzy.' He closed the French windows as if to leave whatever had upset him outside. 'Come downstairs.'

She followed him down to the dining area. 'What's the matter with you?' She was exasperated and her own volume began to rise. 'I want to know what I've done to annoy you. Tony this is unreasonable.'

'You launched yourself at the balcony without a thought for your safety.' He didn't appear to be able to control the panic in his voice.

'I didn't *launch* myself anywhere.'

'That was so dangerous. Don't you realise—?'

'It wasn't. Tony, will you please explain yourself—yelling at me like that.'

'Just stay away from it.' He made for the door.

'You can't just march away from me like that without an explanation.'

He stopped and then turned back. 'I'm sorry.' He raised the palms of his hands towards her. 'Please forgive me... I need to leave.'

'Then you'd better go. Heaven forbid that I should hold you up.' Lizzy was deeply offended. She was also hurt, not knowing what to do with this change in him.

'You scared me—OK? Running to the balcony like that without a thought.'

'What am I six? If you didn't want me to use it you should have kept it locked. How can I stay here if I don't know the rules?'

'There are no rules,' he snapped. 'You're perfectly free to do what you wish.'

'I just did. I went to look at the view and you freaked out. What on earth is this all about?'

Tony paused a moment and then said, 'That's how she died.'

'You mean Louisa?'

Tony's voice quietened to a choked murmur. 'She fell. She was on a balcony and fell.'

'In Paris?' Lizzy said softly.

Tony nodded. 'She was at a party.'

Lizzy was stunned. She stood trembling, unable to speak. Tony's face was suddenly drawn, his eyes full of pain, for there was Louisa, out of the dark shadows of his memory and falling to her death, all over again. Lizzy felt terrible, she had caused this, turned the knife in his wounds. 'I'm so sorry,' she whispered. 'I didn't make the connection. I thought it was a road accident.'

'Yes, everybody did. I let them think that. I was in no shape to get involved with detailed explanations.'

'Were you with her?' Lizzy asked softly.

'No, I was in New York, selling off my interests over there. Otherwise... maybe I could have done something to prevent it.' He stopped and rubbed his fingers across his forehead. Then he braced himself and said, 'I shouldn't have yelled at you. That was unforgivable.' He dragged a tight breath through his chest. 'What kind of host am I? I was supposed to be showing you around.'

Lizzy shook her head and cast her eyes downward to the slate floor. 'I'll be fine.'

Tony spoke as if clear thought had left him high and dry. 'Meals are served in the restaurant over at the villa, but this kitchen is well stocked, you can cater for yourself if you wish. Give Irena a call on the internal phone system if you need anything.'

'I'm sure I can find my way around.'

'Fine,' Tony muttered.

Still staring at the floor, Lizzy said, 'This is a family occasion you should be with them.'

Tony opened the door and then looked back. 'I'm not good company at the moment. I'm sorry. I'll catch up with you later.'

'Could you tell Grace I'll be along to unpack the dresses?'

'Sure.'

The door closed. Lizzy felt sick, lost somewhere between Tony's grief and her own. Louisa was always going to be in his mind and his heart. He had just demonstrated his deep and enduring love that was weaved through every fibre in his body—the Franklyn obsession for just one woman. A pang of jealousy made her realise that her wish to be free of her own passion was just a forlorn hope in the biological warfare of intense, physical attraction. She was shaken to the core. Had pushed the boundaries and allowed herself to be seduced by the magic of the landscape, of Tony's sweet-talking, his gentle gestures and intoxicating kiss. She made that forbidden move, reached for something she couldn't have, and now she must pay for it.

Chapter Twelve

'Grace, what's the matter?' Lizzy asked. 'You look stunned.'

'I am.' She turned on the spot, gazing at the room. 'Just look at it.'

They stood in a lounge, in the Villa Firenze; it had three in all and this was the smallest and the lightest as the sun streamed through the windows. Sofas and chairs were placed into groups. Each one with a round, low table adorned with a flower arrangement echoing Grace's colour theme—cream and lavender freesias and fresh foliage that filled the room with a deliciously sweet scent.

'Beautiful,' Lizzy sighed softly.

'And this is just my dressing room. What will the rest of it be like?'

'Like a well-deserved dream wedding,' Lizzy said. She walked across to the far corner of the room where two white dressing tables had been placed for the occasion. They stood, on their cabriole legs and had oval mirrors shining and reflecting the colours. Each had a stool upholstered in soft, white fabric. There were two dress rails, a full-length mirror and a round table covered with a crisp cloth.

'It looks like a boutique over here,' Grace said. 'My God! How much is it all costing?'

'Don't be so practical,' Lizzy chided.

Grace laughed. 'And you're not I suppose.'

'I'm not getting married in three days' time, am I?'

A frown clouded Grace's face that was, just a second ago, the face of a radiant bride. 'But dreaming about a fairy tale wedding—at my age.'

Lizzy took the little bridesmaid's dress from the box and gave it a gentle shake before hanging it on the rail. 'You think dreams should be the prerogative of teenagers? We're wired to fantasise about our prince charming, about lace and silk. We're supposed to imagine exquisite bouquets, cakes dripping with sugar flowers. And then there's that special dance, with Dad, who really can't bear to part with you, but he knows he must.'

'That's a very poetic speech from somebody who's been to a lot of weddings.'

'It must be the Tuscan air.'

'Come on, Lizzy, I'm thirty-three.'

'You poor, old thing,' Lizzy said with a laugh. 'Do you want me to tie some lavender ribbons on your Zimmer frame?' She scooped up the other twin's dress and hung it up. 'I remember you announcing that you'd cancelled your spring wedding. It gave me the shudders to think about it and I didn't even know you then. Tony wants you to have it all. He loves you. You're his baby sister.'

'Baby sister,' Grace scoffed, 'he's all of five years older than me.'

'Yes, but while you were dissecting your virtual cadaver, in med school, he was already counting his first million, which means he has the wherewithal to make this possible. Your dad's wise enough to see that this place is already geared for it. And your mum's over the moon. So... bring it on.' She took the lid from another box and unpacked Holly's dress. 'Your matron of honour is going to look good in this.'

'She certainly is.'

'When I first met her she hinted that she and Tony had history.'

Grace laughed. 'She was probably just trying to wind you up. He always looked on her as a silly teenager. He still does. When you were engaged to Patrick, did you have a vision of the wedding you wanted?'

Lizzy hung the dress and arranged the fabric to fall correctly, peering at the detail to check it. 'Yes, I did.' She spoke over her shoulder.

'And...?'

'Well... May, Church, family and a few friends.'

'That was your dream? It sounds more like a spring cleaning list than a wedding plan.'

'Yes it does, doesn't it? But that's how we approached everything. I love weddings but I sort of fell into the same way as Patrick. I'd known him for such a long time. I suppose I was accustomed to his passive dominance. Getting married was inevitable rather than a special event so I didn't bother about it much—except...'

'You designed a gown?' Grace guessed.

'Yes.' She removed the lid from Grace's box and began to remove the tissue paper. 'I mean, how ridiculous would it have been for me to have a rubbish dress?'

'I bet it was beautiful.'

'Yes it was. I suppose my own dormant dream needed to emerge somehow.' She stood holding Grace's dress in her arms, and thought back to her own. She was Patrick's fiancée, which meant that she would become his wife. Yet he never intended to make any changes to his own life. Hers would blend into his. To him it was simply a process, a programme like any other he used on the computer; a life that didn't include fripperies or fairy-tale dreams about romantic weddings. 'My dress was a work of love.'

'For him?'

'No, for my work.'

'Do you still have it?'

Lizzy shook herself back down to earth. 'No, I gave it away.'

'*Gave* it.'

'She was very short of money but ecstatically happy about marrying her man.'

'I bet she thought you were her fairy godmother.'

'It gave me some kind of closure on the whole thing. *Goodbye Patrick.*'

Grace became serious; she stood close to Lizzy and stared into her eyes. 'Work apart, something's wrong. What is it?'

'Nothing serious, why don't we finish up here, then you can relax.'

'No,' Grace insisted. 'I think we should talk. It doesn't take a doctor to see that you're trying to cover something up.'

'I'm fine, Grace, stop worrying. Get on with your wedding.'
'Lizzy!'

Lizzy drew a long breath, her shoulders dropped as she spoke. 'I made a big mistake. End of story.'

'Mistake, when, how?'

'I let down my guard—that's what happened. I fell for the romantic scenery, the mutual attraction, the chemistry etcetera.' She stopped for a moment, trying to find the right words to talk to Grace about her brother. 'I pushed my hideous skeleton right to the back of the cupboard and decided, for the time being, not to worry about it leaping out again. I was nervous but things were going along so well. And then suddenly—there she was.'

'Who?'

'The love of his life.'

'He's not still grieving over her, is he?'

'Something happened to remind him. He was devastated, stopped in his tracks. Suddenly I could see her, in his mind, his heart, his eyes—definitely in his eyes. In no time at all she consumed him.' Lizzy tried to distract herself by looking over the dress.

'I'm sorry, Lizzy, I didn't know. He doesn't talk to me about her. He only talks to me about you.'

Lizzy turned to her. 'For a short while it *was* about me. And I was happy, I felt special. Then suddenly she elbowed me right out. I'm sorry to sound so bitter but it really did hurt.'

'I can see that. But isn't it worth putting up a fight?'

'Tony told me that your grandpa had a deep and passionate love for your grandma, and that your dad's the same with your mum, so it seems that Tony inherited the same gene. I'd always be a close runner up. What am I to do? Be there standing by him at all costs, on any terms? I'm too old to be a love-sick groupie. I shouldn't have been tempted. I should have stuck to my rule to keep my distance, at least until my chaotic life was back on track.' She fussed over the gown, tweaking and preening the billowing, white layers like a swan feverishly tending to her feathers. 'The trouble is I'm feeling guilty now.'

'About what?'

'I should have been more sympathetic. He was hurting and I was busy fighting my corner instead of seeing it from his point of view.'

'Nobody gets it right all the time, Lizzy. And Tony's got a broad enough back to understand that. Apart from that he's got family. He should have come to us long ago. We could have helped him through it. I still don't understand why he didn't.'

'I expect time will sort it out.'

'Anytime you want to talk about it, come and find me. You don't have to be brave because this is my wedding. I'm getting it all. I've traded dull, wooden panels in Bowbury Registry Office, for a fairy-tale in Tuscany. And I'm going to Africa, with Charlie. On top of all that I'm even getting a dowry. Nothing is going to spoil it. Not even two lovely people who need their bloody heads banging together.'

'Is that a prescription, doc?'

'If Champagne, blue sky and sunshine doesn't work, then yes, and I'll even perform the operation myself.'

They laughed, returning their attention to the fun of the occasion.

Grace sighed. 'Wow! Look at that.'

Lizzy smiled. 'I always like this bit. Looking along the rail and seeing it all finished.'

'I'm glad you came. It's such fun to have you here. But maybe I made the wrong decision about billeting you in the cottage. Perhaps being with people would be more comfort.'

'I love my billet, as you call it. I have all the *comfort* I need; a fridge full of goodies, Champagne, a huge carton of ice cream and...' a twinkle of mischief came into her eyes, 'some of those little round chocolate lollies to stir my cocoa.'

Grace rounded her mouth and widened her eyes. 'Oooh, can I come and stay with you?'

Lizzy pretended to be serious. 'It depends what you can bring to the fridge, Doctor Franklyn.'

'What else is there but Champagne, ice cream and chocolate?'

'Crème Brule?'

'Then I suggest you get some in your fridge because Tony adores Crème Brule.'

There was a knock on the open door. 'Doctor Franklyn, may I come in?'

'Irena. Hi!' Grace said as the PA approached them. 'Lizzy, this is the genius who arranged everything here.'

Irena, about forty, was dressed in a slim-fitting skirt and a crisp blouse. Her black shoes were smart but plain. Her long, fair hair was wound into a neat bun on the crown of her head. She greeted them with a polite smile and spoke with a slight accent but in a manner that suggested English was a second language. 'I hope this room is suitable. I thought it would be more convenient for you and the bridesmaids. You do not need to walk downstairs in your gowns.'

'It's wonderful,' Grace said, with a radiant, beaming smile on her face. 'My brother kept me up-to-date about your hard work here. I'm so pleased with it all.'

'Thank you, Doctor Franklyn.'

'Grace, please. And this other super-talented woman likes to be called Lizzy.'

'The designer,' Irena acknowledged with a nod. 'I heard about your hard work also.' She looked at the dress rail. 'Now I see the result. Congratulations, they look very beautiful.'

'It must have been a nightmare trying to get all this together so quickly,' Lizzy said.

'I am accustomed to arranging events here. The wedding is a challenging but a pleasant change. The weather will be hot so plans for the outdoor ceremony are going ahead, if that is agreeable.'

'Absolutely,' Grace said. A ripple of excitement ran through her voice. 'Will you be coming to the wedding?'

'No. I have things to do to keep everything running efficiently. I am away from my London office so I have to set up a base here. I operate from an office in the reception area. Please do not hesitate to ask if there is anything you need.' She smiled. 'Lizzy, Mr Franklyn is having drinks by the pool with his parents. He asked if you would join them when you have finished here.'

Lizzy was thrown by the request. Should she accept? Sit by the pool and pretend nothing had happened? Yet she had to get through the next few days so it was grin and bear it time. She cleared her throat and said, 'Thank you, I'll join them when this is done.'

When Irena walked from the room with an air of silent efficiency, Lizzy sighed and shook her head. 'I could be so successful with somebody like that helping me.'

'Tony worries that she's wasted in this job. She used to work in software, designing programmes or something, but she refuses promotion. Not that Tony's complaining she's very valuable where she is.' She looked around one more time and then said, 'I'll go and finish unpacking. Charlie's gone to help his brother with the kids; they're desperate to go for a swim.' She hugged Lizzy. 'Thank you so much. And good luck with… well… you know.'

Lizzy was left alone trying to rehearse some kind of apology to Tony. Her father used to tell her that everything happened for a purpose, even if we didn't like it. She tried to think what purpose was served by putting her through all these stressful events. Jenny and Carrie met somebody, fell in love and now they're happily married. But years with Patrick had clouded her view of men and left her with doubts. Jenny had made it sound so easy. "You can spend time with a guy, enjoy his company, flirt, kiss or even sleep with him without telling him your secrets. You only need tell if it gets serious."

Come on Lizzy, she chided herself. Stop kidding yourself that it's going to get that far. You've had one kiss—one fabulous, heart-stopping kiss. That doesn't mean he's planning a long, meaningful relationship with you. So, one step at a time. He offered you an olive branch, invited you to join him and his parents and that's what you should do.

****

Tony glanced at his watch, yet again, and looked around. He became aware of his fingers drumming on the table; he flexed them then reached for his glass. The ice cubes jingled as he took a gulp of the chilled fruit punch. It cooled his taut throat but his conscience still burned like hot coals inside him. Lizzy had been so thrilled with the view from the balcony, but he'd allowed the unhappy reminder to ruin what was otherwise a special moment. It was going to torment him until he could get together with her to explain, however, it wouldn't condone his outburst, and there was no guarantee that she would forgive him so quickly. He raised his voice to her; he'd never done that to a woman in his life so why today? Why to Lizzy? It was as if the ugliness and the pain from the past crashed into the fragile possibilities of a new start.

'You're very jittery, Tony,' Holly said lazily from beneath her large-brimmed sunhat. 'What's the matter with you?'

'Nothing, I'm fine.'

'I thought you'd invited Lizzy.'

'I have.'

'Doesn't look as though she's coming though, does it?'

'She'll be here. She has more to do than the rest of us.'

'Leaving nothing to chance, I expect,' Ruth said. 'I'm so glad she came. Apart from knowing that she's safe, she's such lovely company, makes me laugh sometimes.'

Tony's patience was thin but he smiled at Ruth. 'Me too, Mum.'

'This break will be good for her,' Nathan said steadily. 'After all that trauma and the hard work, a bit of peace and quiet at last. A busy woman needs a bit of peace to see her through.'

'At least that bruise is fading,' Holly said.

'I'm sure the bruise is the least of her worries,' Ruth said. 'She must be constantly wondering who on earth these dreadful people are.'

'Usually,' Holly piped up, 'these things happen when you borrow dodgy money or gamble—stuff like that.'

'Holly,' Ruth chided, in much the same way she had done since Holly was a schoolgirl, 'you're such a gossip sometimes. Are you suggesting that Lizzy is a compulsive gambler?'

'Well, it's possible.' Holly shrugged. 'Perhaps she has another life. A secret compulsion and that's why she lost her boutique in Bow…'

'If it was just about money,' Tony stopped her in her tracks, 'I could solve it couldn't I? Do you think I'd let all this happen to her—to anybody for that matter, if cash would put an end to it? Do you think I'd sit here…?' He checked his outburst, glanced at his parents and said, 'I'm sorry, I'm a bit preoccupied. Work, you know, I haven't left it behind yet.'

He toyed with his glass as he watched Charlie and his family splashing about in the pool with the children. He smiled at their antics but his thoughts were clambering through the barbed debris left by the cruel twists and turns of fate. Concealing the truth had been a big mistake. It didn't protect anybody from the ugliness of the whole thing. Now it was even harder to face it, to tell his family. But first he must tell Lizzy, tell her the real reason he kicked off about Paris.

When Lizzy approached he went to meet her and kissed her cheek with chaste politeness. He was relieved to see her but tension lingered between them and he was conscious of the fact that the earlier conflict wasn't resolved; it was just patched up for the time being. 'Come and have a drink,' he said softly, and escorted her to the table. He poured the punch from the bulbous, glass jug. Ice cubes and pieces of fruit tumbled in along with it. Lizzy smiled politely and told him how lovely it looked and that it was just what she needed.

'Tony's rather quiet, Lizzy,' Holly said. 'What on earth have you done to him?'

'Nobody's done anything,' Tony corrected her. 'I'm just enjoying this break with the family. It's been a long time since we were all together in one place.'

'Yes, we're very lucky,' Ruth added. 'But I suppose it's no comfort to you, Lizzy, seeing us wrapped up in our family and yours so far away?'

Lizzy sipped her drink and then said, 'I'm really happy for my parents. They're having the time of their lives. They deserve their dream trip.'

'Do they know what's been happening to you?'

'Oh no!' Lizzy shook her head vigorously. 'Before they left we agreed to text them to let them know how we were. That way they won't be drawn into our petty, everyday problems.'

'They're hardly petty, Lizzy,' Tony said steadily.

'I know, but if they knew they'd be home like a shot. I miss them desperately but I don't want them to do that.'

'It's not quite the same thing,' Nathan began, 'but when I lost my father I really missed him. He was my corner-stone. I always liked to tell him our news and some of our troubles. Somebody suggested I should write to him, talk to him in a letter. Of course he wouldn't get to read it but you'd be surprised how comforting it was.'

'You did that?' Tony asked.

'You seem surprised.'

'No, I'm impressed,' Tony assured him.

'Me too,' Lizzy said softly. 'Maybe I should try it.'

'Have you got a dress for the wedding?' Holly asked, as if she was frustrated that the conversation was out of her immediate interest. 'I mean you didn't have much time to shop for one let alone design one.'

'True,' Lizzy said. 'But I almost have one, there's some hand-finishing to do; just a bit of beadwork.' She addressed, Ruth and Nathan. 'I'm sorry but do you mind if I don't come to dinner. I need to get started on it.'

'Course not,' Ruth said, 'but be sure to eat something won't you?'

Suddenly a little voice called out, 'Lizzy!' Eddy scampered up the steps of the pool and ran to her; laughing and calling. Lizzy jumped to her feet and greeted him with a smile and outstretched arms. He threw himself at her and she whirled him around making him laugh even more, making Tony and his parents laugh, too.

'Are you coming in the water?'

'Sorry, Eddy, I can't stay now.'

'Why?'

'I have to fix my dress for the wedding.'

'Why?'

'So I can look pretty.'

'Why do you want to look pretty?'

'So somebody will ask me to dance.'

'I will.'

'You will? Hey that's brilliant.' She put him down, 'Your daddy's calling.'

'Will you come swimming tomorrow?'

'Yes. Go back to Daddy.'

Charlie's brother, known as Ed, since giving his name to his son, called out, 'Eddy, come on, supper time, leave Lizzy alone, you're soaking wet.' He handed Lizzy a towel. 'Sorry about that.'

'No problem.' She put the towel around her shoulders. 'What time are you swimming tomorrow?'

'After breakfast, about eight.'

'See you then,' she told little Eddy.

He stopped, held up his hands and stretched his fingers wide. 'I love you,' he called out to her. 'I love you ten.' Then he stretched his arms wide. 'This much.'

Lizzy smiled and waved her hand. 'I love you, too. See you tomorrow.' She turned back to the table, pinched the wet fabric of her top and pulled it away from her chest. 'His armbands dripped on me.'

Tony smiled. 'Your mother was right. You always end up going home soaking wet.'

She shrugged. 'Old habits... If you'll excuse me...'

'Let me know if you need anything.'

She nodded and walked away with a brief wave of her hand.

****

Lizzy sat at the table, her head rested on her knuckles as she moved her pen swiftly across the sheets of paper like a tickertape sending news to a place miles away. She hardly recognised her sister at that moment as rows and rows of words, that couldn't be said in person, spilled on to the page. She gathered up the sheets, put them into an envelope and addressed it to Carrie and Jack.

She then sat staring at the pale blue dress, spread out on the end of the table, and the little box of beads waiting for her to knuckle down. She had never been so easily distracted from her work. Normally she would have enjoyed this task, considered it the fun part where you transform a basic garment into a work of art. Motivation withered, like blown petals, leaving doubts to fill the space. Do I need to go to the wedding? I'm not family. They know I've been through a difficult time so they'll understand. I can go and do the *Michael Angelo thing* on my own, walk round the flea market. But that would leave Holly to keep Tony entertained. She groaned and tried to think of other things, absentmindedly toyed with her phone, spinning it around, longing to talk to her parents. But she kept to the agreement and eased her frustrations by sending them a text to tell them she was taking a short holiday in Tuscany, and going to a fabulous wedding. They'd love that, her father particularly, he always worried about her. He was OK with her decision to help Carrie, but he never came to terms with the way she closed her boutique.

He had been with her on the day she finally moved out. It made her heart ache to think back how worried he was. She would have been better on her own so she could grit her teeth and get on with it but he insisted on being there for her. She recalled the kindly tone that always rang in his voice, and it didn't change despite the anger and frustration he must have felt. But he *was* angry with her. She knew that.

His footsteps made a hollow, forlorn sound as he walked about the empty premises. 'Are you sure, Lizzy love?' Even *his* gentle voice bounced off the walls. 'You were doing so well.' He looked around and then sighed. 'And now look at you. You've sold off your stock at knock down prices and you've probably lost all your good will. People have short memories. It's not easy to make a come-back.'

'I can't help Carrie, and do all this at the same time. And the whole process is more complicated than I expected. I wasn't prepared for so much. It's hard but I've got to see it through, otherwise I've wasted my time for nothing.'

'You've worked for this since you were so young, a little girl spreading curtains and bits of ribbon about, pretending to make gowns for princesses. It's your livelihood for goodness sake. How can you turn your back on it like this?'

'I don't know all the answers. I don't know what's ahead or how it will affect me. I'm not Super Woman. I can only stumble along and hope for the best.' Her heart was breaking but she had to be brave, play it down.

'Carrie's problems are not your responsibility. She still has choices. She shouldn't have expected you to step in like this.'

'I'm not under any pressure, except... well, you know how she feels. It gets to me. I can't cope with it. I'm not saying that this doesn't hurt but I'd rather close down altogether than see it rot because I can't cope with it all. I'll re-locate—find a nice place in a pretty area. And I promise you, Dad, I'll work my socks off until I get it all back. Then will you feel better?'

'It sounds like a long haul, Lizzy, a dreadfully long haul.' He gathered her up in his arms and hugged her. She pressed her cheek to his chest.

Dwelling on this memory was a mistake. Large, hot tears began to spill from her eyes. Held back too long, through too many painful times, they gushed as if to free themselves from her self-restraint and endurance. She tried to stop them by pacing about. But the first cathartic drops had opened the floodgates for other heartaches to pass. She pressed her hands to her face and tried to feel her father's arms around her shoulders, giving her strength like he always did. She longed for the comforting things about him, his freshly laundered shirt on his way out in the morning and the scent of school coming home with him, his old, gardening sweater where he polished the first ripe tomato of the season before they all ceremoniously sliced it up to share it.

A shuddering breath shook her lungs, as strong arms encircled her trembling frame. She sank into the embrace, but there was no scent of school or tomato vines. This wasn't a fatherly embrace but was, nevertheless, intended to comfort her. She was guided to a chair at the end of the table and a handkerchief was pressed into her hand.

'Sit down, Lizzy; I'll get you some water.'

'I didn't hear you,' she uttered through her tense throat. 'How did you get in?'

'The door was ajar,' Tony said. 'I called, but you didn't answer. I heard you crying.' He set down the glass.

'I'm sorry.' Lizzy sipped the water and then dried her wet cheeks.

Tony drew a chair from the table and placed it close to her. She tried to look away but he took her head in his hands. 'All the troubles you've been through lately, I've never seen you cry. I did this, didn't I?'

'No, of course you didn't,' Lizzy protested. She had been desperately anxious to say sorry to Tony, but she didn't want it to be a tearful, emotional apology. What she longed to do was throw her arms around him, give him a genuine heartfelt, lingering kiss to atone for her lack of consideration, but not while she was blubbing. 'You didn't do it all by yourself, anyway. It's probably delayed shock.' She mopped the last of the tears falling down her face and was relieved that he didn't attempt to dry them for her. 'I'm OK now. I think they've stopped. I suppose my eyes look like blobs of red paint?'

'No, you obviously haven't been rubbing them too much, so they're just a bit... pink.'

'Like a hamster?'

'A very *cute* hamster.'

For a short while nothing more was said. Then, unlike Lizzy's fantasy to show her remorse in a kiss, she blurted out, 'Tony, I'm so sorry. I shouldn't...'

'No,' Tony returned, touching her face with his fingers. 'It wasn't your fault. How were you to know? There are things I should have explained to you before now.'

'But I was insensitive. I could see how hurt you were.'

Tony traced her face with his eyes. 'I won't have you taking the blame. I yelled at you. That was unforgivable, and nothing condones that.'

Lizzy was very conscious of him sitting so close. 'But, looking back on this afternoon, I don't recognise myself.'

'Oh, Lizzy,' Tony sighed and shook his head. 'I haven't recognised myself for over a year. We just have to get though these times and try not to end up in too many pieces.'

Lizzy nodded. 'I really needed a hug. Thank you.'

'I promised to catch you, didn't I?'

'A man of your word.'

'I'm more than happy to put my arms around you any time. The truth is that I'm very attracted to you. I have been since the time we first bumped into each other.'

Lizzy wanted to say she remembered the scent of him, the feeling of belonging right there where he held her, the shockingly erotic sensation from being so close to him. Instead she smiled and said, 'You were very polite. You invited me to have some coffee.'

'That wasn't a courtesy, Lizzy, that was a red-blooded male invitation designed to break the ice and lead to a date. I wanted to see you again. I swung into action but, to my total surprise, you brushed me off. In a charming manner but you made yourself very clear.'

'I didn't know you.'

Tony shook his head slowly. 'You still don't.'

'What do you mean?'

'I realised, when we were sitting there with Mum and Dad, that I was being unfair to you.'

'I don't understand.'

'Being wealthy gives you power, opens doors and offers you amazing advantages.'

'And?'

'Including the ease with which a man can date beautiful women. Somebody who gets invited to high profile events, celebrity weddings, amazing dinner parties on yachts, can always find a trophy for his arm. It's kind of symbiotic, the girls want the exposure and the excitement, and the men thrive on the ego trip. You'd think an intelligent, successful man would know better than to become a stereotypical playboy.'

'You're not a playboy.'

'Not now, but I used to find some kind of gratification in taking out a stunning beauty. It's all part of the success. You do it because you can.'

'What's the point in dating *the girl next door* if you can date a princess?' Lizzy's confident comment was no reflection on how she really felt, sitting there with her hamster eyes still smarting and her half-finished dress spread over the table. 'Why would you need to tell me all this? It's your business; it's not for me to…'

'Hear me out, Lizzy, please.' He ran his hand over her hair and traced his fingers down her cheek. It distracted him for a moment, and then he continued, 'I've never been a man to commit to a long relationship. And most of the women I met had the same attitude. That made them more attractive; we shared the same rules. Dated for a few months then we'd split up.' He shook his head. 'No, that's misleading. I'm kidding myself. Grace told me, a few days ago, that I'd broken up with some of the most beautiful women in the world. Only she put it more bluntly than that. I'd buy flowers and an expensive gift then it was all over. They found somebody else and I—'

'Found more candy for your arm?' Lizzy prompted flatly.

'Actually, I'd keep my own company for months. Find something more realistic to do. That's how I came to build Lakeside. It fixed my discontentment for a while.'

Lizzy's insides were churning. Her heart ached to think of him with these gorgeous women. She had found the courage to follow the possibility of a relationship with him, however brief, but that was now squashed. This was ending before it had begun. She cast her eyes downward. 'It's OK. You don't need to tell me all this.'

'Don't say that,' he said softly. 'I'm trying to explain that I was comfortable with that life. I knew the rules, the protocol, the way things were done among the circle of people around me. Now I'm here in a new chapter of my life, and I haven't learned the rules yet.'

'What rules?'

'I'm not accustomed to dating somebody like you.'

A pain pierced Lizzy's heart and she drew in a sharp but shallow breath. 'I'm not a trophy. Is that what's confusing you? Whether I qualify for the full benefits of a break up?'

'What on earth are you talking about?'

'If this is a prelude to my flowers and my expensive gift, I don't play that game.'

'No,' Tony protested. 'God, Lizzy, no. It's not what I'm saying. I'm trying to tell you that despite my wealth of experience in the world, I'm out of my depth with you.'

His words seemed to ricochet around the beams and leave a stunned silence.

When Lizzy spoke, it was hardly audible. 'Am I so difficult to talk to? Am I such a strange person? Does it irk you that I'm not like them?'

'Of course not.'

'Then why be any different? You didn't seek out timid, malleable girls, easy to manipulate and control, did you?'

'Certainly not.'

'They must have known the score. You didn't promise them the proverbial rose garden.'

Tony frowned, and he looked a little perplexed. 'No.'

'And I know you would never forget that you're a gentleman so they would have enjoyed being treated with respect.'

'Of course they were.'

'Well then. What's to change? Your true colours are intact so why beat yourself up because you enjoyed your success?'

He leaned towards her. 'You're amazing.'

There you go Lizzy, she chastised herself. Now you've convinced him that you're a real pal, such a good sport. One of those broad shouldered, broad-minded women who understands a man's needs to date a lot of beautiful girls. Now he thinks you're amazing. 'You should see me on a good day.'

'Is that a date?' he whispered against her face and then he gently brushed her lips with a brief kiss.

'You should go and be with your family for dinner,' she said softly, then looked back at her dress, 'I still have this to do, and it's beginning to get on my nerves.'

'Why don't I take you into Florence tomorrow, and buy you a dress?'

Lizzy's eyes rounded and fixed on his face as if he'd suggested something obscene. 'Don't look now, Tony, but your old life is showing. Were you going to get me to parade round the boutique so you could see what you were shelling out for?'

'You see?' he said. 'Totally out of my depth.'

'I might need to get something to wear at the wedding, if I don't get this done, but I can manage that all by myself.'

'Am I forgiven?'

'Totally, it was very kind and I shouldn't have been so ungracious.' She smiled and moved from the table. 'I'll pass on the shopping trip, but I'll take you up on that offer from way back.'

Tony looked intrigued. 'Offer?'

'Coffee—tomorrow.'

'You'd make a pathetic gold digger, you know that?'

'Give me time. I might just learn.'

Tony put his arms around her and pulled her close as his delicious, sonorous voice deepened into a secretive whisper. 'Send me away. Kick me out of that damned door or I'll never leave you tonight.'

Lizzy sighed against his jaw. His arms tightened and then crushed her to him as he groaned seductively and pressed a kiss on her mouth. The yearning in Lizzy's heart became a longing in her body and forced her to forget her fears. She raised her heels and reached her arms up to encircle his neck to enable her to meet his hot, thrilling mouth, savouring his obvious, unashamed pleasure in the kiss. Now it didn't matter that he was still in love with his ghost. She was Lizzy Yardley, flesh and blood and in his arms, not his memory.

Shaken and breathless they looked at each other.

'Goodnight,' Lizzy whispered.

Tony nodded, turned from her and left.

Lizzy gasped for her breath as she pushed her back against the closed door knowing that she was in love with a man who could choose from the most beautiful women in the world. This was territory she had tried so hard to avoid but she could no longer find the strength to escape. She could enjoy Tony's charming, considerate affection, even the passion that he had now shown her, all those things that the trophy women had. She could settle for her few months of bliss before her break-up flowers arrived, but she had to endure the fact that his heart, his soul, his enduring love, could never be hers.

Chapter Thirteen

Tony's visit left Lizzy in turmoil. For the first time in her career she was totally incapable of sitting with a fine sewing needle and a box of microscopic beads. The *little kiss ass number,* as Jenny had described it, was looking more like an insurmountable brick wall by the minute.

She went upstairs to finish unpacking. The view through the window lured her onto the balcony. The light of the early evening sun was tinted with a russet glow and it bathed the fields of sunflowers, turning their gold into bronze. She could see that the pool was deserted now. Everybody would be changing for dinner. A groan rippled through her throat as she leaned her arms on the balustrade and reflected on Tony's offer to take her shopping.

Pride! She sighed to herself. Was it so terrible? He meant it to be helpful, not insulting. Just imagine sitting in a Bentley Continental with expensive shopping on the back seat? But Tony was right; you're just not gold-digger material.

Maybe you did right to stick to your principles about shopping in Florence, but you were a prize idiot not to go to dinner tonight. You could have dined beneath that canopy of grapevines, watched the sunset and sipped Champagne in the romantic glow of the garden lights. What's the matter with you? Do you want to spend the rest of your life as Patrick would have you live? Denying yourself everything that would be fun and exciting because you think… you think you're tainted. You're not entitled to fun, comfort or the incredible feeling of a man's arms around you—one that unashamedly admits to being attracted to you.

Tears threatened to return. She fought them back. Not for you Patrick Smith. My tears won't roll because of something you did to me.

Normally, when she felt like this, she would run around the lake to get her mind focused but it was far too hot for anything so energetic. Instead she went downstairs, slipped her letter in her trouser pocket and made for the villa, presuming that there would be a mailbox on the reception desk.

Holly's voice could be heard, chatting quietly to her tablet. She was sitting in the entrance hall, absorbed in her conversation. She seemed startled when she saw Lizzy, and signed off very quickly. 'Got to dash!'

She looked up again. 'Hello there! I see you've dried off. Lively little brat isn't he?'

'He's lovely.'

'I hear you've volunteered for another dousing tomorrow.' She looked around, as if to ensure that they wouldn't be overheard, then she approached Lizzy and said, 'I'm glad I've caught you. I've arranged a poolside party for Tony's birthday.'

'I see.'

'It's a bit of a diversion from the wedding celebrations but Grace agreed that it was a great idea. Tomorrow, about one o'clock, it's a surprise so don't blow it, will you?'

'I wouldn't dream of it.'

'No particular dress code. Wear whatever you like. I know you didn't have much time to get your act together, coming at the last minute etcetera.'

Lizzy perceived the comment to be a complaint for upsetting Holly's well-laid plan to spend time with Tony, but she was unmoved by it. 'Sounds fun.'

Holly raised her palms upwards, 'I had a terrible job to find him a present. I mean… what does a person get for him anyway? But don't worry if you haven't got anything, I'm sure Tony won't expect it.'

Lizzy looked at her behaving like a wife already—Tony's wife, orchestrating the whole thing to give her a chance to play hostess, thus becoming his partner for the occasion. She was so good at this game. 'So if I do find something for him it'll be a nice surprise won't it?'

Holly's face formed a smile like a gracious lady talking to a more humble guest. 'Well good for you. See you tomorrow. Good luck with your dress. I wouldn't know where to start.' She peered at Lizzy's face. 'You should get some cucumber on those eyes they look tired.'

'Thanks I will.'

Holly's tall, slender, fabulously dressed frame glided elegantly across the reception area, towards the stairs.

There was a time, during the past few weeks, when Lizzy would have felt demoralised but after hearing about Tony's fabulous ex-girlfriends and worrying about Louisa emerging unexpectedly, Holly didn't faze her at all anymore and she was suddenly thankful for Jenny's insistence on packing the honeymoon clothes.

'Lizzy!' Irena emerged from her office. 'Can I help you?'

'Hello!' Lizzy pulled the envelope from her pocket. 'I just wanted to mail this letter.'

'No problem, come into my office.'

Irena's workstation was highly organised. It looked more like a whole department than the office of a PA. There was a long unit with two desk computers, printers and other electronic things that Lizzy didn't even recognise. Against the wall stood a large photocopying and collating machine

'Are you still working?' Lizzy asked.

'I always work late when I'm at Firenze.' Irena closed the door. Then she regarded Lizzy with a look of concern. 'Is everything all right?' She indicated to a seating area, three easy chairs set in a group, with a small, low table. 'Please... sit down. I will get you a cold drink. You like orange juice? Or would you prefer wine?'

'Orange juice would be lovely, thank you.' Lizzy sat down. 'Your office is very impressive, quite a collection of equipment.'

'You cannot be efficient without it.' Irena's accent was faint; it was her precise use of English that was distinctive. She took a carton of orange juice from a small fridge and poured out two drinks. 'As you say, the tools of your trade.'

Lizzy held up the letter. 'Do the tools of your trade include postage stamps? I wrote to my sister.'

'It made you sad,' Irena observed. 'You have been weeping—yes?'

Lizzy was taken aback by her intuition. 'I haven't heard from her recently. I was getting worried.'

'Leave it with me, I will deal with it.' She handed Lizzy her drink and then sat down by her. 'I envy you having a sister to talk to.'

'The trouble is I *can't* talk to her. Or even contact her.' A wave of emotion caused her throat to jerk. She swallowed and then continued. 'It seems that she was going away for a while, but that shouldn't mean total silence. She's being very difficult. I'm really annoyed with her.' Her hand trembled as she sipped her drink. 'Anyway that's not your problem.'

Irena smiled sympathetically. 'Other people's troubles are easier to solve than your own. Can you not think of a reason for her actions?'

Lizzy shrugged. 'I suppose she needs a break. I shouldn't be annoyed with her after what she's been through. Years of painful treatment, disappointment and heartbreak, just to have what other mothers have so much more easily.'

'Ah! She has been trying to conceive.'

'It wasn't just the pain it was expensive and very stressful because you just don't know if it's going to work.'

'The desire to have a child would be the driving force, the pain and finances are just a side effect.'

Lizzy nodded. 'It didn't seem to matter what she had to do. She was desperate—obsessed even. It affected the whole family. She just wouldn't give up.' Lizzy paused a moment and then beamed a warm smile. 'But my little nephew came along. He's totally gorgeous.'

'So it was worth it.'

'Oh yes.'

'Perhaps, under the circumstances, it is a good thing she is away considering what has happened to you recently; the ram-raid and the attack at the hotel.'

'I suppose Tony tells you everything.'

'There is no way of knowing that but he tells me what is necessary for me to know.'

'All this aggression must sound very scandalous to you.'

Irena shook her head slowly. 'There are people who could coldly tear your life apart, even if you did not deserve it. I know how you feel. I too have suffered this way.'

'I'm sorry.'

'But these things should not be allowed to leave your life in ruins. I tell you because my life is good now. People can turn misfortune around. You will get through this. You are strong. That is essential.'

'I don't know. I don't feel very tough at the moment.'

'I told my husband that we should leave Ukraine and live in the UK. We would have a better life. The children would enjoy good food and an English education. I have dual nationality so this would not be a problem. He agreed and for the first time in our marriage I trusted him with the money to make travel arrangements. But he did not come home. I had a call to say he would not leave. He thought I would tell him to come home and we would remain in Ukraine. Instead I made the arrangements with the money saved to find accommodation, and three years ago I uprooted my three children from their home and travelled to London, without first securing employment or somewhere to stay.' She raised her brow. 'What right have I to think your situation is scandalous?'

Lizzy was amazed. 'That was extremely courageous.'

'I had never considered my dual nationality to be of any consequence before but it was a blessing. It should have ended in disaster but the day we arrived I chose a company at random, left my children in the reception area and walked into Mr Franklyn's London office. I had scribbled a résumé on a small notepad when I was on the plane. I worked with computers, but I offered to do menial work, anything. I expected to be ordered out but he listened. Said he would find me some kind of employment and gave me an advance on my salary so the children would have a safe place to stay until it was sorted out. I knew my husband for fifteen years, we had three children; he left me with nothing. I knew Mr Franklyn for as many minutes and he gave me so much. It was an amazing gesture. One day, I will repay him, with an equally amazing gesture.'

'You've made his family very happy by organising the wedding so efficiently. They're having such a wonderful time.'

'But you are not,' Irena said with an unnerving frankness. 'And I suspect that it is not just your sister that troubles you. Mr Franklyn was also not happy this afternoon. Quite a coincidence.'

Lizzy sighed. 'We had words.'

'*We had words,*' Irena echoed, shaking her head, 'sometimes, English is so strange.'

'We argued. When he was showing me around the cottage, I dashed onto the balcony and he thought it was dangerous and reckless. So we…'

'Had words,' Irena added. She thought for a moment as if to find a tactful way of continuing her line of conversation. 'Did he explain the significance of the balcony?'

Lizzy's insides quaked a little. 'So you know about Paris?'

'More than anybody, I think. But I thought he was feeling better about it.'

'He can't let her go. I'm sure she was amazing but I'm beginning to resent her for all the pain she puts him through.'

'There is something I think you should see. It is in the public domain so there is no reason why you should not see it.' Irena moved over to one of the computers and made a brief search. 'Come—look at this.'

Shock thudded against Lizzy's chest as she looked at the images on the screen: Tony and a very stylish woman. They were smiling, dressed for a formal evening. 'Is this…?'

'Yes, this is Louisa.'

Lizzy was stunned for several seconds as she looked at Louisa's shiny, black hair and fabulous body. Something clenched around her heart like a vice as she whispered, 'She's so gorgeous. They look incandescently happy.'

'This was in a magazine. People like Mr Franklyn receive many invitations to high profile charity events. He is a good-looking man with a very beautiful woman, so they get their picture taken.'

Lizzy gulped to ease the pressure on her vocal chords. 'No wonder he grieved so much.'

'When he got back from the States, it was all over, including her funeral. Most of the party guests scattered, not wanting to be involved. Those who remained claimed to know nothing. She had no family, only an elderly aunt who was in a care home and did not understand. Mr Franklyn sent her flowers. He visited her but they told him she would gain no comfort as she did not comprehend what had happened.'

Lizzy recalled Jenny's account of that moment when he was unable to write a card. He had told her that there was no way to describe how he felt.

'I want you to understand,' Irena said evenly, 'my work is confidential and I am only showing you this because I want to see him get over this passion. I believe you can help him do that.'

'What can I do? I mean, look at her. What right have I to say he should forget her?'

'I will show you,' Irena said, clearing the image from the screen. 'I offered to continue searching for information but he became angry and told me to leave it alone. He said he was tired of doors slamming in his face. It was over. I felt he deserved to know what happened to this special woman in his life. But he was right, we could learn nothing more. All we know is that she was at a party when it happened. As you saw, she was very beautiful but not famous, so it was not big news. There was just a small piece, in the Paris newspaper, suggesting that it was suicide. Nobody denied it.'

'So they didn't connect her to Tony?'

'No they did not. That was a blessing.'

Lizzy nodded.

'Some weeks later, somebody posted private photographs on the social network, taken at the party just before she died.'

Lizzy gasped. 'That's terrible. What a cruel thing to do.'

'These are not so glossy. They are very shocking. But it is important that you see them. For him you understand?'

Lizzy nodded and looked at the screen. 'It looks like a pretty wild party. But I don't see…'

'You do, Lizzy, but she is not so beautiful when she is intoxicated and clinging suggestively to a man. This next picture is worse. She is stripping off her clothes and laughing, while the other guests look on. She does not behave like a woman in love.'

Lizzy snatched a sharp breath. 'That's her? You're kidding me.'

'We talked, a few minutes ago, about how just one single person can do so much damage to your life, especially when they are not exactly who they pretend to be.'

'I can't believe it, it's so unfair. He probably thinks she's perfect.'

'I do not think Mr Franklyn would like to see his *casta diva* making such an indecent exhibition of herself, do you?'

'He adored her. It would break his heart if he saw this.'

'But it would end his obsession. He would grieve some more but it would pass. There would be justice. But... maybe you will conquer this ghost. He is attracted to you. He makes no secret of that. And at the very least you will find courage in knowing that you deserve him more than she ever did.'

Lizzy returned to her seat, the pictures still visible in her mind's eye. 'Thank you, Irena. Thank you so much for showing me this.'

'Are you all right?'

'I'm more than all right. Now I know that she isn't a saint I can deal with her. And that's exactly what I'm going to do.'

She left Irena's office, ran back to the cottage, purging some of the anger and disgust. She arrived and closed the door, her lungs pulled at her body. Her tears were gone, now there was only resolve burning in her eyes and in her heart. 'You're not going to win, Louisa,' she said out loud. 'Fair enough when you were an angel, a heavenly being who could do no wrong, you had me beaten. But now I know better. So he still worships you but you can't come back to hold him or kiss him, give him the warmth of an earthly love like I can. Maybe I won't have much time with him but I'll have him long enough to stop you hurting him. So, listen up, you two-faced, gold-digger... you're not having him.'

Chapter Fourteen

Tony could hear the sounds of fun and laughter coming from the pool as he left the main villa. A feeling of apprehension came over him as he anticipated seeing Lizzy. Yesterday evening she was so upset, and he had been very frank when he talked of his past; although not all was confessed, that was a mountain he had yet to climb. When he neared the pool the sounds of excited children, playing with their parents, lifted his heart. Then he saw Lizzy as he had never done before. She was holding Little Eddy, who kicked his legs and shrieked with joy as she pulled him along in the water. Their laughter was infectious and it made Tony laugh too. He should have gone to Irena's office by now; a meeting had been suggested, something important, but the sight of Lizzy so relaxed and happy was too good to miss.

The sound of a phone caused him to look around. Lizzy's handbag was on the table; it was open and the phone was visible. Unlike Holly, who spent most of her time talking to friends, Lizzy had so few calls and he suspected that this would be important. He answered it whilst trying to attract her attention.

'Hello there. This is Lizzy's phone.' He snatched up a towel from the back of the chair and started to walk towards the pool steps.

'Who's that?' a woman's voice called out.

'I'm Tony, Lizzy's friend.'

'Is she there? This is her sister.'

'She's swimming. If you could just hold on…'

'Swimming?'

'Yes. I'll get her for you.'

'No, I can't hold on.'

'But she'll be just a minute. I'm almost there.'

'Will you give her a message?'

'I know she'll want to speak to you. She's been desperate to make contact. Please… won't you just hold until I get her?'

'I can't hold any longer. Tell her we're fine. And I'm sorry for not calling sooner.'

'Give me your number I'll get her to call you back.'

'I can't. Just tell her.'

'Is there something wrong? Something we can do?' Frustrated by the sudden silence as Carrie ended the call, he thrust the phone into his pocket and continued towards the pool steps.

'Uncle Tony!'

'Hi Eddy! Having fun?'

'I'm being a boat.'

Ed took hold of him. 'Game over, Eddy.' He ignored Eddy's protest and scooped him out of the water. 'Come on! Give Lizzy a bit of peace.'

Lizzy emerged from the water. Her two-piece beach outfit was simple, brief but not so much as a bikini. He tried to think quickly but the sight of her beautiful body, the movement of her slender legs as she walked up the steps from the pool, robbed him of any clear thought. He was fascinated by the coordination of her limbs as he had been that first morning he saw her running by the lake. She looked fabulous; so relaxed and happy.

Her greeting as she approached was simple, a smile, a brief wave of her hand, but it almost knocked him off balance. It wasn't just her body or the way she caused huge shots of adrenalin to surge through him, he was learning very quickly that she was special.

His efficient, practical mind prepared to explain about the phone call but then his heart intervened and questioned whether she really needed to know about it right away. Would it be so wrong to hold it back for a short while? Keep that wonderful look on her face?

He greeted her with a smile. 'That looked very energetic.' He slipped the towel around her shoulders.

'It's fun being a kid again sometimes.'

He kissed her wet face. Lizzy laughed and dried his cheek with the corner of the towel. She tilted her head and regarded him suspiciously. 'You look a bit preoccupied, is everything OK?'

It was obvious that she had detected something in his eyes. He made a bid to distract her. 'Did you finish your dress?'

'Yes, at two thirty in the morning.' She grimaced. 'That frock has got attitude. I was very tempted to walk away from it and take you up on your offer.'

Tony chortled. 'I don't believe that for a minute.'

'Why not? Perhaps I've decided to become a gold digger after all.'

'Darling, Lizzy, on your most mercenary, selfish day, you couldn't begin to scratch the surface.'

'Well a girl has to start somewhere. Maybe you can give me lessons.'

Tony noticed a marked change in her. She was relaxed and more positive. He dared to hope that this was the real Lizzy coming out from behind her troubles. He expelled a gentle laugh. 'There are much more interesting things we can do with our time.'

Then darts of electricity ran through his flesh as she rested her hands on his shoulders and then slid one hand behind his neck. Her voice became soft and warm. 'Tell me something,' she said with a light in her eyes, 'is there a restaurant like Sanccella's, in this part of the world?'

'Of course there is.'

'Will you take me?' she asked. 'Take me somewhere where there's a grand piano and candles and Champagne? Will you find a place where our troubles have to be left outside the door, and we're not allowed to talk about them? Just you and me talking about ordinary things, books, cinema, music—whatever.'

Tony felt the thrill of anticipation, it was intoxicating. The sounds of the children running back to the villa, faded. He could only see and hear Lizzy, the morning sun on her face, the touch of her hands and the closeness of her face to his. 'You forgot to mention *to-die-for* pasta,' he murmured.

'That too.'

'This evening?'

'After working half the night, I'll never be able to stay awake long enough to listen to the piano or watch the candlelight. Can we make it tomorrow? Or do you have an eve of wedding party?'

'Wedding or no, my family would be delighted to see us going out together.'

Lizzy smiled. 'So that's a date?'

'Too damned right it's a date.' Tony drew a controlled breath. 'Go and get dried off otherwise I'll never get my work done.'

'Work?'

'I have a meeting with Irena but I'll see you later.' He took the phone from his pocket. 'Is this yours?'

'Yes, it must have dropped out of my bag.'

Tony brushed her lips with a brief kiss and dragged himself away.

****

'Good morning.' Tony entered Irena's office.

'Would you like some coffee?'

'No thanks.' He sat down in an easy chair. 'So, what's up?'

Irena drew a long breath as if to form the right words before speaking.

'Irena Ivanovski, lost for words in all of her five languages?'

'This is not easy.'

'Since when did you have a problem talking about work?'

'It is not work.'

'Oh, hell, you're not resigning are you? This wedding is a huge challenge I know but we can work something out.'

Irena held her palms towards him as if to block his words. 'This is not a problem with my work. This wedding has been a lot more fun than a convention.'

'Then what?'

'We should talk about Lizzy.'

Tony stared for a moment, his brow twitching in confusion. 'What about her?'

'We need to help her.'

'You know I'll do anything for Lizzy, but why? She seems very well this morning. In fact I was reluctant to respond to your call. So what's on your mind?'

Irena spoke calmly. 'You would agree that she is not responsible for what has happened to her?'

'Without a doubt.'

'But she is definitely the target.'

'That's the frustrating thing about it.'

Irena's brow twitched but her voice remained even. 'Has it occurred to you that...' she stopped a moment.

'Irena, you're making me nervous. Just spit it out.'

'*Spit it out.*' Irena shook her head. 'I will never understand your use of colloquialisms, they are so confusing.' She looked at him and continued. 'Lizzy was here yesterday evening. She felt homesick. She had written a letter to her sister.'

Tony nodded, 'Yes, my father suggested it.'

'A little more than a year ago, her family was troubled. Carrie, her sister, had been unable to have a child and was becoming desperate.'

'So that's what it's all about. Weeks ago, Lizzy said she couldn't stand Carrie's pain any longer, and that's why she wound up her business.'

'No doubt to give her sister the time and the emotional support she needed. It is possible that she wanted to release funds to pay hospital fees.'

'Do they have to pay for this kind of treatment?'

'They are entitled to some but after a time they have to pay. It is extremely expensive to do this. When they can no longer afford it they might borrow money without paying much attention to the consequences.'

'Consequences?'

'Close relatives being targeted, ram-raids, attacks... are you keeping up, Mr Franklyn?'

Tony stared at her, hardly able to believe what she was saying. 'Are you suggesting that it was Carrie who borrowed money?'

'Do not underestimate the obsession of a woman wanting a child. It is all-powerful and consuming, especially if they have miscarried several babies already.'

'How much money does it take for God's sake?'

'They need not borrow much for it to grow out of all proportion. Although moneylenders advertise their terms, desperate people do not always take note of the details. There are ways of adding on the interest, and it makes it impossible for people to keep up. Some unscrupulous loan sharks, these days, make sure they cannot keep up. Nevertheless it is a debt and would need to be paid to make it go away.'

Tony paused a moment. His brow was knitted, his jaw was rigid. 'Surely this is just supposition.'

'But there is a pattern, is there not?'

Tony recalled his brief, confusing conversation with Carrie. She and her husband were certainly behaving as if they were hiding out somewhere. She wouldn't stay on the line long enough for him to get Lizzy, so she might have been afraid of being traced. 'But even if your suspicions are correct, Irena, it's just money.'

'What is just money to you, Mr Franklyn, is probably a fortune to them. Yet it is the one answer to all this, pay them and it will all be over.'

'How do you suggest we approach this? We have no information to back up your suspicions. Carrie wouldn't even give me her phone number.'

'It is not simple but not impossible either, even crooks keep records.'

'What? What are you talking about?'

'I look for them—and you pay them.'

'What do you mean *look for them*? How on earth are you going to do that?'

Irena shrugged. 'I have Carrie's home address from Lizzy's letter. Not much, but a place to begin. With their address I might be able to trace the loan company.'

'Hacking?' Tony stood up and stared at her. 'Are you serious?'

'I am not English, I do not make jokes. Of course I am serious.'

'What you're suggesting is illegal, even if you could do it.'

'What is a little electronic juggling against Lizzy's safety?'

'It's still illegal.'

'It is not only about the danger. She has fought hard to win back her business. The Press, even your local paper, has taken little notice of it, but if we do not stop all this it could become a very big scandal for Lizzy. What then will she do? Pick herself up yet again? No, Mr Franklyn, I think not.'

Tony shook his head. 'No, Irena, we should tell the police,' he said decisively.

'But they will want to interview Lizzy again. She will find out and will still be able to do nothing.'

Tony slumped back into his chair and sighed. 'What a mess. We have to think of something.'

'I already thought of something,' Irena protested.

'Something legal. And what about the invasion of privacy?'

'I assume you mean Carry's privacy. As for the criminals, they cannot expect such a courtesy. There *is* nothing else. Do you think the police are going to come through with this? They can deal with the thugs because they have broken the law, but these bullies are just minions. The real criminals will always escape. Paying at source is the only way to beat this.'

Tony expelled a long, tense breath and got to his feet. 'OK! OK! I hear what you're saying, Irena, but there must be a better way.' He stopped and scowled. 'Besides, exactly how do you expect to do all this... research? That computer hasn't got the software capable of *juggling*, as you call it.'

'No, but mine has.' She pointed to the other one.

'That's yours?'

'Yes.'

'Like I said, leave it with me for the time being. Just let me think about it.' He made for the door and then looked back. 'Was the treatment successful?'

'Yes, Lizzy has a nephew.'

'Thank God for that.'

'God answered Carrie's prayers but had he answered them a little earlier it would have saved everybody a lot of trouble. The baby is another person at risk. That is why they are hiding, I think.'

Tony left the office. He took the stairs two at a time and returned to his room. He needed to be alone to think. There had to be a way. There had to be something he could do. His money brought help and comfort to many people. That had been easy, he just signed it away but now there was no dotted line; no place to sign away funds to solve this dilemma. His money could be newspaper cuttings for all the use it was at that moment. He thought of all the expensive gifts he had casually bought for women, yet he couldn't even do this one simple thing for Lizzy. His anger and frustration clawed at his gut as he wrestled with temptation. Irena's idea could work but he hadn't had the chance to think through the dangers, the implications to his own family. The battle raged between his integrity and his burning need to protect Lizzy.

Chapter Fifteen

'The wedding planners are really stepping up the action. They've laid a dance floor with a dais for the top table. It's all dressed with tubs of fabulous flowering plants. I wish you could see it, Jen, it's going to be such a romantic wedding.'

'Lizzy, I've *got* flowers. I talk to beautiful blooms all day. I want to know what's happening with *you*. Please tell me you're having a great time.'

'Yes, I am. A bit wobbly here and there but wonderful.'

'And what about the nemesis?'

'She's raised her game, organised a poolside lunch party for Tony's birthday.' Lizzy walked over to the open wardrobe. 'I'm turning circles here trying to decide what to wear,' she said as she nudged the clothes along the rail.

'What's Tony's birthday got to do with her?'

'It's a chance for her to be the centre of attention. And, while she's at it, put me in my place. At least the place she thinks I should be.'

'Is she getting to you?'

'No. She annoys me intensely but it's nothing I can't handle. My main problem is biting my tongue for the sake of the family. If I met her somewhere else I would have packed her off with a flea in her ear a long time ago.' She took a cotton sundress off the rail and looked it up and down. 'So what do I wear? I've got less than ten minutes now.'

'I packed some great clothes, why are you confused? That black halter neck is fabulous, but maybe not for lunchtime. I seem to remember a really classy, jersey skirt—sort of apple-coloured and a silky top, you know, the one with the pretty curvy shapes round the neckline.'

'I'm saving that for tomorrow evening. I want to look classy but not too seductive.'

'Seductive? What's happening tomorrow evening?'

'A date.'

Jenny shrieked down the phone. 'How can you be so casual about it?'

'I'm not casual I'm scared to death.'

'Of what?'

'Everything, how it feels, where it's all going... how it's going to end.'

'Give it a chance to start before you worry about how it ends.'

'I've got this nice cotton dress.'

'Lizzy!'

'What?'

'You're being evasive. You're not going to chicken out, are you?'

'No.' She chuckled and pulled another dress from the rail. 'I've declared war on his ex. She's still hurting him. I can't bear it.'

'You make it sound like she's still there.'

'She might as well be—do you think a sundress will be suitable for a lunch party?'

'Wear the maxi dress. The fabric's fantastic, and anybody can see it was expensive. Those bronze and rusty tones will set off your hair, especially in the sun. You'll look great. Go for it, girl. Knock him out.'

'You're such a tonic, Jen, thanks. We'll speak again soon.'

'Bye, Babe. Have a great time.'

Lizzy began to feel hurried and she went out onto the balcony to see if anybody had arrived at the pool. She couldn't hear clearly, but Holly was there giving instructions to one of the maintenance crew, checking that the sun loungers were straight and the cushions were plumped. All the tables were in orderly array and a small gazebo had been erected to give shade to a serving table.

'Oh, Holly,' Lizzy sighed to herself, 'haven't they got enough to do?'

Grace and Charlie arrived, followed by the children with their parents, and then Tony's mother appeared.

Time was running out. Now she was in danger of missing Tony's arrival. She quickly put on the simple sundress, slipped into a pair of sandals, then looked in the mirror. Her heart sank. Oh no. The girl next door meets Mrs Dalloway. So this is war is it? Louisa, the all-powerful Madonna, versus you with a cotton sun frock? Get your act together, Lizzy.

She tossed the sundress onto the bed then reached for the maxi dress. It rippled when she took it from the hanger and the pattern danced as the wonderful fabric moved, reminding her why she made it in the first place. It dropped into place, like water running down her body. She tweaked the thin shoulder straps, kicked off the flat sandals and stepped into high heels. Her reflection, a little taller than before, smiled back at her. All you need now is the right attitude.

Holly was in her element. This was her show. She was directing it as she glided about in her designer creation of varying tones of aquamarine and mauve, with a gossamer-like overdress that wafted about her as she moved.

'We're not going to shout surprise,' she told the group. 'He wouldn't like it,' she darted a look at Grace, '… apparently. Nathan is going to make sure he gets here.'

It was clear to Lizzy that this party was all about Holly, not Tony. She had set her stage to play the perfect hostess, but Lizzy almost laughed out loud when Tony arrived. He clearly suspected nothing about the celebration and was wearing his wonderful old jeans and his favourite shabby sweatshirt that he wore when he wanted to relax. Tony looked gorgeous in anything, but these clothes stripped away the trappings of his success and left one hell of a sexy guy who didn't need to prove anything to anybody.

The children, oblivious of Holly's carefully structured running order, ran straight to him. They stood looking up at him, wide-eyed and bubbling with excitement. They chanted, 'Happy birthday,' in unison.

'Uncle Tony, we got you a present,' Sarah said.

'With our own money,' Lucy added. She nudged her little brother. 'Go on, Eddy!' she whispered.

The boy held up the package.

'For me?' Tony said, and his warm smile beamed down at them.

Eddy nodded, clearly a little bashful.

'With our own money,' Sarah said.

'I already said that,' Lucy complained.

Tony took the package with great reverence. 'This is a lovely surprise. Let's find somewhere to sit together while I open it.'

Holly twitched at the unscheduled presentation as all the gifts were on an allotted table awaiting the given time. Tony caused yet another scowl to cross her face as he carelessly dragged one of the loungers round at an angle closer to the party. He perched on the edge of it and patted the spaces by his side. Lucy and Sarah responded and sat down. Eddy stood by Tony's knees.

Rising to the children's excitement, Tony built up the moment as the gift was slowly revealed. He gasped appreciatively, not just to be polite, but in a genuine exclamation of pleasure.

'Mummy said you were very busy so we got you a book to write important things in,' Sarah explained.

Lucy pointed to the cover. 'Do you like the butterflies?'

'I *love* the butterflies,' Tony said.

'And I do,' Eddy said.

'What are you going to put in it?' Lucy asked.

Tony looked at each girl in turn and gave Eddy a little nudge. 'I'll only ever write *very special* things,' he said without patronising their young status. He looked around. 'Does anybody have a pen?'

Charlie had one in his trouser pocket.

Tony rested the book on his thigh and wrote, saying the words out loud. 'This special book…'

'With butterflies on it,' Sarah prompted.

Tony nodded. 'With butterflies on it.' He wrote it down and then read it out. 'This special book, with butterflies on it, was given to me by Sarah, Lucy and Eddy, on my birthday.'

'With their own money,' Lucy added.

'With their own money,' Tony echoed and wrote it down. 'It's very important to mention that.' He then dated the passage, smiled and said, 'You're the kindest children I've ever met. Thank you.'

The children, gratified by his reaction, ran off to play.

'Gifts are on this table,' Holly told him hastily as if to try and regain control.

'Gifts?' Tony queried.

'On this table, all ready for you.'

'Hold on, Mohamed,' Nathan called out to his son, 'we'll bring the mountain to you. You look very comfortable there. Come on, Holly,' he urged, his age outranking her self-assumed prerogative. 'You can help me.'

Holly obeyed, floating, somewhat reluctantly, across to the gift table.

'I haven't done this since I was ten years old,' Tony laughed. He selected a small gift and took off the gold coloured wrapping. It contained cufflinks. A swift lift of his brow indicated that they were expensive. He stood to give Holly a chaste kiss on the cheek. 'Very kind, Holly, very generous, thank you.'

Holly seemed to sense exactly where Lizzy was standing and cast a slightly smug smile towards her, claiming a point in the game.

Lizzy smiled back politely. Her fight wasn't with Holly.

Tony returned to his seat and selected another package.

Lizzy loved every moment of this. It was so good to be able to watch him, his interaction with the family, the charm with which he expressed thanks for each gift. She became transfixed with a tantalising glimpse of tanned flesh, visible through the threadbare denim on his knee. She adored this man, his protective ways and his warmth with people, but at that moment she saw him as a lover. It was as if a safety barrier inside her suddenly crumbled and exposed her to his true power to stir her blood until it coursed through her body like an electric storm. She wanted him like she never had before, craved his passion; hungered for his whole body to be wrapped around her as she lost herself in the raging crucible of physical love. She shivered sensuously, from her head to her toes.

'No, Dad, I can't take this,' Tony said as he stood up to talk to Nathan, jolting Lizzy back into the real world.

'Yes you can,' Nathan insisted.

'But Grandpa's watch...' He stared at the gold Half Hunter and shook his head. 'You should keep it.'

'You could buy a dozen of these if you wanted, we know that. But this one means a lot to you. I'd rather see you enjoy it in my lifetime.'

Tony embraced his parents.

'But don't feel that you have to wear it on your waistcoat, like Grandpa,' Ruth said. 'Your dad always carried it in his pocket.'

'Hope you haven't got holes in your pockets, Tony,' Charlie called out.

Tony laughed. 'In my knees, Charlie, but never in my pockets.'

'Let's have some Champagne, shall we?' Holly said, hailing the waiter who was hovering by the gazebo.

'I haven't finished yet,' Tony said, picking up a flat package from the lounger.

'Oh, I think it must be a card.' She looked at Lizzy as if to score another point.

'It doesn't feel like a card,' Tony said.

'Perhaps you should find out,' Lizzy said, smoothly.

Tony flashed a killer smile to her.

'What else can it be?' Holly said.

'Seeing as we're harking back to childhood, why don't you guess, Tony?' Grace urged. 'Remember? We used to do that at Christmas, with our last present under the tree?'

'Come on, Lizzy,' Tony said, reaching his hand towards her. 'I'm going to need some clues.'

Lizzy sat by his side. 'It really isn't that remarkable,' she said. 'My Grandmother gave it to me, but I thought you'd like it—so I brought it.'

'Are you sure you want to part with it?'

'I treasured it out of respect for her, but trust me it's better placed with you.'

'I'm intrigued but I need a clue.'

'OK,' Lizzy said, smiling. 'It's a theatre programme... a particular landmark.'

'RSC?'

'No—same status though.'

'Covent Garden?'

'Yes. It's in perfect condition. It was Gran's twenty-first birthday treat. She loved the Opera, that one in particular.'

'Which one?'

'I'm doing all the work here,' she laughed and gave him a nudge with her shoulder.

'Come on,' he coaxed, 'I'm getting very impatient to see it.'

'Tosca, and that's the last clue you're getting.'

Tony's voice lowered and he tilted his head, still being very persuasive. 'Your grandmother's twenty first birthday. That would be circa…?'

'What a flirt,' Grace called out. 'Don't fall for that one, Lizzy.'

Lizzy kept quiet as her eyes challenged him.

'Come on,' he coaxed, 'give me a decade at least.'

'Sixties.'

'I'm very happy with this, whatever it is,' Tony said. 'But if it was dated 1965…' He was almost breathless when he added, 'Then I would be a very happy man indeed.'

'Oh, really?' Lizzy said, pan-faced.

'Tony, you're drooling,' Grace laughed.

'You bet I'm drooling.'

Lizzy became a little uncomfortable with all the attention focused on them. 'It wasn't meant to be a big deal. It's just a token. I heard you playing a CD at Larchwood,' she said, thereby delivering the last vital clue to Tony.

'So, Covent Garden, the sixties, Tosca, Maria Callas.' He paused, his eyes shining. 'I can't believe it.'

'Yes, it was her last…'

'Her last performance in an opera,' Tony said. He carefully opened the wrapper and looked at the programme.

'The signatures are genuine, Gran got them herself.'

'It's signed?' He shook his head. 'It doesn't get any better than this.'

'Oh, Tony,' Ruth sighed, 'how lovely.'

'A true gift,' Nathan said.

'Something you haven't got,' Grace added. 'Well done, Lizzy. If you had any idea how long he's looked for that.'

Tony hugged Lizzy, kissed her face and whispered privately in her ear. 'Thank you, sweetheart. Thank you so much.'

Lizzy was shaken and had to pull herself together quickly. All eyes were on them. 'My pleasure—really.'

'I'm almost speechless,' Tony said to the party. 'All these gifts are amazing.' He shook his head and returned his attention to the notebook. 'All my adult life I never had a gift from children using their own pocket money.'

Holly spoke up. 'The buffet is ready, under the canopy.'

The group dispersed. Tony stopped to show the children his watch. Holding it to their ears so they could hear it tick. The sound lit their faces.

Lizzy strolled away to try and recuperate her senses. She stood quietly watching the stillness of the pool.

'Every time!' a voice surprised her.

She turned to see Holly's cold stare. 'I'm sorry, what?'

'No matter what happens, Lizzy Yardley comes up smelling of roses. You really don't have to try, do you?'

'I don't know what you mean, Holly.'

'Your little catalogue of achievements.'

Lizzy shook her head in confusion.

'Oh, come on! You, came to the rescue to save the wedding, you bonded with the kids. Oh, and let's not forget that touch of tragedy in your life that brought you here. Then, the jewel in the crown, you casually produce a rare item for Tony's collection.'

Lizzy began to find Holly's game tedious. 'It was a coincidence. It's only an old theatre programme.'

'That just happened to be the one he's been searching for. Did you know that he started his collection years ago? And he won't use his power or his fortune to force the items from collectors? There's no fun in that you see.'

'No I didn't.'

'It adds to the thrill of the hunt, the way it was before he became so wealthy.'

'I can understand that.'

'You even managed to find a halfway decent dress for the party. Did your fairy godmother come in the middle of the night?' She shook her head slowly. 'Like Cinder-bloody-rella.'

Lizzy looked at Holly's cold eyes and her tight-lipped bitterness and wondered just how far this woman would go to get what she wanted. She then told herself that she didn't have time to fight two women, particularly as Holly was making no progress in her mission at all.

'Can I go and get some lunch now?' Lizzy asked, trivialising Holly's complaint.

'You might be the family pet for the moment, Cinders, but you haven't got to the ball yet. While you're trying to make conversation on the miss-fit table, I'll be on the family table playing catch up. See what your fairy godmother can do about that.'

Lizzy was unperturbed. 'I'll look forward to it. I like meeting new people.'

'With a bit of luck you'll bump into another geeky stationery dealer and elope.'

'Another what?'

'Well that was your type until you bumped into Tony.'

'You've got a good memory.'

'I get around.' With a lift of one brow, Holly drifted over to the buffet table, as her dress drifted and floated around her like a venomous Portuguese man-of-war.

She was becoming more and more rude and bitter by the day. She wasn't after Tony's heart or his money; she wanted the status, the profile, just like all the others.

'Hey! Daydreamer.' Tony surprised Lizzy. 'Love the dress. You look fabulous.'

'Thank you. So do you.'

'I don't think Holly was very impressed. Nor my mother for that matter. She said I looked like a hobo.'

'I love those clothes.'

'Really?'

'Oh yes.'

'So you don't mind giving a birthday kiss to a tramp?'

Lizzy smiled. 'I thought you'd never ask. I wore my high heels specially.' She was tempted to give Tony a lingering kiss for Holly to see, but she couldn't use him that way. She smiled and pressed a brief but warm kiss on his mouth. 'Happy birthday, you fabulous hobo.'

Tony slid his hands beneath her hair and rested them on her naked shoulders. And this,' he whispered, 'is for the gift.' He kissed her again. It was brief but hot, and a hum of pleasure rose from his vocal chords.

A waiter approached with a tray of drinks. Tony took two, gave one to Lizzy then raised his glass. 'To the only woman who loves my favourite clothes as much as I do.'

Chapter Sixteen

Tony perched on a lounger, writing in his notebook by the amber spill of the garden lights. Tendrils of guilt wrapped around his contentment as he pondered on Carrie's phone call this morning, and whether he should have told Lizzy about it. He sighed at his deception, now he had two secrets instead of one. He looked at Lizzy, as she slept peacefully, stretched out on the next lounger. She lay on her back with her face turned towards him. Every now and then she passed her tongue over her lips and then closed them again. The rich fabric of her voluminous dress fell into soft curves over her body and rose where her knee was slightly bent. Despite the innocence of her sleep, he fought a powerful urge to reach out and run his fingers along the ridge of her collarbone. Or press his mouth on the delicious roundness that rose and fell below it. He had often heard men tell about the pleasures of watching a woman sleep but he could never relate to that particular pleasure until now. These days, there never seemed to be a time when his body wasn't burning for the want of her. He drew in a long breath and then blew the air out through pursed lips, making a faint whistling sound. It did nothing to cool his heated thoughts.

'Mr Franklyn?'

Tony looked up. 'Are you still working, Irena?'

'I just finished. Have you enjoyed your birthday?'

'I most certainly have. It was a great party.' He gestured to her to sit down. 'Holly claimed to have organised it but I suspect you did it.'

Irena sat at the end of Tony's lounger. 'She is a bossy lady. Your family is very tolerant.'

'She's the daughter of a very respected and valued friend. It gives her diplomatic immunity. She didn't come to dinner though. That's unusual. Every time I turn round she seems to be there.'

'Miss Parker had something in her room. She had to make some phone calls.'

'Charlie was on form talking about his internship and things he did to stay awake.' He paused to look at Lizzy. She was still very much asleep. 'Lizzy was exhausted; up half the night fixing her dress. Charlie's anecdotes about sleep deprivation, made her even more tired. She walked around to try and wake up a bit. When I caught her up she was lying there.' He smiled and turned back to Irena. 'I haven't the heart to wake her yet. Sleeping under the stars for a while won't do her any harm.'

Irena nodded. 'I came to give you a gift.'

'You too? Everybody's being very generous today.'

'It is not the kind you can wrap up. I have something to tell you.'

'OK.'

'My assumption was correct. It was Lizzy's sister and her husband who borrowed money. They were very deeply in debt.'

'How do you know?'

'I targeted a shortlist of loan companies. After a while I got lucky. You might think it an invasion of privacy but it was just a column of numbers.'

Tony expelled a long steadying breath. 'Are you sure?'

'Yes.'

'I don't want to tell Lizzy if it isn't absolutely true. It'll break her heart. And God knows what that will do to our… friendship. We need to work out what we can do. Put a PI onto it… find Carrie.'

'But the money lenders will also have a PI looking.'

Tony's voice strained in his throat. 'Then we'll have more than one. We've got to find Carrie before they do. If we can get hold of her, we can pay it.'

'Investigators would approach it in the same way as I have, except that you would be paying them to do it.'

'I can't give you permission to…'

'Why ignore a problem that has a straightforward solution?'

'I agree it's the best way but it's still illegal.'

'But morally acceptable. Can you not see the justification in what has been done?'

'Been done?'

'Yes,' Irena said firmly. 'It is done.'

'What?'

'I was not acting on your instructions, Mr Franklyn. I know you were not willing to pursue this so I worked alone; nothing can be traced to you or your company.'

'The company's strong enough to ride it. I was concerned for you.'

'There is no need to be. The degree of violation to the moneylenders is a matter of opinion. It is paid.'

'With what? How did you transfer the cash without my input?'

'I used funds that were no longer needed.'

'I don't know what you mean. I might have a lot of money, Irena, but I know where it all is.'

'Not quite all. What about the,' she cleared her throat, 'the, *out of town,* account?'

'What on earth's that?'

'The one you put in my control last year. You said you were going to the US for some weeks and you wanted to secure expenses for Miss Warren, that your accountant would be calling me when she needed financial support.'

'Ah, yes,' Tony muttered, 'of course.'

'It was not something you wished to address after the Paris incident, so you have been paying into it until now.'

Tony cleared his throat. 'I'm sorry, Irena, I should have sorted that out.'

'It is no problem for me. I paid the debt and donated the remainder to charity. Then I closed the account to cover my tracks. That will not cause any suspicion because the lady is deceased.'

Tony decided that any more thinking was a waste of time. It was done. Trying to rationalise the situation now was unproductive. 'Your dedication is admirable, but I didn't expect you to take such a personal risk.'

'I think perhaps you wish me to resign?'

'Course not,' Tony scowled. 'Personally I also feel that the end justifies the means. And if only Carrie was a little more communicative we could have asked her for the details and paid it legitimately. Just out of interest, how much did it take?'

'Fifty thousand for the debt and twenty for the charity. A lot of money, I know, but you had already given it away.'

'It's all relative, probably not as much as the children paid for my notebook. They used their pocket money.' He paused for a moment. 'And you, Irena, you did an incredible thing.'

'It needed to be.'

'What do you mean?'

'I have been indebted to you for three years. You saved my children from hardship and confusion. I did this for Lizzy, because I wanted to do something for you—something equal to the risk you took by employing me that day.'

Tony nodded. 'I remember when you first arrived. You must have been exhausted, but there you were, smartly dressed, and offering to work; so impressive—unexpected.'

'Not all Ukrainians arrive with snow on their boots, singing, Orchi Chornia.'

Tony chuckled. 'Irena, you made a joke.'

She sighed. 'Did I? My English blood is showing.' She thought for a moment and then said. 'About Miss Warren.'

'What about her?'

'Will you get over her? Maybe one day the pain will go?'

Tony breathed steadily for a few moments and then said, 'It isn't so much getting over it as the impact she had on my life. It's my time with her that I can't forget so easily. It was life-changing and it stopped tragically. It put my whole existence into confusion. That's why I still feel the pain.'

'What about sleeping beauty?'

Tony fixed his eyes on Lizzy, her hair had fallen over her cheek; her hand hung limply over the edge of the lounger. 'She masks the pain. She always has, since the first moment I saw her.'

'Do you want me to tell her what has been done?'

'No, but I'm about to spend a sleepless night trying to work that one out. It won't sit comfortably on her shoulders. She'll be upset for her sister—embarrassed for herself. Her independence will be shattered because she'll want to pay the money back. But, tell her I must. She needs to be ready for when Carrie calls again, to tell them they can go home.'

'The Police will be delighted. They were never going to catch the money lenders and they already have the thugs.' She stood up. 'Is there anything more I can do?'

'No, it's late. Time you stopped working.'

'Don't worry I will. I shall have a glass of wine and watch a movie.'

'Which one?'

'Brief Encounter.'

'You like that film?'

'Yes, especially the music. Goodnight, Mr Franklyn.'

Chapter Seventeen

'Hey, beautiful!' Tony's voice pierced the early morning stillness.

Lizzy's heart leapt as she climbed the steps of the pool. She attempted to calm it down by telling herself that, at her age, she should have more control even if she was crazy about him. 'A guy could turn a girl's head with a greeting like that,' she called back.

Tony was standing by the lounger where Lizzy had left her things. 'Well, what's a man to do when he sees a Bond girl emerging from his pool?'

Lizzy grimaced as she squeezed water from her ponytail. 'Bond girl? You're the one who's armed and dangerous, standing there in your fabulous casuals.'

Tony picked up her towel and handed it to her. 'You're very brave. The water won't have heated up yet.'

'It was a bit chilly.' She mopped her face and arms, then hugged the towel to her chest. 'I didn't expect to see anybody around so early.' She laughed. 'Not even Eddy.'

'So you thought it was safe to come out in your bikini.'

'It's new. I wanted to make sure it would behave properly in the water before I wore it in public.'

Tony smiled and there was a distinct twinkle in his eye. 'Trust me, it's perfect.'

His smiling eyes and his compliments nourished her ego. Words of love and affection jostled to be released from her soul but she was afraid to reach too close to his heart. He wasn't the boy next door he was a man of the world and very eligible. Sure he was attentive and demonstrative but any overzealous declarations could lead to a very polite and gentlemanly finale to her short but dramatic time with him. She filed the words away in a special compartment in her heart, smiled and told him, 'You say all the right things.'

He pressed a brief kiss on her mouth. His lips felt hot after the cool water in the pool. 'I'm going to pick up my two cousins at the airport.'

She smiled. 'The notorious Gallier boys?'

'They're the ones. Fraser's worried about Eliot. He says he's OK, but, like you, he's still recovering from a traumatic event.'

'He was attacked?'

'We don't know. He can't remember.'

'Poor man,' Lizzy said softly. 'Does he need to be alone? I could move out.'

'No, he's fit enough. Do you remember that day you collected the strawberries?'

Lizzy nodded. 'You weren't very pleased.'

'Only because I fancied you like hell and felt it inappropriate to make a pass at you. Anyway, I'd just come back from Cape Town. I went with Fraser to bring Eliot home. He'd sustained a head injury. Woke up in a hospital and hadn't a clue where he was or why. His normal memory came back within a couple of days and physically he was recovering well. But even now he can't recall what he was doing there.'

'You must be very worried about him.'

'He says he's come to terms with it. I hope he has.'

'So I'll get to meet them?'

'I'm not sure I should let you.'

'Why?'

'I can't say that I've noticed myself, but I have it on good authority—namely Grace—that Eliot and Fraser are incredibly *fit and sexy as hell.* And eligible,' he added.

Lizzy expelled a soft laugh. 'Well we're only going to be here another forty eight hours or so, that doesn't give me much time to break their poor hearts. A guy would have to be in love first.'

'I know at least one young man who's crazy about you.'

She smiled. 'Eddy, you mean.' Affection rang in her voice. 'His little heart is safe with me.'

Tony was silent for a moment and then, as if somebody took the sunshine away and left a dark cloud over them he said, 'I'm really sorry but we need to talk.'

The words chilled her body. Her insides churned at the swift change in him. She put her best mask of control in place. 'Something wrong?'

Tony's brow was puckered. 'We should go to the cottage.'

'It sounds very serious.' She wrapped the towel round her waist then perched on the lounger. 'Is it—serious?'

'Yes, I suppose it is. I wanted to tell you before I left for the airport. Shall we go to the cottage?'

'You said you hadn't much time,' she blurted in a panic. 'You've made me nervous now. I'd rather hear it straight away.'

Tony nodded and sat by her, his eyes focused on the ground, elbows braced in his thighs and his hands clenched against his chin. The muscle in his jaw twitched characteristically. 'OK, we'll talk here.'

'Are you going to ruin my day?' Lizzy's voice was quiet. 'It started so well.'

Tony clasped her hand. 'I hope not.'

'I've never hidden from life. I've always faced it head on, so don't try and protect me now, Tony, just say it.'

He nodded. 'The first thing to say is that I answered your phone yesterday, while you were in the pool. It was Carrie, but she wouldn't wait. I tried. I'm sorry.'

'So what else's new? Don't worry about it.'

'I was being a coward. You were so happy and relaxed I chickened out. But I should have told you yesterday.'

Lizzy shrugged her shoulders. 'Told me what? That my illusive sister rang to play *catch me if you can*?' She looked at his face. Her eyes challenged him. 'You're not keyed up because of that. There must be something else.'

Tony cleared his throat and began again. 'When you told Irena about Carrie, and her long, painful attempts to have a baby...'

'She told you that?'

'For good reason I can assure you.'

'OK, carry on.'

'Irena's approach to life is very straightforward. She doesn't waste time looking for a better way or a more suitable time to deal with a situation. If something needs doing... Her idea is to go straight for it and solve it.'

'I've noticed that. But solve what? What has that to do with my conversation with her?'

Tony's hand tightened on hers. Their fingers locked together. He was seemingly searching for the right words, but each one seemed to catch in his throat as he delivered the barbed truth: the reason for the violence, the damage to her boutique, the threatening note. She listened, too shocked to interrupt.

'Of course this couldn't be confirmed without a certain amount of prying,' Tony continued. 'She had to begin the trail with their home address. Find the loan company. But Irena truly believed that the end justified the means.'

Lizzy felt an overwhelming urge to run from him, take this family shame with her and hide it away. Previously she could only guess as to why Carrie was behaving this way, but this news debunked her theory. She stood up to leave but Tony grasped her hand.

'Lizzy please sit down, there's more to tell you.'

'Oh God!' She sank back down and dropped her face into her hands. 'Where did she find these people?' she asked through her fingers.

'You don't have to look very hard, they're out there waiting, working out ways to hook up desperate people who need quick money. Put them in a situation where they pay interest on crunched, mythical, barely legal figures. It's easily done, Lizzy.' He braced his arm around her.

She dropped her hands to her lap and stared at them as they twisted together. 'I know the treatment cost a lot of money but she's good at business. She was even going to help me. Why would she make such a stupid mistake?'

'She was desperate. You must have known that. Why else would you have sacrificed so much to help her?'

'The same reason I always help her. But it's never enough is it?' In her mind she saw what was left of her business slipping through her hands, not just temporarily but completely. Carrie needed money—lots of it probably. 'It's always been this way. She expected her wish list to get ticked off a lot quicker than anybody else's. A new Barbie doll, pink bike with ribbons on the handlebars, trendy clothes.' Words began to spill rapidly from her mouth as the implications raced through her head. 'I must get hold of her. Find out how much she needs—I'll make her tell me. We need to work out a plan. See my bank manager and…'

'Let me explain, Lizzy,' Tony said. 'I told you that Irena didn't stand any nonsense about this. Waiting wasn't an option. Once she'd worked out the solution she didn't leave it to chance. So, yesterday she found her way into their files and paid the debt.'

The word debt resounded through her head. 'With your money?'

'Yes. I didn't actually give my blessing for these acrobatics in cyberspace; nevertheless it was a great relief once it was done.'

'So now we owe you.'

'Of course not, it's over.'

His words only served to feed her embarrassment, make her want to hide away. 'Well it's obvious my sister can't pay, so somebody's got to.' Her breath squeezed through her tightened throat. 'How much…?'

'Lizzy…'

'Please… I need to know.'

Tony sighed and shook his head in protest. 'This is ridiculous,' he muttered. 'Approximately…'

'You didn't knock that on the head with *approximately.*'

'Irena found the money in an obsolete account. I didn't even know I had it. Fifty—fifty thousand is all.'

Lizzy's body suddenly wilted. 'Oh God!'

'Lizzy, listen to me. I would have given a lot more than that. When I saw you look at your beautiful work lying around in glass and dust, I was so angry. And the other day when I saw that bruise on your neck I was burning up with rage. I wanted to crush these despicable thugs for hurting you. It was so unjust after all you'd done for me. I failed to protect you. Please let me do this.'

Lizzy sat for a moment staring into the pool. It was calm and still; no waves or ripples. She was conscious of Tony's patience as he sat silently beside her, respecting her moment of shock. Goose bumps came up on her flesh and she shivered.

Tony pulled off his sweater. 'Here.'

'I'm fine. You have to go to the airport.'

'Come on, I've got time to pick up another one.'

Lizzy slipped her arms into the sleeves and caught the illusive but fine scent of his cologne. As she put the sweater on it was warm; on her arms, her back, her breast, sinking into every pore of her flesh. Her whole being sighed at the touch of it as she wrapped her arms across her body to hug it closer; Tony's protection; from the cold, from the violence, from ruin.

'Better?' he asked gently.

She nodded. 'I need to talk to Carrie.'

'Yes. Will you apologise for the invasion of her privacy?'

'Apologise?' The word was like a slap across the face to wake her out of her shock. 'I'm not going to tell her *everything.*'

'She has a right to know the truth.'

'The truth? I should be honest with her, when she's been so evasive with me?'

'You have every right to be angry with her but don't let it cause trouble between you. Give yourself time to take it in.'

Lizzy shook her head and fixed his eyes with hers. 'But this is so typical. She blunders along on her own terms knowing that somebody, usually me, will get her out of trouble. Look what people have had to do for her. Irena's stuck her neck out and the whole thing's cost you a fortune. Just how many people does she need to get through life? Well this time she'll have it on my terms. I'm going to follow Irena's example. What's the point in waiting around for her to call? I'm taking control of this. I'm going to find her.'

'Irena's rule book works fine for her, but it won't work for you. If you lay into Carrie now, whatever she's done, you'll hate yourself for it. Think it through, sweetheart, please.'

'I can't trust her with the truth. She'll blow it. She'll tell somebody one day. I'm sorry, Tony, I know you like to be straight with people but it's too risky.'

'How will you find her if she won't answer your calls?'

'I'll text Mum and Dad. She's bound to be keeping in contact with them—sending them brief messages. She wouldn't ignore them otherwise they'd want to know why. Mum will make her call me.'

'Won't that worry them?'

'No.' She stood up and picked up her bag. 'They'll throw their eyes up to the sky and assume that she's just being Carrie.'

'Lizzy,' Tony stood up and put his hands on her shoulders. 'Don't let it get to you. You've been through enough.'

She looked at him. Tears brimmed in her eyes, partly from anger but mostly from a feeling that her playing field just became uneven once again. She had become more secure with Tony, over the past couple of days, gained her independence, felt more equal but this changed everything. 'Irena said that she always wanted to do something for you. Repay you for what you did for her and her children. Now I know how she felt. I'll keep you posted.'

'Keep me *posted*?' The mood in his eyes darkened. 'What am I, a casual acquaintance? What do you want, Lizzy, a going steady badge to prove that I'm here for you?'

'I'm sorry I'm too embarrassed to stay.'

'Let me come and make you a hot drink. We can talk some more.'

'You'll be late. Don't add any more to my guilt list, please. I'll catch up with you later.' She slid her arms around his neck, hugged him and said, 'Thank you.' He snatched her to him and kissed her hard on the mouth before releasing her. It stirred her, set her body alight and her heart reaching for him. She turned and walked away knowing that he would never know how much she wanted to stay there in his arms.

'That sweater looks better on you than me,' Tony called after her.

'Don't you believe it,' she answered over her shoulder. Then she stopped and looked back. 'Is the offer still open for that *going steady badge*?'

Tony expelled a gentle laugh. 'Sure, I'll pick one up while I'm out.'

****

Lizzy texted her mother and it wasn't long before it resulted in a call from Carrie.

Her voice was high pitched and breathless. 'You rang Mum.' It sounded like an accusation. 'We weren't going to bother them while they were away.'

'I didn't *bother* them. I sent a text like we agreed. At least I found out that you'd changed your phone. Why didn't you give me your new number?'

'You don't understand, Lizzy.'

'I'm probably the one person on the planet who does, Carrie. I have to talk to you. It's very important.'

'I can't.'

'You must. You need help.'

'What makes you think that?'

'Didn't it occur to you that sooner or later somebody was going to work it out?'

'Don't push me, Lizzy. You don't know the half—'

'Half?' Lizzy gasped at Carrie's attitude. 'I know it all. And you've got to listen.' There was no time to argue. It had to come short and fast before Carrie fled again. 'You've borrowed money. Tell me who these people are. How do you make your payments?'

'That's private.'

'You're in too deep to worry about privacy. We have to pay it off.'

'Stay out of this, Lizzy; it's none of your business.'

Lizzy's control creaked but she held on. 'They made it my business weeks ago.'

'What?'

'When they couldn't find you, they found me. They drove an SUV through my boutique window.'

'Maybe that was just an accident.'

'Get your head out of the sand. A few days ago a guy dragged me by my neck and tried to bundle me into a car. That wasn't accidental. It's taken this long to realise but now I know it's your debt.'

'Oh God! It's so out of control. I can't bear any more of this.'

'You have to deal with it. I'll help you but you'll have to cooperate. Give me some details, your account number and password.'

'What can you do about it?'

'Just do it, Carrie.'

'I can't... I can't do this.'

'Isn't it time you saw the world from other people's point of view? Have you any idea what's been happening on your behalf? Somebody has even offered to pay it off for you.'

'Who would do that?'

'A friend—a very good friend. It can be done electronically. You can be free of it right away.' She was not about to tell Carrie what had already transpired, but with the banking information the timescale of the transaction could be fudged to protect Irena and Tony. However justified the research was it was risky. 'There's no time to ask questions, just get me the reference numbers or are you waiting for them to find you and snatch Jamie?'

There was a silence. Lizzy felt her body tighten with the stress of waiting for a response, half expecting Carrie to hang up leaving no chance of contact.

Eventually Carrie relayed the number and the password along with the on line information for the loan company. 'Why is your friend doing this?'

'It's what he does. He helps people. This will be done immediately, so you can relax—celebrate if you like.'

'Is it really over?'

'Yes. I have to go now. You're not the only one who's suffered over this.'

'Don't go, Lizzy, talk to me, I've had a terrible time. I've missed you so much.'

'You've missed me, Carrie? *You've* missed *me?* Doesn't it ever cross your mind that I might have needed you? That you might ask what *I've* been through?'

'But you're stronger than—'

'Don't play that familiar card with me. It must be great to pick up your feet and say, "You're the strong one Lizzy, you do it." Lock yourself away until somebody comes to bail you out.'

'But you always do, Lizzy. You always seem to stay on your feet while I'm falling over.'

'On my feet? My business is in shreds and splinters. I've got to start all over again—for a second time. I'm on the brink of a relationship with a guy I adore but he doesn't know about last year and the thought of telling him freaks me out.'

'Why can't you tell him?'

'I don't know how he's going to take it. Who would know that Patrick was capable of reacting that way? That strength, that you claim I have, won't be nearly enough to face it if Tony does the same. I'm already embarrassed over this loan business.'

'It's his money? Oh God, Lizzy! I made an awful mess of this. What am I going to do? How can we pay it?'

'He probably won't take it. I'll leave you to work that one out all by yourself. You've got your dream, it's my turn now. I don't know how much time I'll have with this relationship but I *will* have it.'

'Lizzy—'

'Go home. Kiss Jamie for me then get on with your life. Give me some space to pick up the pieces of mine.'

Chapter Eighteen

'I just wanted to say thank you,' Lizzy said to Irena. 'You took a personal risk and I'm so grateful.'

'For the sake of my children, I would not put myself in jeopardy if I thought it would be discovered. But I now have your sister's details on file so it all looks perfectly innocent.' She smiled. 'So now you drive to Florence, to celebrate at Sanccella's?'

'Sanccella's, in Florence?'

'The original restaurant is here. Mr Franklyn says he fell in love with it and then discovered the one in London.'

'Are they both the same?'

'The only difference is that the pianist is Italian, and he sings romantic arias and ballads to charm the ladies.'

'Tony can do that all by himself, without singing.'

'He is a solitary person at Firenze. He stays in the cottage, sometimes goes out for dinner—but always alone.'

'So we're breaking the rules.'

'You most certainly are. I hope you both have a wonderful evening. A little relaxation is deserved I think.'

Holly's voice rang from the staircase as Lizzy left Irena's office. 'For goodness sake, am I to be the only one here this evening?'

'Surely you won't miss me,' Lizzy commented.

'No but you've commandeered Tony, leaving me without a soul to talk to all evening.' Holly spoke as if the world had done her a disservice.

'What about Fraser and Eliot? I met them this afternoon, they're wonderful company.'

Holly approached. 'There's a vineyard on the market and they've gone to look at it. Said they won't be back 'till late. The Franklyns are meeting up with my parents. Charlie and Ed have been banished for the night,' she rolled her eyes to the ceiling, 'tradition and all that. Even Grace is deserting me in favour of a quiet supper in her room. That leaves me with her sister-in-law and the brats.'

Lizzy was amazed how Holly could make her needs sound far more important than two families put together. 'Glenda's a very accomplished woman I could chat to her for hours. And the children are lovely. They're fun if you'd join in their conversation—listen to what they have to say.'

'About princesses and little trains with numbers on? No thank you. I'll follow Grace's example.'

'Sometimes it's good to be alone for an evening.'

'Fine talk from one who definitely won't be alone tonight.'

That comment gave Lizzy a sharp jolt to her stomach. She had only been thinking about the restaurant and what to wear. Now she was wondering what they would do when dinner was over? Her hands began to tremble just to think of the possibilities. She raised her chin a little more and bluffed her way out of it. 'I haven't thought about it.'

'I'm sure you haven't,' Holly drawled. 'I'll just have to see who's on line. Social network is amazing, isn't it? You can link up with—well—all sorts of people.' She made it sound intriguing, as if it meant something significant. Her eyes ran up and down Lizzy's outfit but she didn't comment on it. 'Have fun but don't take all this gentlemanly charm too seriously. You must know that you're just a handy compromise for the wedding.'

The words pierced Lizzy's self-esteem like an arrow and reminded her that she was on borrowed time with Tony; however, she rode the jibe and remained composed. 'I know you want me out of the frame,' she said, 'but I haven't noticed Tony making a move on you. It can't be a lack of opportunity you're rarely more than a couple metres from his elbow. Trying to make me feel two inches tall isn't going to help you drag him up the aisle.'

'That's *your* game plan I suppose.'

'I have no plan, and I want no part in your private little contest.'

Holly lowered her voice. 'That's disappointing. I was so looking forward to a final showdown, a chance to play my trump card.'

'You're like a bossy school-girl playing out a fantasy. Maybe I'm a compromise, but he chose me, even though you were available. Nothing will change that, no matter how many aces you can find up your sleeve.'

'I only need one,' Holly said over her shoulder as she walked away. 'Excuse me I might as well enjoy the evening sunshine for a while.'

Lizzy heard Tony's voice at the top of the stairs. She was comforted as it reminded her that she was his choice of companion, not Holly, no matter how much she schemed. Her heart danced with anticipation as she waited.

'Where are you going, Eddy?' Tony called out at the top of the stairs.

'To find the cat.'

'What cat?'

'He was outside. I saw him.'

'You can't go on your own, Eddy. Come on I'll take you back to Mummy, she'll be worried about you.'

'I want to see the cat.'

'I'll help you find him after the wedding. It's bedtime. We've all got a very busy day tomorrow.'

'Do I put my special waistcoat on?'

'Yes. We all have a special waistcoat, don't we?'

Their voices became fainter and then could be heard no more. Lizzy smiled to herself at the way Tony had taken to being an uncle. It seemed as if he'd already had years of experience. She was still smiling when he came downstairs.

'You're here,' he said, as if he'd made a discovery, 'I was going to call for you at the cottage.' He seemed a little uneasy as if he had violated some kind of protocol.

'I came to see Irena. There was no point in going back.' She chuckled. 'Besides, my father's not there to quiz you and tell you what time to bring me home.'

Tony smiled and kissed her face. The contact was brief but there was just time to close her eyes and inhale the scent of him. 'You look gorgeous,' he told her.

Lizzy couldn't remember when she last felt so happy. It seemed she had stepped onto a cloud that ferried her into a dream as she smiled at the chauffeur who held the door of a shining black car. The conversation was polite, mainly with reference to sight-seeing, as there was no partition between them and the chauffeur.

When they arrived, they walked beneath the awning outside the restaurant where small, round tables and wicker chairs were laid for alfresco dining.

Inside the restaurant the chink-chink of brisk table service, the gentle chorus of conversation punctuated with ripples of laughter, washed over Lizzy like waves of music. She absorbed it, her flesh tingled, her heart fluttered, her artistic eye drank in the mellow colour tones created with the subtle lighting.

The centre of the extensive room was arranged for larger dinner parties. Around the perimeter were smaller, round tables nestling within snug arcs of plush, red, upholstered seating; each one a cosy den for more intimate dining. These were laid with crisp white linen, candles and a small arrangement of flowers.

The piano was situated on a carpeted dais that was dressed with large, potted ferns. The pianist, complete with white tuxedo, was playing a theme from a romantic movie. Lizzy had to smile to herself for this was just as she imagined it.

'Mr Franklyn, good to see you.' The maître d' greeted them and beamed a smile at Lizzy. 'And you have a lady with you tonight. Come, I find you a nice quiet place.'

He led them to a table where a waiter poured Champagne into delicate glasses. Lizzy watched it feeling that she was already intoxicated by the atmosphere. She looked at Tony and beamed a radiant smile. 'I love it.'

'Then we're off to a good start.' Tony reached for his drink. 'It's your turn to think of a toast.'

Lizzy raised her glass to his. 'To Sanccella's because, like the lake, it's always there.'

Tony smiled. 'And *we're* here, at last.'

'It's a great word, isn't it?' Lizzy said. 'It should be adopted as a term to recognise special times in people's lives. You know, like... congratulations... way-to-go... mazel tov...' She wrinkled her nose. 'Oh God! I'm talking such rubbish. I suppose you think this is what I'm like without problems to keep me in check.'

'Problems?' Tony took her hand. 'You mean those ugly things with their noses pressed to the window?'

Lizzy smiled and nodded.

'I'll let you into a secret,' Tony whispered. 'I think *everybody* should talk rubbish on a first date.' He squeezed her hand, 'I guess this is breaking the rules but I just have to say how impressed I am with the way you've handled everything. It took a lot of courage. And if I'm allowed to be, I'm very proud of you.'

'Carrie insists that I'm strong.' Her brow tweaked. 'She makes me feel like an Amazon, but I'm not that tough. I'm just a regular person.'

'Perhaps it's because of the way you reach out to others when they need somebody. And, in the most charming way, you make people feel better.'

'Oh God! Now I'm Florence Nightingale. You think I should have been a nurse?'

Tony laughed. 'Absolutely not.' He raised her hand to his lips. 'With the skills in these fingers you would have made a brilliant surgeon.'

'There isn't much call for beadwork in brain surgery, and I'd look ridiculous in green scrubs.'

'Nonsense! You'd look sensational.'

Lizzy ran her hand over the sleeve of his pale grey jacket. 'So do you.' She expressed a little sigh of pleasure. 'This suit is so fine, wonderful cloth, great cut.'

'Does that mean you've gone off my old jeans and sweatshirt?'

'Never. The way you dress gives you an edge, but,' she lowered her voice, 'when you're wearing your old gear I see an incredibly sincere, attractive and dare I say, sexy guy.'

'All of those things, in one old sweat shirt?'

Lizzy smiled and nodded. 'A man who's comfortable in his own skin—that's a very potent quality.'

Lizzy's words resounded in Tony's head and then plunged downward to cause mischief with his self-control. His libido had already hit the ground running when he first saw her this evening. It wasn't unusual for him to feel these natural reactions on seeing a very attractive woman with a great body, yet these typical responses were not the only ones he felt. There was something else far removed from lust; a warm, sensuous experience making him want to wrap his arms around her and just savour the consuming pleasure of holding her close, to kiss just for that moment and not as a prelude to making love. Yet had they reached that stage where this kind of affection is readily shared? That understanding that gives people the confidence to be demonstrative. He looked at her glossy hair that fell to her shoulders, her eyes that reflected the candlelight, a taunting mouth that was going to tempt him all evening, and he felt good. He leaned towards her and whispered. 'What do you think happens when potent meets the positively irresistible?'

Lizzy uttered her answer, almost against his lips. 'This early in the evening we look at the menu.'

'Hmm, I suppose you're right.'

Lizzy listened to Tony's tales of his boyhood, when he and his cousins were invited to stay at Larchwood during the school holidays. 'So your improvised boat capsized and you had to swim for it. What were you thinking?'

'We really believed it would float. Well, it did for a short while. It just had no ballast.'

'It seems strange that somebody living by the water didn't have a proper boat.'

'Grandpa had a small craft but that wasn't nearly so much fun as inventing one.'

'How old were you boys then?'

'Eliot was about twelve... Fraser a few months older.'

'And you?'

Tony cleared his throat. 'That pasta really was fabulous, wasn't it?'

'Come on,' Lizzy chided, 'tell me the truth.'

'About fourteen. Grandpa made us fish it all out again and drag it back.'

'That sounds gruelling; soaking wet and defeated.'

'Stella made us hot chocolate.' He narrowed his eyes. 'Didn't you ever do something foolish like that?'

'Me, do something as silly as making a canoe out of sawn off bike wheels and a plastic sheet?'

'Confess it. You must have done something.'

'I cut my sister's hair.'

'Everybody does that.'

'What about deliberately binning my history homework?'

'That too, you're going to have to dig a bit deeper than that.'

'When I was about eight—I shut myself in the shed.'

'Was it an accident?'

'No, I was hiding. I'd glued some coloured string onto my best coat because I thought it looked pretty. Carrie told me I was in *big* trouble, so I hid. I don't know why I would do that, my parents never issued punishments. I think I was just ashamed that I'd done something stupid.'

'Not so stupid for a child destined to become a designer.'

'I suppose the same could apply to your prototype boat.'

'One thing I learned from that was the importance of staying afloat.'

****

By the time they had exchanged other childhood tales and shared college anecdotes, Lizzy felt relaxed and happy. To her great relief, Louisa's ghost didn't show. The only problem was that time seemed to be in a big hurry.

Tony had ordered desert, said it was part of the Sanccella experience and was to be a surprise. Lizzy gave in to his charming argument and agreed to sample a little of it—whatever it was. She felt flattered by his sheer enjoyment of the evening.

When the dish was placed before her, Lizzy stared at it. 'This isn't desert it's a work of art.'

'Try it, you'll love it.'

'But I've got a dress to squeeze into tomorrow.'

'How can you resist this? Small pieces of peach drenched in a fine liqueur, stirred into soft, luscious Crème Brule, with chopped hazel nuts, honeycomb and garnished with delicate, chocolate leaves.'

'I mustn't,' she protested, her willpower working on two levels; one to resist the food and the other to resist kissing his mouth that hovered so close to hers. 'I'll just have to admire it… and… imagine how it would… taste.'

'Just a little,' Tony insisted. 'He navigated a spoon over Mr Sanccella's masterpiece and carefully harvested a morsel of each flavour. 'I know you want to resist,' he said, looking her in the eye, 'but willpower just isn't enough when you're faced with temptation on such a grand scale.'

'That's very true,' Lizzy agreed.

Tony offered the spoon to her mouth and her lips drew in the sweet, edible pastiche. Her taste buds flipped, she savoured it then passed her tongue lightly over her lips.

'Good—yes?' Tony whispered.

'Wicked. As you're so fond of Crème Brule it must be your all-time favourite.'

'It is but I'll just cut to the coffee.'

The pianist began to sing a haunting, passionate aria. They stopped talking and listened. Lizzy watched the candle; it was burning low. The evening was racing by, and while she was enjoying it so much there was no chance of it slowing down. Her eyes remained fixed on the dying flame until the last flicker of light sank into the pool of liquid wax and drowned, leaving her to wonder if her glimpse of happiness would do the same; burn away after shining so brightly? She couldn't bear to lose him, not yet. But how could she fight to keep hold of somebody she hadn't yet won? What was a *handy replacement* to do?

The aria ended. The people applauded. The waiter brought the coffee and set it down gently. It brought Lizzy back down to earth.

'You seem distracted,' Tony said.

'I was enjoying the singing.'

'With a frown?'

'I was watching the candle, it's burned away.'

'That's OK, sweetheart, we can get another?'

'No, it's fine. It made me realise how quickly the evening's gone by. I've had a fabulous time.' She smiled. He'd called her sweetheart. Not necessarily significant but it felt amazing.

'Good,' Tony whispered, 'I suppose we'd better pour this coffee.'

Lizzy wanted to hold on to this moment. That look in his eyes was for her, not Louisa, not Holly or any of those beautiful women from his past. She held his gaze and he seemed in no hurry to move. Lizzy hovered at a mental crossroad. She could drink coffee, call the evening over, and then go back to the cottage. Or she could take some control over the next few moments.

'I can do coffee,' she said.

Tony smiled and gestured towards the pot. 'As you wish.'

'No,' she said, 'I meant that I can make it… at the cottage… for both of us.' Her heart was racing as she made her bid to hold on to him for a while longer.

'I'd like that.'

Her courage failed her for a moment. 'Of course it doesn't have to be coffee, if you'd rather something else like orange juice…'

'Coffee's fine, after dinner. I only drink orange juice first thing in the morning.'

With newfound courage she seized the moment and said, 'I have a whole bowl of fresh oranges.'

Tony's eyes fixed on hers as if to seal the bargain. 'I'll call the chauffeur.'

Chapter Nineteen

The sound of a child screaming and sobbing greeted them on their return to Firenze. Voices attempting to communicate above the shrill, heart-wrenching cries came from just inside the main entrance.

Tony called to the chauffeur to wait, and then he took the steps two at a time. Lizzy followed, her heart pounding, her throat suddenly dry.

In the reception area, Grace was trying to talk to Eddy, who screamed and writhed as Glenda, his mother, tried to hold him.

'Grace?' Tony called out. 'What's happened?'

'Eddy's injured his arm. He followed room service out of the door and ran down here. Glenda followed just in time to see him fall down the last three stairs. I can't tell how bad it is, but he needs an X-ray. It's probably broken.'

'Eddy began to scream out. 'I want my daddy… I want my daddy.'

Glenda lost her grip on him and he wriggled free.

Tony hooked his arm around Eddy's waist and in one swift action picked him up. He held him firmly but was unable to contain his thrashing limbs as he shrieked for his daddy.

'Eddy,' Tony said, 'Eddy, listen to me.'

'I want my daddy.'

'I'll get him for you, but you have to calm down. Come on now, stop kicking. I know your arm hurts but you need to stop this so we can help you. Stop it now, Eddy.' The boy gasped and then gulped, and Tony took advantage of a momentary silence. He held him close and said gently, 'That's better. Good boy. We're very proud of you.' He turned to Glenda. 'I'll ask the driver to get the courtesy vehicle then we'll have room to bring Ed back with us.'

'I don't expect you to come, Tony,' Glenda said. 'I'll be OK. Ed and Charlie will meet me there.'

'Until then you should have somebody with you. There's no need for you to deal with this alone.' He handed Eddy back to her. 'Be a brave boy while I talk to the driver—OK?'

Eddy nodded and gulped in a sudden, quivering surge of air.

'I'll be right back,' Tony called over his shoulder as he left.

Lizzy noticed the twins looking on, pale and shaken; trying desperately not to cry. She went to comfort them. Felt their arms clinging to her, their fingers clenching her skirt. 'I'll take the girls back upstairs.'

'Oh, Lizzy,' Glenda sighed, on the verge of tears, 'we've ruined your evening.'

'Of course you haven't, I had a wonderful time.'

'Eddy's been hyper all evening, wanting to go and find a cat. He's usually the quiet one but he's so excited—all three of them are. Half past ten and they haven't slept yet.'

'I'll get them to bed. Perhaps they'll sleep in tomorrow. They don't need to be in the dressing room until eleven o'clock.' She looked at the girls. 'Come on you two. Show me where your room is.'

The girls settled quickly and Lizzy sat on the sofa in the adjoining room. She flipped through a magazine, unable to concentrate on actually reading it.

There was a knock at the door. It was Irena, but it took Lizzy a few seconds to realise as she was casually dressed and her fair hair was loose and falling past her shoulders.

'The driver called to let me know what had happened,' she said quietly. 'Mr Franklyn has just left with the boy and his mother.'

'Poor little Eddy. It must really hurt.'

'These things happen to children. After worrying the adults and changing everybody's plans, he will return triumphant, and wearing a plaster cast as a symbol of his bravery. His mother, of course, will not revel in his glory.'

'She couldn't help it. He was determined to find a cat.'

'There is one that lives at the caretaker's house. He waits outside the kitchen for extra food. Doctor Franklyn was going to come and take over from you but I insisted that she go and rest. And now I say the same to you?'

'I'm fine. You've got a lot to do tomorrow.'

'For me it is a day of organisation. For you, it is a special time. People will want to talk to you about the wedding gown. You must be prepared to take advantage of this as you celebrate with the family. And for that you need to look your best.'

'Thank you.'

A frown tweaked on Irena's brow. 'I had a visit from Miss Parker, trying to change the seating plan.'

Lizzy laughed. 'So she actually did it. She threatened to get me transferred so I wouldn't sit by Tony.'

'What a ridiculous woman. Did she really think Mr Franklyn would tolerate it? He made it clear that you were to be seated with him and his cousins? That has always been the case. She is a little jealous, I think. But she is wasting her time if she thinks she can turn Mr Franklyn from you.'

'Do you really think so, Irena?'

'I do not make up these things. You should go now and get some sleep. The hairdressers and the beauticians will be arriving at nine thirty.'

Lizzy returned to the cottage and lay on her bed, staring up at the ceiling, reflecting on her date, reliving moments that she would treasure all her life. How would Tony sleep: on his side with his arm around her, or would he lie on his back so she could watch him as he breathed? She imagined resting her hand gently on his chest as it rose and fell. She reached her arm across the bed where he might have been but for Eddy's accident, the sheet was cold. It then made her wonder if he would steal away in the early hours. The thought made her heart twist a little.

The next thing she knew she awoke to the sound of her phone buzzing. She snatched it up from the bedside table.

'Hi, sweetheart,' Tony said softly. 'Sorry, did I wake you?'

'No,' she lied. Her insides reacted but she was unsure whether it was the term of endearment or the fear of hearing bad news about Eddy. 'How is he?'

'He's had an X-ray. It seems to be a clean break. He's gone into the treatment room with Ed and Glenda. He looks a bit dazed but he's calm.'

'Thank goodness.'

'Now the panic's over,' Tony said, 'I'm thinking about where I might have been right now.'

'Me, too,' she said running her palm over the bed sheet, 'but it wasn't to be. You're needed there.'

There was a brief silence and then he spoke in a low whisper. 'Am I not needed there with you?'

His direct question threw her. Of course she needed him, wanted him, there was a space right there beside her; an even bigger void in her arms where he should be. She was desperate to embrace her time with him. How could she not be truthful?

'Yes you are, but I'm not a four-year-old with a broken arm.'

'True, but I promise you, Lizzy Yardley,' he said in a low, seductive voice, 'I won't be parted from you tomorrow night.'

'Our second date?'

'You should get some sleep now. I'll see you tomorrow.'

Chapter Twenty

Two hairdressers, one female, very stylish and business-like and one male, flamboyant and totally enjoying the environment of the flowers and wedding gowns, set up their portable salon. Two beauticians used the dressing table.

Lizzy was ready, save for her dress and shoes, and moved about in her maxi-dress while she checked everything yet again.

Just as predicted, Eddy came to show her his plaster cast, and told her that he was going to ask everybody to write on it.

Gradually the dressing room began to take on the atmosphere of a wedding as the time moved on and hair was styled, headdresses weaved into place, and makeup was skilfully applied.

Lizzy dressed the twins and put them on their best princess behaviour. Ruth ran through the flower girl routine with them once more. For two very excitable, exuberant girls, they were uncharacteristically calm and attentive.

Lizzy held the wedding dress and beamed at Grace. 'Shall we do this?'

Grace smiled. 'You're a star, Lizzy. I wouldn't have had all this but for you.'

'Oh hush!' Lizzy said and she held the gown as Grace stepped into it. 'This is my favourite part. I love being able to dress the bride. Make sure it's all as it's supposed to be.'

'Have you seen Tony today?'

'No.'

'He drove off somewhere earlier. I don't know what that was all about.'

'Perhaps he wanted to get something for Eddy, after his traumatic evening.' She stood back, nodded smugly and then smiled.

Grace was radiant. 'Will I do?'

'You'll more than just do. You look stunning. Doesn't she Ruth?'

Ruth blinked at a tear in her eye. 'So lovely.'

'You look so pretty,' Sarah said.

'Yes, you do, aunty Grace,' Lucy added.

Grace looked at Lizzy. 'Get yourself ready,' she said. 'Mum will help Holly.' She laughed. 'She's been doing it for years.'

Holly, still in a robe, soaking up the pampering of the beautician, drawled that she wasn't ready yet, as if there was some kind of pecking order to getting dressed.

'Holly,' Grace called out to her, 'come on. I have to go soon and you need to supervise the girls.'

'What?'

Ruth went to her and brusquely started to usher her away from the dressing table. 'You're supposed to be helpful. Being chief bridesmaid isn't just about dressing up. You've got duties so come away from that mirror.'

Lizzy changed into her *kick ass* dress, as Jenny had dubbed it, and it slipped over her slender body as if it was made for her and not for another woman somewhere. Having chosen high heels so she would feel taller when she was with Tony, she felt good.

She then took some photographs for her portfolio and left her camera on the dressing table ready to collect later.

There was a loud knock at the door. Ruth crossed the room and answered it. Nathan asked if he could come in. Everybody called out to say he could. His arms were outstretched, and his face was aglow with love. He sighed at Ruth. 'Well, darling woman, look at our baby girl. And I have to give her away.'

'Rather you than me,' Ruth said. She kissed him.

'You look very handsome, Dad,' Grace said.

'Got to look the part,' he answered. 'Tony's waiting by the French windows,' he told Ruth. 'He'll escort you to your seat. You, too, Lizzy.' He went to the French windows and opened them up. The gentle, polite sounds of the waiting congregation rippled along the heatwaves.

Ruth hovered by Grace a moment longer.

Lizzy went outside, Tony greeted her and she wondered if he could get anymore gorgeous.

His eyes gleamed as he said, 'My God, Lizzy, you look beautiful.'

Ruth joined them. He offered one arm to Lizzy and his mother took the other. 'I'm the lucky one,' he said, 'I get a gorgeous girl on both arms.'

'You sound like your father.' Ruth laughed.

'I'll take that as a compliment.'

They walked to the garden; the guests were all seated in two traditional blocks. They took their place on the front row.

Tony nodded to Charlie, where he stood with his brother and the clergyman.

Lizzy felt his hand clasping hers as the chamber orchestra began to play and the little nieces appeared. They giggled at sighs of, 'Ah,' coming from the congregation. Then they nodded to each other and walked like princesses, scattering the petals to make a path fit for a bride. The music stopped and then changed telling all that Grace was about to appear and inducing them to stand.

Lizzy's heart swelled when the music started again, and Nathan escorted his daughter to the platform framed by billowing shrubs and adorned with cream and lavender blooms.

Charlie watched, his face aglow, his eyes full of love.

I want that, Lizzy's heart sighed, I want that kind of love, the mutual language between two people who can convey their feelings without a word.

She was always surrounded by wedding gowns and brides but had never been touched so deeply before.

'Don't tell me it's all gone pear-shaped. Please tell me you're having the time of your life,' Jenny urged.

'I'm having a ball,' Lizzy answered. 'The wedding was wonderful, a real fairy tale. All the traditional things, like dancing with her dad and throwing the bouquet...'

'Did you get it?'

'No.'

'Who did?'

'Don't ask.'

'Not *her*?'

'And she didn't waste the opportunity to gloat, as if it was some kind of sign.'

'Well she might have got the flowers, but you're the one sipping Champagne and dancing with the gorgeous, sexy guy?'

'True—well *three* gorgeous, sexy guys actually.'

'What?'

'Tony's two cousins are here.'

'You don't fancy them all, do you?'

'Course not. But they're such fun when they're together. Very close, like brothers, always there for one another.'

'Well, what are you talking to me for?' Jenny said laughing. 'Get back there.'

'I'm going, I'm going! I'm just making my way past the pool. I've been back to change for the evening party.'

'What are you wearing?'

'A full skirt and top. I've been dressed in chiffon and beads all day. Everybody's dressing down a bit.'

'Good for you. Have you worn that bikini?'

'Yes. And before you ask, he was very complimentary.'

'I should hope so. Is it still hot?'

Lizzy looked around. It was still twilight, but the garden lights were lit. The sound of music mingled with happy conversations. 'Yes really warm but it'll be dark soon. Tony's going to be waiting in the garden. This is the most romantic thing I've ever done in my life. But I'm so scared, Jen.'

'You'll be fine. Have a bit of faith.'

'I can see our table now.'

'Is he there?'

'Yes, he's dressed more casual now, talking to Grace and Charlie. Eliot and Fraser are there, too… Oh my God!' she gasped.

'What?'

'I left my camera on the table.'

'Surely you don't think somebody's going to take it?'

'No, Grace and Charlie are looking at my photos.'

'What's wrong with that? You've probably captured some nice ones today.'

'I haven't deleted anything for ages. Goodness knows what might turn up.'

'You make them sound like naked selfies.'

'There's one of Tony.'

'Naked?'

'Well, no, only his chest and perhaps a bit… a bit lower.'

'How low?'

'His… well… his hips and… abs.'

'Can I have a copy for my screen saver?'

'It's not funny, Jen. He doesn't know I took it. He'd been working out in the gym. I just know he'll think I was being a cheap, peeping Tom.'

Jenny laughed. 'Sounds as though you were.'

'He's going to be so offended. I'd better get there before they find it.' She put her phone in her evening purse and walked briskly.

Tony greeted her with a kiss on her face and whispered,

'You look lovely.'

Lizzy smiled but she was preoccupied, trying to work out how she could politely recover her camera from Charlie and Grace, who had their heads together scrolling through the shots.

Charlie looked up. 'I have a very photogenic wife.'

'Wow!' Grace exclaimed. She grinned at Tony. 'I have a very photogenic brother by the look of it.'

Lizzy's heart jumped and pounded. 'That's not meant…' She reached for the camera but Grace had already passed it to Tony, who looked at the picture, tilted his head and then frowned. 'Not my finest hour.'

'If you looked back further, you'd see that I was taking shots of flowers and foliage in the garden. When I passed the pool it looked so amazing… the sunlight made it… it was artistic—like a…'

'Like a what?' Grace teased.

'A Hockney painting.'

'I never saw you as one of those guys in a Hockney, Tony,' Charlie said. He shrugged his broad, powerful shoulders. 'But who can argue with the artistic eye?'

Lizzy sighed; frustrated that she couldn't explain herself properly. 'It was the pool, the blue sky and the gold, not Tony.'

Fraser took the camera and fixed his eyes on it for several seconds. 'Whether you were compelled as an artist or a woman doesn't matter,' he said. 'Don't apologise for this, it's a great shot. You should keep it.'

Tony put his arm around Lizzy's shoulders. 'Of course you should. Besides, I'm guilty of doing something similar.'

'You've taken a secret photograph of Lizzy?' Grace said.

'Not a real one, just a mental snap shot—a memory.'

'Oh dear,' Lizzy said, 'what was I doing?'

'I'm intrigued,' Grace said, her body language urged him to tell more.

Tony hesitated a moment, then looked at Lizzy and clasped her hand as it rested on the table. 'Back in May, you all know I was in a bad way—grief stricken they call it don't they?' He stopped talking and his brow pleated above his nose.

Lizzy held her breath, unsure of what was about to happen. She glanced around at each of them and could see that they had become serious. This wasn't a joke. She knew how desperately the family had wanted to know more about this time. They waited and Lizzy could feel them as they spread their virtual arms around him.

'We were all concerned about you,' Eliot said. 'It must have been hell.'

Tony nodded and then began again. 'I couldn't sleep or work. One morning, after a very uncomfortable night on the sofa, I got up and looked at the lake. It was one of those times when a blanket of mist hung over the water.'

'I love the way it does that sometimes,' Grace said with a tone of nostalgia in her voice. 'It's like a canopy.'

'Yes, I remember,' Fraser said.

'It was weird,' Eliot added, 'kind of grey and mysterious.'

'To me, at that time, *everything* was grey,' Tony said. 'But I noticed movement in the mist. It was like a ghost. Gradually it became clearer and then I saw Lizzy.' He looked at her, smiled and squeezed her hand. 'She emerged from that greyness and for the first time in weeks I saw colour, her clothes, her skin and her hair. She ran clear of the haze and along the footpath to the larch wood. As I watched her I felt a little warmth glowing inside me. The next day I saw her again. I wasn't ogling her,' he hastened to add. 'I wasn't in a fit state to do that. But I was transfixed by her movement; her limbs, the swing of her hair with each stride, everything moved so rhythmically, like a beautiful, finely tuned mechanism. Such precision at a time when my life was so jammed up and out of sync. Each day she brought a little more colour, more warmth... so reliable.' He stopped for a moment but nobody spoke to break the silence or to distract him. 'After that I waited every morning and there she was, at seven o'clock on the dot. Her tenacity and sense of purpose pulled me from where I stood in the dark and I began to function again.' He tapped his forehead with his fingers. 'I, too, have a picture—in here.' He looked at Lizzy. 'I was a coward. I couldn't admit I'd been watching you.' He squeezed her hand. 'But now we're quits—yes?'

'Yes.'

'What a lovely story,' Grace said, with a romantic ring in her voice.

'I've never heard Tony waxing so lyrical,' Charlie said.

'I'm jealous actually,' Eliot admitted. 'What I'd give for an experience like that; a girl to run into my life and put some light into my head.'

'There's still time for it to come back,' Grace assured him. 'Memory is a strange thing. Something could trigger it any time. Something might remind you of your time there.'

'Is that right, Doc?' Eliot said, his soft, blue eyes smiled at her.

'Yes it is.'

Music began to play. Eliot turned his head to listen for a moment, and then he looked at Lizzy. 'Will you dance with me? It's a nice slow one so I won't tread on you.'

Lizzy accepted the invitation, pleased to have overcome her embarrassing moment over the photograph.

'Tony's memory didn't make you happy,' Eliot said, 'are you offended by it?'

'Course not. I'm glad I was able to bring some comfort, even if I didn't know at the time.'

Eliot's eyes fixed on hers. 'But something bothers you.'

'You're very perceptive.'

'I don't know about that. I'm an architect, I only know how to make buildings, but I know you're in love with him. You're also insecure about it.'

Lizzy nodded. 'You won't tell him will you?'

'Neither will you by the sound of it.'

'I wish I could. I wish I knew how he'd react to it.'

'He wants to be with you. When you're not, he looks around to see where you are. I'm not saying he's a control freak, but he behaves as if something's missing when you're not there.'

'Perhaps there is something missing. Maybe I'm his lifeline. I help him forget his lost lover. When he feels the pain he can think of that image of clockwork precision that pleases him so much, so he can function when I'm around.'

'That incident, in Paris, left him powerless to drag himself from one end of the day to the other. I know how that black space feels. A few weeks ago I woke up in a hospital. I had no idea why. When I found out that I was in Cape Town, the shock was terrifying. I knew who I was but not why I was there. Tony and Fraser came to the rescue. It was such a relief to make contact with somebody outside of my nightmare, somebody who could pull me along for a while.'

'You guys have always looked out for each other why didn't he call you when Louisa died?'

'There's something about it that doesn't make sense. It seems that it was a tragic but straightforward accident but why hide away? Why not tell somebody? He left us all on the outside. Then he found you to haul him through that first barrier. It's obvious he needs you. But do you love him enough to see it through?'

'I tried very hard not to love him because I'm so scared of it.'

'You can't protect yourself by sitting on the fence. Either go for it with all you've got or bail and move on.' He smiled. 'We'd better do a twirl or something; we're being watched.'

Chapter Twenty One

Lizzy had never imbibed to the extent of losing control of her behaviour and tonight she had been even more mindful of temperance despite the steady flow of Champagne and wine on offer. It had been difficult enough to handle the intoxication of being hopelessly in love. The only reminder that she was on earth and not up in the clouds was her sore feet; every heartbeat brought a painful throb to remind her that they had walked, stood and danced in high heels all day. The last celebration was over. She had survived being a reluctant part of a female triad: Holly's ridiculous game and Louisa's haunting hold on Tony. With shoes hooked on her fingers, clutch bag in the other hand and camera slung over her shoulder, she walked towards the cottage, mentally re-living the past few days.

You've had a ball, Lizzy, she told herself. You're old enough to know that life isn't a permanent fairy tale, but for now it certainly feels like one, except for your feet.

Despite the night air the grass was still dry and brittle, it crunched as she trod, and gave no comfort. The pool looked like a huge, curved mirror set in the ground. The reflected lights gleamed gold in the stillness of the water in contrast to the silver moon.

Lizzy put her things on one of the loungers. Tony was walking the grounds with security so she knew he wouldn't be along yet, but she looked around to ensure she was alone. She unhooked her suspenders and peeled down her stockings. Much as she had enjoyed wearing them it felt good to be free as she pushed them into her shoes. The flagstones were more soothing than the crispy grass but the pool, even though it would now be cold, looked a more promising mode of comfort for her throbbing toes.

Go on, Lizzy, she told herself, Tony won't see, he's tying up loose ends. He won't be here for ages yet. He won't come back until he knows that all's well.

Her skirt was ruched around her thighs as she sat on the top step of the pool and stretched her legs out into the chilling water.

Despite the temperature it was soothing and drew a long sigh of relief from her lungs. Her movements broke up the clarity of the reflection and amber streaks travelled on ever widening ripples. Hands braced behind her she dropped her head back and stared at the night sky. All the painful twists and turns of her eventful journey, the junctions and forks in the road, had brought her to this place where the night scented flowers and the hint of pine from the cypress trees fuelled her anticipation of the hours ahead—her promised night of love.

Tony stopped in his tracks when he saw Lizzy; her skirt gathered over her thighs, head back allowing her hair to hang freely. Wanton because of what it made him think and feel, yet innocent because she believed herself to be alone. As if she hadn't driven him crazy all day; every time she looked at him with those fox-like eyes, her warm smile lighting her face, the touch of her hand on his arm when she spoke to him and the slow dances, more like excuses to hold each other close than to move to music.

'Hey, beautiful!' he called.

Lizzy turned. 'You startled me.' She got up to greet him then noticed that his clothes were grimy and his face smudged. 'What happened to you?'

'That wretched cat got trapped in a fuel store. Apparently it was crying out for some time but nobody could find it. Dad tracked it down eventually but I was the one elected to rescue it.'

Lizzy laughed. 'Nonsense, you volunteered.'

'I'm sorry,' Tony said, staring down at his clothes, 'it isn't very romantic when your man comes home all hot and grimy and in dire need of a shower.'

'In the old days your woman would have the tin bath ready by the fire and a big jug of hot water to pour over you.'

'That sounds promising.' He felt her arm as it slid around his back, her lips pressed softly to his neck. The kiss, however soft, made every nerve end in his body buzz with pleasure and he thought of the night ahead, the sighs and tremors of making love, the complete nakedness of bodies and souls alike. It was a wonder to him that a man could reach the age of thirty eight and only meet one woman who made him feel quite so in tune with the world. How she merged into his very being and fit so snugly inside without even trying or even knowing that she did. The way she nestled against him induced him to put his arm around her, grime or no grime. He pressed his lips to the top of her head and lingered over inhaling the scent of her hair. 'We've worked hard and long to make this wedding happen for Grace and Charlie, this is our time now—you and me.'

****

Our time—you and me. The words resounded in Lizzy's mind as she stood in her moonlit room. While Tony was in the shower, she felt the huge void in her life's experience. Patrick being the only protagonist in her history, one that failed to fill her with expectation. Tonight she felt inadequate, not knowing if Tony expected her to follow him, or whether raunchy showers were just something in movies and novels; she had never actually met anybody who'd talked about it. It was tempting but would he be shocked? Would she ruin the whole thing? Their relationship had yet to prove that it could stand a disagreement or two.

'Oh God!' she whispered to herself. 'Have you been so locked in your work that you didn't learn these basic things about life? Do something positive, make a decision. Don't stand here like a Victorian, teenage bride preparing to shut her eyes and think of England.'

Secure in the knowledge that Tony's shower was still running, she stripped right down to nothing and then slipped into a heavy satin robe, uttering her thanks to Jenny for packing it. She brushed her hair—that was positive; he loved her hair.

So shall I sit on the bed, lie on it, get under the covers? One thing's certain you must steer clear of the balcony.

The moon cast a shadow of the balustrade across the fine, lawn curtains; a row of ghostly, hourglass figures stood like a guard of honour as if to remind Tony of the tragedy.

No, you're not having him tonight, he's mine, and all I have to do is pull the drapes to block you out. She reached for the curtain.

'Shutting out the moonlight?' Tony had emerged from the bathroom dressed in a towel that was hitched around his middle.

Lizzy was startled, lost for an explanation and afraid that he would see the menacing shadows.

He looked at it and shrugged. 'It always does that. Does it bother you?'

'No… I thought…' She stopped, afraid to ruin this moment. He was so beautiful. His wet hair sprang slightly into curves falling carelessly over his brow. 'Nothing…'

'Stop worrying about it,' he said as if he knew what she was thinking but wouldn't spell it out. 'You seem nervous.'

'I'm—'

'Changing your mind?'

'No, course not.' As he moved closer she inhaled the heady dampness of his flesh. 'I know it sounds ridiculous for somebody of my age… but I'm not accustomed to… to this… new relationships, that is.'

'Then I'm a doubly lucky man to be with you.'

'I'm probably hopelessly out of touch.'

He scooped her up and said, 'I'm pretty old fashioned myself.'

It wasn't the way he spoke that made her forget her misgivings. Nor was it the way he carried her to the bed and perched on the edge, looking at her. There was a moment when he kept his eyes focused on her face and slowly raised her foot to kiss her ankle, and that was when she banished her fears and all the negative reasons why she should have resisted him. His mouth felt hot as her limbs were still chilled from the pool. She had never before considered her ankle to be a particularly sensitive part of her. Nor her shinbone as his lips moved slowly along its shining ridge, speaking a secret, silent language to her flesh that clearly understood and whispered back. She shivered at the lingering kisses encircling her knee. He was so masterful yet humble and he made her feel beautiful, for why would a man kiss a woman's ankle or her knee if she wasn't?

They kissed with increasing hunger, explored each other's lips and mouths with the sensuous, giving and taking of mutual pleasure. Lizzy was home, right there in his arms, locked against his body.

Her silky robe was slipped from her shoulders, revealing the tell-tale reaction in her breast. Tony pressed his lips to them and then his mouth journeyed downward to her ribs and the hollow where her hip bone rose slightly. His kisses journeyed back up to her breast, leaving his hand to linger along her thigh. Her deep, compelling love cavorted with the pleasure, and she was consumed with unashamed hunger for him as she expelled long, erotic sighs in unison with his masterful foreplay. She circled her arms around him, clung to him as they united. Intoxicated by a potent cocktail of chemistry, physical attraction and love they reached the delicious ease to the hankering of their bodies. Lizzy's whole body shook. Tony sighed heavily and she expected him to fall to his back, but he seemed reluctant to relinquish the closeness and he held her against him.

Lizzy embraced the mellow oneness of their sated bodies, of feeling their two hearts pounding furiously and then slowing into a common beat. She lay unashamed, in the arms of her lover who not only held her naked body, but also cradled her naked soul. Nobody could take this away from her now. She had given him her love. She was complete.

Chapter Twenty Two

Tony was on the phone, discussing the travel details for the journey home. Lizzy watched him move about the kitchen as he talked; phone in one hand and coffee in the other. It seemed a well-practised habit.

'We'll be by the pool for a while,' he said to Irena. 'We're having one last get-together with Grace and Charlie. I'll pop in and see you after that to check everything's OK. Oh, and thanks, Irena, you did a great job here.'

Despite her night of love, Lizzy had woken early. A night with Tony Franklyn, was a giddy, exciting experience but not without its *morning after* twinges, especially as she had slept alone for over a year. As Tony was sleeping very soundly she crept into the bathroom, ran a bath, threw in all manner of aromatic salts and perfume then sank into it sighing as the soothing hot water flowed around her body. She stretched out in the hot, foamy, aromatic water and closed her eyes.

'I woke up next to a space in the bed.' Tony's voice put an end to her solitude. He stood in the doorway, a towel hitched around his waist, hair tousled and falling over his forehead, his jaw a little darker than yesterday. 'You deserted me for a bathtub?'

'No,' Lizzy said, 'I just changed the venue.'

Lizzy shook herself out of the daydream. Tony's sonorous tones were still echoing in the cottage kitchen, only now he was discussing the agenda for his first meeting back in London. He glanced across to where Lizzy sat at the table sipping her orange juice, and mouthed the words, 'Won't be long.'

Lizzy smiled and shrugged that it didn't matter. It's OK, you gorgeous thing, she said to him in her mind. You just carry on, I'm happy I can watch you walk about, listen to your sexy voice, feel it sending chills down my back. Did I say any of that to you last night? I must have said something crazy the way you made me feel. Have you overcome your grief or have you, at last, learned to live with it? Some things still don't add up. Why did you stay so long in the US? This morning you complained about the empty space in the bed and you hardly know me, so why would you tolerate the long separation from Louisa, if you loved her so much? For that matter, why didn't she go with you?

'What's going on in your mind?' Tony asked.

Lizzy had drifted off into her thoughts and didn't realise that his phone call had ended. 'I'm sorry, what did you say?'

He regarded her suspiciously. 'Your mind is miles away and you're spinning your glass around. What are you thinking about?'

'I thought that question was a woman thing.'

'That's just propaganda.'

Lizzy mentally reshuffled her thoughts to come up with an honest response. 'I was just thinking... wondering about the way chance acquaintances become important people in your life. Do we have a say in it, do you think? Or is it all laid out before us?'

'I suppose you can plan your life, even control it to a certain extent, but fate will always have the last word.' He became silent and glanced down at floor as if he was about to say something but needed to think it through first.

Lizzy was suddenly nervous and tried to guess what it would be. That last night was wonderful? Or that weddings draw people together but now it was time to get back to reality? She knew he'd be a gentleman, he'd be kind, but it would still be the end of her extremely brief but wonderful interlude with the love of her life. It then occurred to her that she had none of those little nonsense keepsakes that one gathers during a relationship. No pressed flower, no coloured pebble that might have caught her eye on a stroll, no selfies to laugh back at her on rainy days. Nothing to put with her brownie badges in her memento box in the wardrobe. A barbed suspicion snagged around her heart and she stood up, not wanting to hear bad news unless she was on her feet.

Tony approached her and took hold of her hands. 'Darling, Lizzy...'

'Are you going to break my heart—so soon?'

'I hope not.'

She raised her head and attempted to make a joke to ease the tension. 'Well don't keep me guessing. What kind of man does that to a girl?'

'The kind of man who believes he's in great danger of falling in love with... *the girl*.'

Lizzy was stunned into silence. She stared at him. This wasn't expected. She was prepared for a disappointment, not a declaration of this nature.

'Aren't you going to say something?' he said softly.

'You're *in danger*?' she said. 'It scares you so much?'

'Yes, it does. I told you I'm out of my depth with you and I'm afraid.'

'Me, too.'

'So we can help each other... yes?'

'Yes.'

'Shall we join the family?'

Lizzy wrinkled her nose. 'They'll all know, won't they?'

Tony smiled. 'Yes, they will. They'll be delighted.'

'Come on, you two,' Grace called when they approached the pool.

'Morning, everybody,' Tony called back.

'Sit here, Lizzy,' Nathan said, 'then I'll have a beautiful girl either side of me.'

Ruth nudged him affectionately.

'I've heard that somewhere before,' Lizzy said as she sat down. She nodded to Holly, who was seated opposite; her wide-brimmed hat and sunglasses made it difficult to know if she had responded.

Tony sat by Grace and kissed her cheek.

'Oooh, you smell nice,' she said, 'what is it?'

'Aqua Firenze—very special.'

'Expensive?'

'Priceless.'

Lizzy feared that Tony's secret joke would make her cheeks burn red but was saved by Nathan passing her a glass of punch. She was glad of the chilled drink to hold on to.

'Are your parents joining us, Charlie?' Tony asked.

'They've already gone—spending a few days in Rome.'

'We were just saying how good the children were,' Ruth said. 'Especially little Eddy, bless him.'

'I must say that a plaster cast on your arm is a great social asset,' Charlie said. 'He had a perfect excuse to speak to everybody. That cast is full of signatures. And he ended up with a pocket full of cash. Ed didn't know whether to give him a pat on the back or tick him off for hustling.'

Grace laughed. 'And here's me, *working* for a living.'

'Would he like a job?' Tony said. 'I can always use a smart guy like that.'

'Ed took him round again to give it back but the few people he could remember wouldn't take it. He's going to give some of it to charity.'

'That's a good example,' Ruth said.

'Find the middle ground,' Nathan added.

'Poor Glenda,' Lizzy said with a tone of sympathy in her voice, 'she was so upset.'

'These accidents happen,' Grace said. 'Mind you I don't know how I'd feel if it was my own child. Having young ones around makes you think what your own will be like.'

'Oh no!' Charlie teased. 'Married twenty four hours and my wife's getting broody already.'

'No, I mustn't, not until I get back.'

'Is that a state of mind or is it physical?' Holly asked.

'It's both,' Lizzy spoke up, authority in her tone. 'It's everything.'

'You sound very sure, Lizzy.'

'I am.'

'But you're not speaking from experience, are you.'

'Not mine but my sister's. She was totally consumed with the urge to be pregnant. Wanted a baby so much she couldn't think of anything else—nothing was more important.' She couldn't imagine why Holly would butt into a conversation about babies but knew there must be a motive lurking somewhere, she wouldn't have otherwise joined in.

'So it doesn't run in the family?'

'What are you talking about, Holly?' Ruth chided.

'Well, Lizzy doesn't want to be bogged down with a kid.'

A sickening feeling filled Lizzy's stomach. She knew Holly's strategy by now, she was about to strike right there where she would gain the best advantage. Her moment had come and the family conversation had played right into her hands. Lizzy knew she had to act, but she couldn't get a foothold on the situation because she didn't know what Holly was going to do or say next. 'If I had a child I wouldn't consider myself bogged down. When the time comes, I'm sure I'll be able to cope.'

Grace turned on Holly. 'Children aren't your bag either so why don't you just shut up?'

Nathan leaned and spoke privately to Lizzy. 'Don't listen to Holly,' he whispered. 'If she can't be the centre of attention she strikes up a ridiculous conversation to wind everybody up. She's always done it.'

Just when it seemed Holly's line of conversation had ended she spoke up again. 'But actually, having to raise one of your own isn't like playing with everybody else's like a big sister.'

Lizzy remained calm but a painful feeling of resignation filled her entire being as she realised what Holly was going to disclose. How she found out was a mystery, but then she had clearly made it her business to winkle something out that would discredit her opponent in this game she insisted on playing out to the bitter end.

'The children are innocent,' Lizzy said, 'don't bring them into all this...'

'Into what?' Tony asked.

Holly shrugged. 'Just a little game we've been playing.'

'It's *your* game, Holly, not mine. I never joined in. But it's obvious that you're going keep challenging me and press on regardless whatever the cost.'

'Wait a minute, what's going on here?' Tony asked.

'I told you,' Holly answered, 'it's just a game—'

'It's a showdown,' Lizzy interjected, and then her soul chilled with resignation. 'A very carefully planned moment, and I suspect quite a lot of research has gone into it.' She fixed a cold stare on Holly's face. 'I can understand why you want to discredit me, Holly, but how could you do this to a family that's treated you like a daughter since you were at school?' She held her stare. 'Well go on, you've got that trump card you boasted about why not get it on the table where everybody can see it?'

Grace glanced at Lizzy, as if she had perceived what was happening. 'Wait a minute! Nobody's doing anything because Holly's going to shut up.'

'What the hell is this about?' Tony asked, looking from one to the other.

'Nothing, this conversation is finished,' Grace insisted.

'You talk as if I'm the one out of line,' Holly complained.

'You are,' Grace returned. 'Nobody's interested in your opinion.'

Lizzy said no more. She couldn't run from this even if she'd been defeated. She had always faced life head on and this would be no exception. Holly was now in full swing. She took off her sunglasses like an actress in an old movie, ready for her big speech. 'It's not *my* opinion,' she said, 'it's *his*.'

Tony was becoming intolerant. 'Who are you talking about?'

'Patrick Smith—Lizzy's ex. He sells stationery on line…'

Tony's face was like thunder. 'I know what he does. But why would *you* need to talk to him? What do *you* want with stationery?'

'He posted something on my timeline.'

'Something personal about Lizzy?'

'It's hardly personal now is it?'

Tony scowled, his fist clenched on the table. 'Does this man have no decency at all? It was bad enough scribbling insults in Lizzy's treasured book, but that's outrageous.'

Lizzy's heart twisted. She had forgotten that. The words pierced her brain like needles.

Dream on, Lizzy! I heard about your boutique taking a nosedive. It's judgement on you. I told you one day you'd pay for what you did. I hope it was all worth it.

Tony had thought that Patrick was angry because she'd walked out on him, but he was about to find out the real reason. She stared at the table and waited.

'Now I understand why he wrote that,' Holly insisted.

Grace grimaced at Holly. 'Enough! Nobody wants to know Patrick Smith's opinion.'

'It's illegal to publish scandal on the social network,' Tony said.

'It isn't scandal if it's the truth,' Holly drawled. 'He said he couldn't marry a woman who gave her own children away. There—now you know.'

Lizzy gasped. There it was, Holly's trump card. The anger in Tony's face changed to shock and then she could see the look she expected to find in his eyes: the horror, the disgust, the pain.

'That's not true,' Grace snapped angrily. 'Lizzy tell them.'

Lizzy began to feel numb. 'Why should I?' She rose to her feet. 'I don't owe anybody an explanation.' She perceived Tony's move to go with her, but she raised her palms toward him. 'Please stay with your family. I can't talk to you now. I need to be alone for a while. I'm done with all this bitching. Having to watch my back, not knowing what Holly will do next. There's no more you can do to me, Holly. So what are you going to do for fun now?' She looked around at the stunned faces. 'Forgive me while I back out of this childish cat-fight with as much dignity as I can.'

'Wait!' Tony clamped his fingers round her hand to restrain her.

'Let me go, Tony, please…'

'Somebody had to tell them about your kid,' Holly said.

'I didn't have *a kid,* as you put it so crudely,' Lizzy spoke to Holly with fire in her eyes but ice in her voice. This cold, calculating, unfeeling woman had stolen Tony from her after all. He was too well-mannered to behave exactly like Patrick, but she had seen the evidence of his true reactions in his eyes. 'Sorry to disappoint you, Holly, especially as you'd cultivated your cyber friendship with Patrick so carefully—skilfully even—But I never had a baby.'

'Then what's he talking about?'

'I was a donor. I donated an egg to my sister because her heart was breaking. She couldn't get pregnant.'

There was a gentle taking in of breath around the table but nobody interrupted her.

'They're just microscopic things, and wouldn't have become a life anyway because I didn't plan to have children at that time. Thank God, otherwise my children would have a malicious, bitter man for a father. It wasn't straightforward. I had so much time away from work that I decided to close it down and worry about it later. Just to get the record straight, that was the *nosedive* that Patrick wrote about. But it was worth it. One of them held on and Carrie was pregnant at last. Jamie, my beautiful baby nephew, beat the odds. When I saw him I knew that he was way more important than a whole string of boutiques.' She fixed her eyes on Tony. 'So anybody who thinks I did wrong can go to hell.'

She dashed off. Tony called after her. 'Leave me alone,' she called back. 'Just leave me alone.'

Chapter Twenty Three

By late afternoon Lizzy was back at Larchwood. She had endured some challenging days in recent months but this was by far the worst. The family had been so apologetic about Holly's attack on her, and saw it all in the same way as her own family did, but the whole event left her cold and disappointed.

Tony had said he had to check on the travel arrangements so she saw nothing of him for the rest of the morning. When she did see him he was pre-occupied. She reasoned that if he was really falling in love it would have taken more than Holly's malicious meddling to cause this sudden change in him. It was as if it all jolted him back to reality. He never spoke on the flight back but sat alone dealing with a pressing problem with his work.

But for Eliot, who was travelling with them, the return journey would have been gruelling. They had both suffered a physical attack, leaving them at one of life's crossroads so they seemed to understand each other. Eliot said he had never felt the same about his work since his trip to Cape Town, and that it was strange how one chance event could change everything beyond recognition.

'And you still don't know why you went?' she asked him.

'Not a clue. What do I know about Cape Town, all my work's in the UK?'

'Maybe it'll come back to you.'

'It's time I stopped worrying about it,' he said. 'It was only a period of three weeks and who knows what could be lurking in that darkness. I might not even like it. It was suggested that something so traumatic happened that I blanked it out. But what about you, Lizzy, what will you do now?'

'My plans seem to have glanced off the track. I just can't see myself at Lakeside anymore. Nor Merevale for that matter.'

'But you and Tony… you're OK, aren't you?'

'I don't know.' She looked back to where Tony was sitting, peering closely at his laptop. 'Something's changed.'

'But the man was positively incandescent at the wedding. Everybody was commenting on it. Saying how good it was to see him more settled. I mean with somebody… you know.'

'Yes—I know. But everybody gets romantic at weddings, especially in a place like Florence. It was lovely, but it's time to give him some space.'

Having arrived back at Larchwood, she was at a loss as to her next move. Much as she wanted to seek refuge in her room it threatened to be a long, sleepless, heartsick night so she went to the studio in search of a mindless task to pass an hour or so. There were some work things that needed to be packed away ready to move on, even though she hadn't yet decided where. It had been such a pleasure to work here, the space, the beautiful view from the huge windows, the ability to just step out of the French windows and onto the terrace. Sharing the excitement and anticipation, with the Franklyn family, had been such a privilege.

She recalled the sound of the twins galloping around, being flying horses. The echo of her own footsteps reminded her of when she closed her business in Bowbury, and her vibrant, beautiful boutique became just another empty shop to let.

Back then she knew what her plan was, even though it came at a high price, but now things were not so clear. She felt the intense stress in her shoulders and she winced with the pain that gripped the back of her head like a vice. She decided to go outside and get some air.

There was a slight breeze nudging the larch trees, dotted with yellow leaves; summer was preparing to step aside and let in the early autumn.

Face it, Lizzy, she told herself as she trod carefully down the terrace steps, it's not as if we had an agreement, just a joke about a going steady badge, so there's nothing to break up. It just burnt out like a beautiful, exploding firework. You felt so empowered this morning because you had a lover. A fabulous hot, passionate lover who took your body to sensuous heights you never even fantasised about or even dreamed of. How could you, you didn't know feelings like that existed. You didn't know the pleasures in sharing a breakfast of cold orange juice and long, fabulous kisses? Or did you dream it all? Imagine that he'd laughed and said that even though your lips were cold from the drink, they could still burn him up? No wonder you thought you were sharing something good and lasting—how naive. What happened to that *danger* of Tony falling in love? Maybe guys do that. They have a great night with a woman and imagine themselves more deeply involved than they really are.

By the time she reached the lake the breeze was stronger and it whipped up the surface of the water making it choppy and grey. A pair of mallard flew in, and skidded on the surface; their voices echoed like mocking, raucous laughter. She walked slowly past the bulrushes that stood tall, like brown-hatted guards watching over the lilies. Even this steady walking pace made her head thump and she sat down on a fallen tree trunk that had been trimmed and left as a seat. She could see her home across the lake, it looked bleak. Jenny's studio lights were on indicating that she was still working. Lizzy found comfort in that image of her friend and decided to visit in the morning.

'There you are,' Tony called out as he approached.

Lizzy was abruptly jolted out of her thoughts and she stared in surprise.

'Sorry, did I scare you?'

'Yes, I wasn't expecting to see you.'

'I saw you from the kitchen window. Are you all right?'

'I was restless after the journey,' she told him. 'I needed some air.'

He tilted his head and a frown puckered his brow. 'You look pale.'

'Just a headache.'

'Quite a bad one by the look of you. And you're going to get cold.' He started to pull off his jumper.

'No, I'm fine,' Lizzy protested hastily not wanting to re-live that morning in Florence, when the warmth that lingered in his sweater wrapped around her and made her body sigh for the want of him.

'Why don't you come back and I'll get you something for that headache.'

'I'll be OK. I'll sit here for a while and then I'll take myself off to bed. That should sort it out.'

'Take *yourself*—you'd rather be alone?'

His question was direct and came as a surprise. She was silent for a moment and then decided to follow his example. 'I thought that was the order of the day.'

'What do you mean?'

She hesitated.

'Lizzy? Tony prompted. 'What's this all about?'

She knew Tony wasn't going to dismiss it now. Far better to say what was really on her mind. She looked up at him and asked, 'Why the big chill all of a sudden?'

'What?'

'You sat alone on the plane. What was that for?'

'I was working. I know it wasn't very hospitable of me but I had pressing things to sort out.' He looked puzzled. 'I explained all that.' He regarded her suspiciously. 'You're not convinced, are you?'

'I don't doubt you needed to do the work. But we spent all that time together, even a whole night, and then suddenly you had a million things to do and none of them included talking to me. Why did you hide from me all afternoon?'

'I wasn't hiding. You asked for some space. This is the most ridiculous conversation I've ever had with you.' He sat beside her and spoke quietly. 'What's happening here, Lizzy?'

'I don't know.' She drew up her knees and rested her arms across them. 'It seemed easy when we were in Florence.' She shook her head. 'I really can't... I just don't know anymore.'

Tony's voice remained steady. 'You regret what happened at Firenze?'

She shook her head. 'Of course I don't. But I feel that there's something you need to say.'

'What we have to discuss isn't the kind of thing you rush into and certainly not when you've got a blinding headache. It's far more important than that. We'll talk it all through properly tomorrow.'

'What do we have to discuss anymore?' Lizzy said softly. 'Holly dragged my skeleton, kicking and screaming, from its cupboard this morning.'

'You're not the only one with a secret, Lizzy, and I can assure you that mine is a lot more shocking than you imagined yours to be. We agreed to discuss this properly after the wedding—didn't we?'

Lizzy nodded.

'Holly's childish trick seized our prerogative to do that, but I'm not going to allow it to dictate what we do now.'

'It worked though, didn't it? Her plan was to discredit me, make you see me in a different light. If she couldn't have you then she would stop me. Patrick's posting was a timely gift and she knew how to use it.'

'That headache's making you insecure. Nobody thought badly of you, the opposite in fact. The whole family's very proud of you. That's over now. Why are you still worried about it?'

'Because, for an instant, you hated what I'd done but your integrity quickly put you back on track.'

'Of course I didn't hate it.'

'I could see it in your eyes. I wasn't surprised. I'd seen that reaction before.'

Tony glowered at her. He was horrified. 'You really believe I could behave like that idiot?'

'Something went through your mind,' Lizzy insisted.

'And you misread it,' Tony snapped. 'So I should be arrested for my thoughts because you imagine you can read them?'

Confusion, pain and disappointment bombarded Lizzy like an army of sensations, twisting and stabbing at her soul. Tony's cooling attitude was bad enough, but now he was angry with her. This was unbearable but she was certain about it and wasn't about to be beaten down. 'I didn't claim to have read your thoughts. Come on, Tony, I'm not making all this up. It was obvious that you didn't like what you heard, and things haven't been the same between us since. Why can't you be honest about it?'

'We can do this tomorrow.'

'Today's good for me,' Lizzy told him firmly. 'Something offended you this morning. You're reluctant to tell me so I know I'm right and it hurts not knowing.'

Tony drew a long, tense breath and clenched his hands together. 'What I heard this morning was unbelievable. The woman I was falling in love with had given a child away.'

'It wasn't true,' Lizzy cried out in exasperation.

Tony sprang to his feet. 'For a split second it *was.*' His voice echoed across the water.

His outburst shocked them both and there was a silence, save for the evensong of the waterfowl as they prepared to settle for the night.

Tony sighed and he rubbed his fingers over his forehead. 'Lizzy, please, let's not fight over this.' He sat down again, weary and shaken. 'Maybe I was judging you, I don't know, I don't have an answer for that. But I was angry.'

'With me?'

'With everybody imaginable. I was bitter and jealous because of the terrible irony of that moment.'

Lizzy was confused; she fixed her eyes on his face and spoke softly. 'Like what?'

'You had a choice.' He gulped as if it caused him a severe pain to do so, then he cleared his throat and added. 'You could decide whether to keep your baby or not. I wasn't given that choice.'

'I don't know what you mean.'

'My daughter was taken from me in the cruellest possible way—for her and for me.'

Lizzy was shaken to the core. Her face drained even more. There were no words to respond to it, but she had to try. Tony had a daughter, a little part of him and she was gone. Was it a custody thing? How could somebody who could access so much high calibre legal support, lose a custody battle that was so final? 'A daughter? When—how?' she whispered.

'Louisa was pregnant and very close to her due date when she… when she fell from the balcony.'

Lizzy's lungs juddered and she and grasped her arms across her waist. She hadn't considered that the child was dead.

Tony braced his arm around her shoulders. 'My pain—that reaction you saw was about *my* child not yours.'

'I'm so sorry,' Lizzy's whisper was almost inaudible. 'I can't imagine how you suffered.'

'I think you can, Lizzy, you feel other people's pain.'

The light was fading as if to reflect that chilling moment when Lizzy began to comprehend the full extent of Tony's grief. The thought of his pregnant lover falling that way must have been excruciating, but to add the death of his unborn baby was horrendous. She tried to speak but the words jumbled up and danced on her tongue. 'It… it must have…' Her voice faded and she shook her head, unable to form a coherent sentence.

'Come back to the house now?' Tony urged, swinging into protective mode. 'You don't look well.' He tightened his arm around her and they walked together.

As they entered the house via the French windows, Lizzy suddenly saw how pathetic she'd become. The love of her life was trying to come to terms with a terrible loss and she was limp and pale and annoyed about his attitude on the plane.

For goodness sake, she told herself, get over it and give him some support. This isn't about you it's about him. Do what you're good at, face it head on and get on with it.

They walked through the banqueting room. The ancestors stared down as usual and the headless knight still hung in the threadbare tapestry. This drab room wasn't conducive to trying to comfort anybody but she reached out to him. 'You must have been through hell all these months. I wish there was some way I could make this more bearable for you. But I'm here if you need me.'

Tony frowned. 'Of course I need you. You're the one person who got me through all this.'

'But you're not through it, Tony, are you? You're just patched up. This is going to take more than just gritting your teeth.'

'I'm doing fine. As long as I can be with you, I can hack it.'

'Is that what I am, your shield?'

'We've got to fix that headache you're not making sense at all.'

'Yes I am.' She stopped walking and spoke directly. 'We get along really well. And last night was amazing—for both of us, but...'

'Now you're talking sense,' Tony agreed looking at her affectionately. 'It was very special.'

'But I'm not Louisa, am I? That's why our relationship hits these difficult patches. I'm not your lost love.'

Tony's face clouded. 'I don't want Louisa—I want you. At least that part of you that doesn't think she's second best. For goodness sake, Lizzy, the only lost love around here is the one that's slipping through my fingers right now.'

'But maybe you need more time than you think to get over Louisa.'

Tony took several seconds to answer. Then he fixed his eyes on her and said, 'I was sorry to hear about Louisa's death but I wasn't in love with her. I-did-not-love-her.' He added accentuating each word.

His staccato admission left her stunned. She felt she should have been relieved and happy. There was no ghost, no faultless angel standing in her way now, but the news of the lost child overshadowed any joy in that.

'We dated a few times,' Tony said, 'a couple of dinner parties, one or two business things. I offered to take her to the opera but she passed on it. We attended a high profile charity do—she loved that one. Somebody took our picture for a magazine. I wasn't surprised, she was very beautiful. But after a few weeks she got careless and let her true personality show. Then she wasn't so attractive. I was never in love with her. I just let people believe what they wanted. The bottom line was that I couldn't cope with losing the child. I just wandered about in a black fog.'

An unexpected shudder ran through Lizzy's body. She wished they could move out of this depressing gallery but Tony had started talking and she feared he might stop if they moved on.

'I can see that you're surprised,' he said. 'Let's just say that I didn't share her penchant for wild parties so we split up. Three months later she came to see me in my London apartment. Told me she was pregnant. I couldn't believe it of course. I always took great care... well it didn't seem possible. But she gloated as she gave me a little picture of the scan to prove it was real. I looked at that image and a powerful feeling engulfed me. My child, my flesh and blood.' He looked at Lizzy, and a faint flicker of a smile crossed his lips. 'Likely to be a little girl, so she said. Offered to get a DNA test but I couldn't agree to that. She was confident that we'd get married, and she could live the high profile life that she coveted. I never courted it, but it was unavoidable at times and she'd tasted it. But I wasn't about to raise a child in a loveless marriage and certainly not one that would definitely fail miserably. I offered to buy her a house, here or London—both even, if that's what she wanted. I thought we could parent the little girl between us. People do that all the time. It then became apparent that the baby was just to hold me to ransom. Bold as brass and just as cold she said she would terminate it and get on with her life. I panicked. I'd never had so little control over anything. This wasn't a piece of property it was my daughter, imprisoned inside this terrible woman. She was over four months pregnant, fit and healthy with no career plans, other than making a good marriage. There was no good reason to terminate so late. I threatened legal action before I could even think about whether it was possible to force her to see it through.'

'Did you do that, take her to court?'

'No. On reflection I couldn't put a pregnant woman through that. It was her body after all. Who was I to dictate what she did with it? Besides, she might have won. What would I do then, marry her? Commit myself to life with a woman I detested when I couldn't even commit to any of the decent women I knew?'

'So what did you do?'

He paused for a while. 'I took the easy option. I used money. Louisa accepted a deal. I was to have complete custody and raise the baby here, alone. She balked at all the restrictions but she loved the sound of the money.'

'What kind of restrictions?'

'Providing she took proper care of herself, attended regular check-ups at the clinic and sent reports directly to me, I'd stick to my part of the bargain which was to pay for all her expenses, including her aunt's care, plus monthly instalments of cash. I gave Irena control of the account. She had no idea what it was all about, but she never questioned what went on in my love life. I bought lots of things for women; cars, jewellery, even property. This was just another day at the office for Irena. Talking about it now it sounds like a terrible way to deal with it, but I had to get the baby from her. I didn't trust her one inch and she knew how much I wanted it. Once I'd stitched it all up as tightly as I could, secured every angle, every loophole, I swung into action—big time. I went to the US, sold all my interests over there and drastically cut my workload. I fully intended to have time to be a good father, but then a good father would have stayed closer to home and kept his eye on Louisa.'

'You couldn't be everywhere at once.'

'Instead of returning home to a fool-proof plan it was all so elusive. I was legally the child's father but I wasn't Louisa's next of kin, so nobody informed me. When I couldn't find her, I went to see her aunt, her only relative, but she was very frail and couldn't understand. The staff told me about the accident. It seems that her aunt was contacted but...' He dropped his shoulders and sighed. 'For God's sake, couldn't she just have waited another four weeks?'

'Did you go to Paris to bring the baby home?'

'I couldn't do that. She died with her mother, there was nothing to bring home?'

'Nothing, not even a document, a certificate?'

'What do you mean?'

'She was going to live here, be part of Larchwood. Any evidence of her existence should be here, with you.'

Tony stared at her. 'Nobody could tell me anything. There were closed doors, people saw or heard nothing.'

Lizzy was desperate to ask more questions but hated hurting him like this. Yet something wasn't quite right and she couldn't keep quiet. 'Tony, you must have rights as a father. You can't be left like this. You should have gone to Paris. You might have—'

'Stop it, Lizzy!'

Lizzy thought of that baby, a viable child that would now be the same age as Jamie. She had held him from the moment he was born; warm and vulnerable, but Tony's child was not so fortunate. 'I can't see this the way you do.'

Tony was losing patience. 'So how do you see it, Lizzy? You who only just found out about it can come up with a better solution than mine?'

'With only four weeks to go it would be very obvious. Surely the coroner would have recorded it? You could have at least had that instead of a big, dark, empty space.'

Tony's eyes glared and he slapped his chest hard, with his hand. 'I know how big and dark that void is. It's right here, inside me. It sits there day after day. My only peace from it is you and now even that's falling apart.'

'But you can't be sure that Louisa was still pregnant.'

'For God's sake,' Tony's voice ricocheted across the gigantic oil paintings. 'I had a team of lawyers, advisers, medical reports; she *was* pregnant. I did everything I could.'

'You did the maths,' Lizzy lashed back, tormented by the bitter truth that Tony was facing the rest of his life without actual confirmation of his daughter's death. 'You added up all the logic, the lawyers, advisers, doctors, administrators, so the answer must surely be *one deceased baby.*'

'Are you trying to twist the knife? Make me suffer because I won't go to Paris to bring back a ghost? Why can't you let it go?'

'There are doubts.'

'What are you talking about?'

'Pictures, I saw them, on a web site. I didn't want you to know about them.'

'Why shouldn't I know about them?'

'I thought it would hurt you to see such images. She was hanging all over this guy. And there was another shot where she was topless and dancing on a table. She had an incredible body. There's no way she was pregnant in those pictures.'

'That could have been any party from another time. It's what she did; the flirting, the stripping and the dancing on the table. It was like a calling card. That's why I couldn't stand to be with her anymore. Stop grasping at straws, Lizzy. It's over.'

'Because nobody would tell you what actually happened, it's over? Your little girl is entitled to…'

He glared at her, his eyes burning with anger. 'Entitled to what, a better father?'

'Of course not.'

'Then what did I miss? What is it that I've denied her?'

'An identity.' Lizzy thrust the words right at him. 'A bit of paper to say she died because if you don't have that she didn't exist. She's a nonentity.' She stared, through her tears, at his hot, angry eyes. The pain in her head was piercing her nerve ends.

'What do you expect? For Christ's sake, the funeral was over before I got back.'

'Who's funeral?' Lizzy cried out.

'Louisa's, who's do you think?'

'And your daughter's? Where does it say that she had a funeral? I know how you've suffered, but she was a viable life, a whole person and you need her home where she was going to be raised. Make her a garden or plant a tree, a bush, anything—a special place where you can acknowledge that she was real.' She dragged a breath through her tightened lungs. 'How else will her future siblings learn to understand that they had a big sister? What will you say about *the child, the baby, the little girl?* For heaven's sake, Tony, you didn't even give her a name.'

Tony dragged his palms down his face and he braced his body as if to ride the shocking truth that spilled from Lizzy's mouth.

Lizzy's head pounded, her heart ached to have been so cruel but some kind of maternal urge made her stand and fight for the child. Something wasn't right about all this. In his grief Tony had missed it. She couldn't judge him for that. 'Tony, I'm so sorry. That was a terrible thing to say. Please forgive me.'

'It's OK,' he said. His breath was laboured as if he had been running. He approached her, his face deathly white. 'If you'll excuse me I have more work to see to. You need to get something for that headache, and then you should go to bed.' He pressed a polite kiss on her cheek. 'Goodnight,' he said curtly and left her in the company of his ancestors.

Chapter Twenty Four

Jenny handed Lizzy a mug of tea. 'I know you can get a bit sharp tongued once in a while but that was harsh, Babe.'

Lizzy sighed. 'It was positively cruel, I know. He must have been feeling really terrible, as if he'd failed in some way. I should have been supportive not challenging. What kind of woman does that?'

'The kind who's been through hell and back herself.'

Lizzy clasped her mug in both hands and sipped the tea. 'I had a thumping headache and I panicked. I started thinking about those pictures, it made me doubt.'

'He's right though, Lizzy. If Louisa was prone to behave that way then it could have been any other party. People put things on the internet but they're not necessarily accurate. You shouldn't really be telling me all this. Will he mind?'

'I doubt it. You know more about his private life than anybody else. All the people he's sent flowers to. All those break ups. '

'Now I know why he was so gutted that day he came in and couldn't write a card. It must have been excruciating because Joe came to help him to the car.'

'You never told me that.'

'He seemed to be getting over it when he met you.'

'I was afraid that Louisa conned him for the money, played on his integrity, but he had lawyers checking everything out, direct contact with the clinic she attended. I'm going to have to admit that she must have been pregnant. And, if he'll let me, I'll apologise.' She set down her mug and raised her hand to her face. 'Poor little baby. It makes me want to hold her—make her better.'

'Did you tell him that?'

'No.'

'You should. He'd understand because he'll be feeling the same. Why don't you go and find him and tell him.'

'We haven't spoken since the row yesterday. I don't even know where he is. Gone to London I suppose. Back to his business, his comfort zone. He can lose himself in that and move on.'

'He didn't tell you where he was going?'

Lizzy shook her head.

Jenny frowned. 'Strange though. He's not a vindictive person. He wouldn't sulk either. Why don't you call him?'

'Not during office hours. He'll have his business head on. Reminding him about Paris won't do him any favours if he's in a board meeting or something.'

'It isn't just that, is it?'

'What do you mean?'

'So he's one hell of a catch, but that doesn't mean you can't have him.'

'I don't care what kind of catch he is.'

'But you can't ignore the fact that he's got a lot of money and a shed load of sex appeal, so whether you care or not that's who he is—what he looks like to the outside world.' She shook her head. 'So you're still wondering why he's attracted to you. You think you should back off and leave the field clear for Mrs tall, blonde and beautiful to come along. You know he's falling for you. He's told you as much. But have you told him?'

'No.'

'Why not? Don't tell me, it's the old *I'm out of his league* rubbish. Look at everything you've done, everything you've been through these past few months. You can put up a better fight than this. Before you went to Florence, you looked through your window and told me that you were afraid of staying because you'd see Tony across the lake, playing with his children. That you couldn't bear the thought of knowing they wouldn't be yours. But you've got a chance now so hold on to it. Call him. Tell him you love him. Say you're sorry. And tell him that thing about wanting to hold his baby.'

'I don't want to upset him again.'

'None of that will upset him.'

'I must go. I know you're busy because I saw your studio light on last night.'

'Just some table centres for a lunch party at the hotel.'

'Thanks for the chat. You always make me feel better.'

'Not today though, eh?'

'I'm much happier than I was.'

'Well don't forget your flowers,' Jenny said and picked up a small spray of yellow roses.

'Jenny, no, you can't afford to keep giving me freebies.'

'Oh that's no problem,' Jenny smiled smugly. 'He paid good money for these.'

'What?'

'No card though because he phoned in.'

'So what do they mean? Goodbye?'

'Course they don't mean goodbye. He said they were to cheer you up because you weren't well last night. He said he wanted bright yellow ones, the colour of sunflowers because you liked them so much. Go and call him. At least if your courage falls through the floor you have an excuse. Thank him for the flowers and say they cheered you up.'

****

When Lizzy called Tony's London office, Irena said she hadn't seen him since he left Florence.

'But you must not worry,' Irena added. 'Occasionally he does this. He will have switched off his phone so do not waste your time calling; it will only frustrate you. When he needs to think, he finds a quiet place, turns off his phone, and works it out. Then he will come back with a solution.'

'That's what he does?'

'Yes.'

'So this isn't unusual?'

'Not at all.'

'So… I just wait?'

'Yes—you wait.'

Chapter Twenty Five

Paris, Tony could hardly believe he'd actually come here as he stepped from his plane; but come, he must. Lizzy had shocked him to the core. Her voice echoed inside his head, *you didn't even give her a name.*

He sat in newspaper offices and combed through their records. Tragic though the accident was it didn't seem to attract much press attention, and there was nothing to take home.

After badgering the police, who had more to do than dig around in an open and shut case, he found the same doors slamming in his face.

He walked the streets of Paris, achieving nothing except weariness of spirit and body. Having run out of bureaus and record offices and listened to advice about learning to move on, he was at a loss as to how he could take home a token of his child's identity; proof of her life. He wanted to call Lizzy, hear her voice, feel her presence wrapping around him, masking this pain, but he denied himself the luxury. He walked past the Paris Sanccella's restaurant, busy and bustling. It reminded him of their date which seemed months ago and not just a few days. He felt warmed by the memory of Lizzy's eyes reflecting the candlelight and he walked on and found a small café. He took a piece of card from his pocket and stared at the address written on it. His insides sickened at the thought of going anywhere near it but all other possibilities were exhausted. His failure to do this, six months ago, had come between him and Lizzy. So he would do this for her, bring home a ghost, plant a tree in the garden, go through the motions of conventional closure, and then face the real task of actually living with it.

By the time he made a move to find the house, it was early evening. When he arrived he stood and looked for a while. It was just a house and he wondered how it could look so conventional. He tugged at a bell-pull; it jangled.

The door was jerked open briskly, by a young woman, freckled faced and with unruly, frizzy hair pulled back into a silk scarf.

'Hi! Can I help you?' she said cheerfully. 'Oh, sorry I mean…'

'It's all right, I'm English.'

'What a relief,' she sighed. 'My French is still awful, but I married a Frenchman, so it's got to improve. What can I do for you?'

'Forgive me for interrupting your day. I don't mean to upset anybody and I realise that this is a terrible impertinence.'

'Oh my God, you really are English, aren't you?'

Tony smiled. 'Guilty as charged. I have a very strange request and I quite understand if you decide to shut the door.'

'Well, give it a try,' she said. Her smile lingered, lighting her face.

'My name's Tony Franklyn. I'm here to lay a ghost.'

The light faded from the woman's face and a frown replaced it. She stared. 'Oh God! The woman at the party.'

Tony gave her a business card and a brief outline of the background to reassure her that he wasn't a journalist.

'Come in! Come in!' she said. 'I'm Sam Jordin.' She rolled her eyes to the ceiling. 'My dad was convinced I was going to be a boy. He had the name picked out since I was just a foetus. It's a dad thing, I suppose.'

'Absolutely,' Tony said, guilt twinging at his conscience as Lizzy's words hit him once again. Even through all his pain he never named the child. 'If you want some other kind of ID I have my passport if that helps.'

'It's OK. I can take care of myself, and quite honestly you don't look too scary.' She ran her eyes over his clothes and said, 'Nor do you look as though you need to rob me. More to the point I haven't anything to take.'

'I don't know any details,' Tony explained as he followed her, weaving between cartons and storage boxes on the floor, 'but I needed to see where it happened. I'm ashamed to say that I didn't see the point until now.'

'I don't know anything either,' Sam said when they reached the staircase. 'But you're welcome to look around. As you see we've only just moved here. We wondered why it was in our price range. Then we found out that there was a party here and a woman had…'

'Fallen from the balcony.' Tony ended her sentence out of kindness because she was clearly upset on his behalf.

'Yes, I'm really sorry. The previous owner was traumatised by the accident and just wanted to get away from it. Her friends closed ranks to protect her. Were you related?'

'No… we dated for a time. But…' Tony hesitated and then he spoke more positively. 'This is very kind of you, Sam, and I feel I should be honest with you. It was my ex-girlfriend that died but she was pregnant.'

Sam put her hand to her mouth. 'I'm so sorry,' she said through her fingers. 'Nobody said anything about that.'

'I came back because my new girlfriend pointed out that the baby has no identity, nothing to prove that she existed. Louisa was just four weeks from her due date you see. Nobody recorded it or mentioned it. I wouldn't have intruded otherwise.'

Sam led him to what she described as the biggest room in the house. 'I suppose that's why they had the party here. It was a studio, they were both artists.' She hovered a moment and then said, 'I'll leave you alone. Would you like some coffee—tea?'

'No thanks. I just need a moment.'

The room was large and empty. Tony approached the balcony doors. His hands clamped on the handles, unable to move further. After a time, anger rose inside him, he pushed them open and stepped onto the balcony. 'God, Louisa,' he said aloud, 'you had the rest of your life to have fun. Would it have been so bad to hang on a little longer?' He looked down to the patio below, then turned from it, closed the doors behind him and went back downstairs.

Sam met him. 'Are you sure you wouldn't like something to drink—maybe something stronger?'

'I'll just visit the garden if that's OK, then I'll be on my way.'

'Sure.' She opened the door. 'Just ring the bell if you need me. Good luck.'

They shook hands as Tony said, 'Please don't let this spoil your day. At least I can go back to my girlfriend and tell her that I really have turned over every stone, and found nothing. I hope this will be a happy home for you.'

'We'll make sure it is. We scraped every last penny we had to buy the house. It just needs some furniture and lots of kids. We've got all the names sorted.'

Tony nodded. 'Like your father.'

'In the meantime we'll manage on love and cardboard boxes.'

'Love and cardboard boxes,' Tony echoed, smiling faintly. 'That sounds perfect.' He turned to leave but looked back, 'What will you call your first daughter?'

'Sam smiled. 'Stephanie, crowned with victory. I guess that means a winner.'

It was growing dark. Tony stood on the lawn; it seemed irreverent to stand on the patio. He almost wished that the accident was on the road, like everybody had assumed. This was bizarre.

His eyes burned as he looked up at the balcony. 'Well, little girl, this wasn't part of the plan was it?' He stopped as the pain gripped his heart, his abdomen, and his face creased with the agony. He clenched every muscle in his body and clamped his jaw as he willed himself to look at the patio, a sorry resting place for one so cherished. He dragged a breath through his throat. 'It's all so bleak thinking of you dying here.' He paused and turned about as if to recharge his courage. Then he chastised himself for not being stronger. He was the daddy he should be the strong one. He stood firm and said, 'Your mother loved Paris. She wanted to be here, so that's fair enough. But I won't leave *you* here. The truth is, darling child, she wasn't ready for you. But I was. And I still want you with me; it just won't be quite like we planned. Lizzy told me I should do this. I thought it was crazy but she's right. So come along now, Daddy's taking you home to Larchwood.'

'Mr Franklyn... Tony,' Sam called to him. 'I called the previous owner to ask if she'd see you. She couldn't face that, but she told me quite a lot about it and asked me to pass it on to you. Can you come back inside? I'll make some tea.'

****

Lizzy decided to take Irena's advice and wait, instead of trying to make contact with Tony. It was very difficult. She had grown accustomed to being in touch with him constantly while they were in Florence. The day passed slowly and she went to her room with a bag full of mail that Jenny had taken in for her. A tedious job seemed a fitting end to an equally tedious day. She changed into pyjama bottoms and a T-shirt and sat on the bed winkling out the genuine mail from the flyers and leaflets.

A letter, from Carrie cheered her up. It contained a little snapshot of Jamie, playing in his paddling pool. Her sister was remorseful, that was no surprise, but she also said that her experience had made her grow up. She wanted to be friends. Lizzy stuffed the junk mail into the wastebasket, found a pen and pad then returned to her bed.

A faint knock on her door gave her a start. 'Who's that?' The doorknob turned. 'Hello!'

Tony entered the room. He looked drained, like a ghost. It was as if he was sleepwalking but he was fully clothed.

'Tony, are you OK?'

He said nothing. He flopped on to the bed and a huge sigh gushed from him as his head sunk into the pillow.

'Tony…?'

He closed his eyes and immediately began to sink into an exhausted sleep. With his last waking breath he uttered, 'I went to Paris…'

Chapter Twenty Six

It had rained in the night and the earthy freshness of the new day filled the air. Tony walked along the gritty path of the kitchen garden to pay his respects to Bryn, the gardener; a courtesy that Grandpa Franklyn had taught him long ago. He needed to do something uncomplicated, a simple task to help get his thoughts together.

The trip to Paris, yesterday, was an attempt to return Lizzy's metaphorical white feather. He'd been on the receiving end of some sharp comments from her, from time to time, but none that drilled so painfully into his conscience as that. But the visit had unexpectedly thrown light on the bitter darkness of the past few months and had completely changed everything. It was no surprise to learn that Louisa, who had made a fine art out of gatecrashing, had tagged along with somebody she met at the hotel. She had a lot to drink and started to boast, celebrating the fact that she'd *made a killing* out of being pregnant. It seemed that nobody wanted to listen to her and she became more and more loud and ill-mannered; told people about the financial deal and even referred to her benefactor as *the father who stumped up a fortune.*

Louisa's words, seemingly from beyond the grave, made him shudder, but he breathed in the freshness of this new day, smelled the wetted peat and the produce where raindrops had lingered on the foliage. It was wholesome and innocent and far removed from the echoes of Louisa's callousness. He walked past the greenhouses and the rows of cold frames, stepping back into Grandpa Franklyn's time, wrapping the comforting memories around him. He thought how swiftly it all passes and how easy it was to bounce off the surface of life without really living.

Bryn touched his cap with his fingers. 'Morning Boss.'

Tony hated this rank, bestowed on him by his staff; something started by Joe. It made them all feel comfortable so he lived with it.

'Everything all right Bryn?'

'Grand, thanks. Just getting the plums sorted.'

'Is it time for them already?' Tony looked at the trays filled with the purple, sumptuous fruit, fit to be named after a queen. He thought how it might feel to have a career like Bryn's, governed by the seasons as opposed to market shares and exchange rates. 'They're a credit to you, Bryn.'

'Not just my doing,' Bryn protested. 'It's a good year for them. A bit o' luck with the weather and some hard work by the bees, in the spring, that usually does the trick.'

'And then the wasps come along to do the damage,' Tony added and swatted at one that was buzzing around his head.

'Bit of a pest but they probably do something useful somewhere else. You can't get through life without a sting or two, can you, Boss? That's what pays for the good things.'

Tony nodded as Bryn's words summed up his feelings at that moment. 'I'll remember that.'

'Well, look at Larchwood,' Bryn added as he gazed around him. 'We older ones had some bad years with your uncle.' He touched his cap and added, 'If you don't mind me saying, Boss. But you got Larchwood back on its feet.' He expelled a heavy but contented sigh. 'All it needs now is a family; kids like you and your cousins, running your grandma ragged when you came for the holidays.'

'Were we that bad?'

'No, just lads growing up.' He chuckled. 'Stella baked cakes and they were gone before she'd even made the tea. And you…' he added, raising his old brow.

'Me?' Tony said with a laugh, enjoying the glimpse back into the carefree years of his boyhood.

'Rooting through my tool shed, looking for things to make gadgets.' He winked and jerked his head for Tony to follow him into the greenhouse.

Tony glanced up at the vines sprawling and weaving along the roof, and ducked his head as he walked beneath them. The grapes, fashioned into broad shouldered bunches, had begun to show a faint shade of purple in the green.

Bryn stopped at his workstation, an old oak table containing an orderly array of seedling trays and pots. 'Remember making this, the *Tony Franklyn rotating planter?*' Bryn spoke about the gadget with respect and an air of affection.

Tony's heart pulsed to see that Bryn valued it. His head slowly shook. 'You still have that?'

'I certainly do.'

'Does it still work?'

'Course it does. It's a bit creaky but it can still do its job; like me.'

'I'll make you another one—a better one. I have much better technology now.'

Bryn scowled. 'A young lad, with better things to do with his holiday, had the good nature to design this for me when I had a bit of trouble with my shoulder. And I know you mean well now, Boss, but this one's fine.'

Tony felt that his offer had violated some kind of feudal protocol; noblesse oblige was a tricky practice. He changed the subject and moved to a more recognised interaction. 'Stella's not here today but she's sure to want some of those plums back at the house.'

'Your young lady came for them yesterday and she fetched the strawberries, back in June. She likes it here, she said.'

'Yes, I remember her bringing the strawberries.' He recalled it very clearly. He was angry with her for doing it, but he wouldn't have missed the sight of her standing there looking as delicious as the fruit in the basket. Her flushed cheeks and hair blown about her face put ideas in his head that had no right to be there at that time.

'Nice girl.'

Bryn jolted him out of his reverie. He smiled and nodded in agreement then turned, left his memories in the greenhouse and prepared to face the present once again. It seemed easy in Florence. It was all going so well, but back here in Larchwood it wasn't so simple. In Paris, Sam had confirmed that Louisa wasn't pregnant at the party. Now Lizzy wasn't the only one asking the question, *what happened to the baby?*

Lizzy sat in the kitchen window seat, her back rested on the shutters, her knees pulled up to support a small sketch pad as she attempted to get back into the swing of work. Whatever had happened, there was an empty shop on the other side of the lake that made her feel like a tiny bird with a baby cuckoo in her nest, hungry, demanding all of her efforts just to achieve the most basic results. She was uninspired, unmotivated and conscious of a vacuum where her creativity used to be as she ran her pencil aimlessly around a sketched figure, yet to be dressed. Guilt still weighed heavy in her heart. The echo of her ill-chosen words would give her no peace until she had apologised. Of course Tony would play the gentleman card, tell her it was understandable and not to concern herself about it, but she wasn't going to accept that. She would be mistress of her own guilt and would apologise if she had to clamp her hand over his mouth and make him hear it.

She reflected on the way he came to her room and collapsed on the bed. She watched him sleep, fully clothed, even with his shoes on; Tony Franklyn would never do anything so undisciplined. It made her realise just how exhausted and drained he was. She listened to the soft sounds of his breathing and longed to cross the physical and emotional space between them, kiss his face and tell him how she loved him, hold him through his sleep. When she woke up this morning he'd gone, leaving her to wonder if she had dreamt it.

Giving up on creativity and unable to see past her frustration, she tossed her pad to the floor. It landed with a loud slap befitting all she cast off with it. An anxious sigh squeezed from her lungs and she clamped her arms across her chest. Her fingers buried in the folds of fine wool of Tony's sweater; the one he put on her that morning by the pool; a long, long time ago it seemed. She meant to give it back one day but for now it was a prop to lean on during this time of uncertainty.

'I'm sorry, sweetheart, but we really must go to Bowbury, to see DCI Brent. We can't leave it any longer. He needs to know what happened about Carrie's loan. Can you get the information together?' Tony's familiar, sonorous tones reached across the kitchen, to her ears, her heart and her soul, all in one moment and the hours of waiting were over. His tone indicated that he had forgiven her, but this was her chance to apologise and without another thought she dashed to him, wrapped her arms round his neck and gushed her apology unashamedly against his face. 'I'm sorry... I'm sorry... I'm so sorry. Please forgive me.'

Tony's arms tightened around her. 'There's no need to...'

Lizzy stepped back and looked him in the eye. 'I knew you'd say that,' she complained.

'You were right to say what you did.'

'Rubbish! What I said the other night was cruel.'

'It was entirely my own fault.'

'I knew you'd say that, too. I've been in agony since that row. You didn't call yesterday so I couldn't apologise. Come on, Tony; don't be so gracious about it.'

'You want me to swap that sweater for a hair shirt? Well I don't have a spare one. I'm using it.'

'For goodness sake, all I want... I'm trying...' He smiled at her making it more difficult to have her say. She became tongue-tied. It annoyed her and in desperation, called on her feisty alter ego to fight her way out of it. 'I was a complete bitch and you know it,' she blurted.

Tony held his fingertip to her lips. 'Now wait a minute. I don't want to hear that.' He looked at her for several seconds, and then he took her face gently in his hands, his eyes poured love into hers. 'I won't hear a bad word against the woman I love, is that clear?'

'Love?' she echoed softly.

'I've wanted to tell you for some time. I almost did in Florence, but I had this ridiculous idea that I should wait until our lives had regained some kind of order. Then I could take you somewhere beautiful and romantic, Lake Como, the sunflower fields in Tuscany, a golden beach somewhere, and say I love you, Lizzy Yardley.' He shook his head. 'And here we are, in the kitchen; a great plan that turned out to be. But I've denied you the truth long enough.'

Lizzy's heart thudded. She couldn't speak. All she could do was stare in awe at those eyes that she could read so well.

'I told you the other day that I was in danger of falling in love with you but that was ridiculous because I was already in love with you, and have been since you came out of the mist, like a guardian angel and turned my life around.'

Lizzy widened her eyes. So she was still his salve through bitter times. 'If you're in love with an angel then walk away now. I'm not a pure, white, heavenly being without faults or blemishes.'

'I didn't mean to suggest that.'

'Then tell me that you love me, the outspoken, feisty, independent woman who's too proud to be gracious about your generosity. Tell that woman how you feel because angels fall, don't they? What would happen then?'

Tony's eyes shone, her words did nothing to deter him. 'I'd catch you. I promised I would, didn't I?' He smiled. 'I love you—feisty, outspoken, tenacious and independent.' A frown creased his brow. 'I admit I haven't yet learned to deal with your pride about accepting help—give me time. But I won't ever deny myself the memory of my first sight of you. That won't ever go away just because you're afraid to be special.'

Lizzy was a little mesmerised by his words and his gaze. She smiled and spoke softly, not wanting to break this mood. 'That first time I met you, and you stopped me falling into the palm plant, I felt your arm around me and your voice saying, "It's all right I've got you." It was as if I belonged right there, close to your body, locked in your arms. I hadn't a clue whose arms they were, or whose voice whispered but those words were so powerful. I was frightened to death of my own reactions. The feelings were too strong—too sudden. I'd never experienced anything like it before. I tried to avoid you, assuming it would wear off. I refused to go to Florence, thinking that I could get on with my work and by the time you got back I'd be free as a bird. I could carry on avoiding men to make sure I wouldn't be hurt or insulted again.'

Tony nodded and smiled. 'I was scared too. But now I'm not and I can admit to you that I absolutely and utterly adore you.' He wrapped his arms around her so tightly that it felt as though they circled her twice as their bodies stood as one. He buried his face in her shoulder where her hair rested. It was like an act of humility, as if to pay some kind of homage to his lover.

Lizzy embraced it all, her arms holding a man who could have had almost any woman in the world, but who, at that moment, had laid his naked soul at her feet.

Tony looked at her face and then took her by the hand. 'Before we go to the police station, I have something to tell you.'

'Oh no. Is it going to hurt?'

'Perhaps,' he said, as he led her to the window seat. 'But we're both on the same side, we'll face it together.'

As Lizzy looked at him, his brow puckered, the muscle in his jaw twitched. She knew that although they had overcome the complexities of love, they had yet to settle their differences with fate.

'What's the matter?' she prompted.

'Louisa,' Tony answered with a faint sigh.

The sound of the name sent daggers of anger through Lizzy's body. Tony had endured months of suffering that he didn't deserve, and she wasn't going to allow any more pitfalls or obstacles to perpetuate his pain. If she was his guardian angel, then she had leave to speak out about it. 'Surely we're not going to let her hang around like some kind of crazy wife you keep locked up in the attic, or a ghost who won't let you free?'

'No, darling, that's not it,' he said softly. 'I learned, in Paris, that what you said was true. It was gruelling, but you were right, the baby had no identity and I owed her that.' He shook his head. 'It struck me hard to realise how carelessly and easily I gave her life.'

'Nature doesn't work with integrity, Tony, making a baby isn't a crime.'

Tony was silent for a moment but he smiled faintly and then said softly, 'Stephanie. I called her Stephanie.'

Lizzy's eyes warmed as she looked at his face and nodded. 'Stephanie, that's lovely.'

'I believe it means crowned with glory—a winner. I named her after a very special child, one that isn't born yet but is already loved.'

Lizzy nodded gently not knowing what he really meant but she didn't question it. 'I really like it.'

Tony told her how he trekked round record bureaus and police stations, searching for a glimmer of information; and how he was left with nothing but the fearful task of going to the house where it all happened. He talked of Sam, the young woman, who was determined to turn the scene of a tragedy into a happy home again and fill it full of the sounds of children. Lizzy then understood about the name.

'I actually stood beneath the balcony,' Tony said, almost unable to believe he'd really done it. 'I talked to her. I couldn't imagine doing that when you suggested it, but it felt perfectly normal.'

Lizzy moved closer to him and linked her arm through his, hugging it tightly. 'I didn't mean to put you through all that pain again, Tony. I'm so sorry.'

'I had to go, my love, it didn't matter who prompted me.'

'You don't need to talk about it now. Give yourself a chance to recover.'

'There's no time. The visit changed everything.'

He spoke about Louisa's behaviour at the party and that the pictures on the internet were genuine, Louisa wasn't pregnant at that time.

Although Lizzy had suspected it, she was shaken. Yet this wasn't a time for drama, she had to be calm. She was part of Tony, his comforter, his lover—his love. Her new role was not to shy away from it but to go towards it with her whole being. 'Was she conning you, sending false reports?'

'No, they were accurate. I knew how she hated the restrictions of pregnancy and she was probably bored because one day she set off to drive to a fashion fair in a market town, she never said where and the guests took little notice of her by then. So I've no idea where it was, it could be anywhere in the UK. On her way she started to feel pains and had to check into the nearest hospital… The baby was born six weeks early.'

Lizzy's insides quaked. She suppressed a gasp of surprise but said nothing. She just put her arm across Tony's back, leaned against him and listened to his voice.

'Louisa must have used her own name. Had she told them about me and my custody rights, they would have traced me. As it was, nobody knew Stephanie was mine.'

'But if Louisa was in France, so soon after the birth.' She gulped to try and relax the tightening in her throat. 'Was she free to leave because Stephanie didn't make it?' Now Stephanie had a name, it seemed more upsetting.

Tony clasped her hand. 'I don't see how it can mean anything else. Sam found out that Louisa was only there a couple of days. She checked into a health clinic for two weeks then flew to Paris in search of some fun. She didn't even know anybody there. It must have been a reaction to all the restrictions.'

Lizzy's heart twisted, it seemed so final, so cruelly certain that Stephanie didn't thrive. 'I'm so sorry.'

'It's a small but welcome comfort to know that she didn't die from the fall.'

'When you told me about it, I just wanted to go and pick her up, hold her, make it all better and I had some idea of how you must have felt.'

'I must keep searching for her and give her what she was entitled to in the first place—her name and a father.'

'There must be a record of her birth on line. We don't even need Irena's skills. If people can find their ancestors then surely we can find…' She stopped a moment and took in a steadying breath.

Tony put his arm across her shoulders. 'Yes,' he said, 'we'll start with that. The records should show where she was born. If we find that out then we can go to the hospital to learn more.'

'We'll find her,' Lizzy whispered.

Tony nodded but he couldn't speak.

'Maybe the police could help, you know, give us a clue as to where we begin.'

Chapter Twenty Seven

'What makes you so sure she didn't survive?' DC Grant asked.

'Just deduction based on all the other information we have,' Tony said.

'But if she was still alive after the mother checked herself out,' DCI Brent reasoned, 'then she'd be an abandoned child, treated as a foundling. The police, in that area, would try very hard to find the mother.'

'I can't believe a woman would do that?' Lizzy said.

'She wouldn't necessarily have to be a bad mother,' DC Grant said. 'She could have post-natal depression.'

'I suppose it would be kinder for us to assume that,' Tony said. 'But I'm afraid her subsequent behaviour did nothing to suggest it.'

'There's bound to be reports and files somewhere in the system,' DC Grant said. 'I'll have a look and let you know if I find anything. You never know she might still be fighting her corner. In that case she's a missing person. She should be in the system somewhere.'

Tony's body suddenly tensed and his brow puckered. 'They won't have put her up for adoption, would they? Don't tell me she survived only to be given to somebody else.'

'Not yet, premature babies don't usually start to develop until they reach their actual due date,' DC Grant said. 'It takes them a while to catch up so she would have been in hospital a long time.'

'Then what?' Tony asked.

'With foster parents, they'll place her with a mother who is experienced with premature babies. She'll understand her and all her stages of development. So don't worry about that.'

Lizzy felt Tony's whole body sigh with relief and she grasped his hand.

A frown flickered across DC Grant's forehead and she said, 'Do you think Louisa Warren toed the line during the pregnancy? If she was prone to drink it might be possible that Stephanie will have other problems aside from the premature birth.'

Tony nodded. 'I understand, but if that's the case, she'll get everything she needs to help her overcome it. But nothing showed up in the reports from the clinic. Louisa was very keen to see it through to secure the money; I don't think she would have risked it. The premature birth must have been a coincidence.'

DC Grant flipped through her notes. 'It was one hell of a quirk of fate,' she said. She turned to DCI Brent. 'Can we assume that Stephanie's a missing person until we find out more?'

'You'd better get on to it.'

DC Grant gathered her notes and left the office.

DCI Brent shook his head. 'Walked straight off the catwalk onto the beat, that one. She's a bit mouthy but a good cop. Wants to make a difference; to women mainly, that's what she's all about. She'll find your little girl, and she won't sleep until she does.'

Chapter Twenty Eight

Jane Clarke, the social worker, met them in a waiting room and they sat down. 'I'm sorry you had so much grief, Mr Franklyn,' she said, 'especially as you'd taken such care to protect the child.'

'I'm afraid I thought I'd covered every angle to secure her safety, but it wasn't to be.'

'You couldn't possibly have foreseen what was going to happen. Of course there was a search for the mother, but unfortunately nobody was looking for you.'

Tony nodded. 'That's what we assumed.'

Lizzy clenched his hand, their fingers weaved together. 'It was very traumatic for Tony,' she said.

Jane Clarke nodded. She placed a file on her lap and read from the notes. 'The nurses in ICU named her Hope, because she was fighting so hard to survive. She's referred to as Hope in this file, but we'll put a note in to say that you wish her to be known as Stephanie. We also informed the foster mother. You've probably worked out that Stephanie is six months old now. Her development is a few weeks behind, but, as the nurses said, she's a little fighter. It's early days yet, but at the moment she seems to be on-track to reach a normative stage of development.'

Lizzy and Tony stood up and embraced each other. Then they gushed out words of gratitude.

'So what happens now?' Tony said.

'That's up to you.'

'In what way?'

'She's legally yours, you don't need permission to take her, but you haven't met her yet. I would recommend that you take it slowly, visit a couple of times; spend some time with her in familiar surroundings before you take her.'

'Then that's what we'll do,' Tony said. 'We'll find a hotel and stay on here for a few days.'

'Shall we go and find her then?' Jane Clarke said with a smile.

Tony felt the tight grip of tension across his abdomen as they followed the social worker along passages and through fire doors until they arrived at a purpose built playroom. Blue carpets fitted into every corner and there was all manner of colourful equipment—tiny tricycles and sit on trains and tractors. There were one or two coloured, plastic balls scattered about.

A woman stood by the window. She held a baby in her arms and was talking to her as she pointed to things outside. She turned and Tony's eyes fixed on the baby, the bright blue eyes, soft fair hair formed into little C shaped locks. He was so overcome with a father's love he could hardly breathe. She was his daughter, his little girl; the child he believed had died six months ago. But there she was, alive, and thriving, a tiny person looking across the room at him.

'Look who's here,' the foster mother said. 'Shall we go and say hello?'

Tony wasn't dealing with this very well. He could cope with a serious manufacturing glitch or juggle huge problems in the boardroom, but this moment drained him and he had to dig deep to find the strength to stand on his feet. But his composure returned, given to him by Lizzy's voice and the touch of her hand on his shoulder.

'She has your eyes,' she whispered.

'Oh God! She's wonderful. I can't believe…'

'Stephanie,' the foster mother said cheerfully, 'it's Daddy.'

'Hello, sweetheart,' he whispered. He hesitated when the foster mother began to hand her to him. 'Perhaps she'd rather not be held yet.'

'Children who have spent a long time in hospital have been held by a lot of carers. She'll be a bit nervous but you're her daddy.'

An emotional sigh quivered through his throat as Stephanie Hope Franklyn, was placed in his arms. He stood still for some time as the baby protested. Then he talked to her, walked her around the room, looked at the colourful pictures and posters. She began to make happy little sounds as they moved. Tony's eyes watered and a tear escaped and rolled slowly down his cheek. It caught Stephanie's eye, she seemed curious and she pressed her tiny finger on it then let out a squeak.

Lizzy went to them. 'Your daddy loves you, Stephanie Hope, he loves you so much, and so do I.'

'Are you going to hold her?' Tony asked.

'In a little while,' she said softly. 'This is your time, what you've dreamed of. It's your recompense for all the pain.'

It was like a dream, walking around with his child, sitting on the floor poised to catch her if she fell over, watching her reaching for toys, examining them with her eyes, her fingers, her mouth. Lizzy joined in and they became a family.

Lizzy felt ten feet tall as they entered the restaurant that evening. Tony was still shaken but so happy. They were escorted to a table and they sat down, still in some kind of daze. 'You look a bit pale, are you all right?' Lizzy asked.

'I'm fine. I'm just working out what to do with all this good news.'

'It doesn't get any better than this, does it?'

'I don't think I could cope if it did.' He looked at her, his eyes mellow and adoring. 'You've worked your magic again.'

'What do you mean?'

'Rescuing me, looking past my stubbornness, my confidence that I knew the score, making me see what I had to do. I might have gone through my life without ever seeing Stephanie. Instead I'm going to see her tomorrow, and the next day and then we're taking her home.'

Lizzy scoffed. 'Why do you insist that this is down to me? You would have found her. Something would drive you to do it.'

'You've given me so much and you ask so little in return.'

'I ask that you love me, that's everything.'

'I do, darling, I really do. But for goodness sake won't you let me buy you something? What would you like: a car, jewellery, a bolt hole somewhere in France? How about a nice boat to explore the lake?' He leaned towards her and smiled. 'Go on,' he urged, 'let me buy you a car.'

'All right, but I still want my badge. I've been waiting for it since we were in Florence.'

A smug smile crossed Tony's face as he reached into his inside pocket and pulled out a small package.'

Lizzy laughed. 'You got it?'

'I bought it in Florence.' He held her hand as it rested on the table, fixed his eyes on her face and said, 'Will you go steady with me, Lizzy? For, say, just a few decades to begin with?'

'I'd love to be your steady girlfriend.'

'Then, my darling,' he said as he slipped a ring on her finger, 'whether I deserve you or not, we're going to be married.'

Lizzy's eyes widened. She looked down at her hand and the glistening diamonds. 'It's so beautiful.'

They leaned over the table and kissed. Suddenly there was a round of applause from the next table and calls of congratulations.

'Is there anything else you'd like?' Tony asked, 'now that you're going to be my wife?'

'Do I get Grandma Franklyn's reading room?'

'It's already yours.'

'And can I keep the sweater?'

'Of course. Anything you want, just ask.'

'Can I sometimes borrow your favourite jeans and tatty sweatshirt?'

Tony laughed. 'Er... I don't know about that. It's a big ask.'

'And some more....' Lizzy paused and looked at him with a glint in her eye.

'Some more...?'

'Children.'

Chapter Twenty Nine

Tony strolled steadily along the sand and his mind reached back to when Lizzy sat by his side, on the plane, and told him about this place and the cottage between the mountains and the sea.

On hot, summer days, you won't find a better beach anywhere in the world. The water looks blue, and the sand gets hot under your feet. The waves dazzle you when you run towards them. The sea seems to make a special sound on those days, sort of muffled and soporific.

He watched Lizzy and Stephanie, as he followed their mingling and meandering footprints at the edge of the tide. They stopped occasionally and examined seashells and bits of coloured seaweed. He still found it hard to believe that his little girl survived. Now she could run about with her mummy, and chatter in a language that was a blend of English and toddler-speak. Lizzy still had no idea how much he loved her. Saying *I love you,* a million times a day wouldn't convince him that he'd conveyed it to her. He still remembered Little Eddy, at Grace's wedding, when he told Lizzy that he loved her *ten,* which was the highest number he dealt with in pre-school. He could count other numbers but they were words he learned to chant, ten he understood because he had that many fingers and toes, it had value. He'd spread his arms as wide as he possibly could, to show her. It was the ultimate measure, for his arms could go no wider.

Now there was a new Little Eddie. He looked around him and now and then he let out a squeak or a chuckle when something caught his eye or the breeze ruffled his hair.

Tony breathed in the sea air, hugged his son and smiled at his daughter as she ran about, then returned to Lizzy to show her what she'd found. Lizzy glanced back at him and smiled. He smiled back at her, his amazing wife, his lover, his steady girlfriend. He felt blessed. He was a Franklyn, destined to love deeply, passionately, like his father and his grandfather but with no ultimate yardstick to measure it. How then could he tell her how much he loved her? All he could do was be there with his million *I love yous,* his adorning gazes, his shoulder to catch her tears, his arms to hold her through the night.

She still loved to run around the lake and it always reminded him of that first morning. Just an ordinary May morning, but it was one of those moments in time that fate plants in a person's day like a tiny seed destined to grow into a new beginning; this whole new beautiful beginning.

The End